THE CHEMISTRY OF DEATH

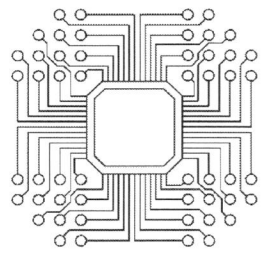

REBECCA CANTRELL

ALSO BY REBECCA CANTRELL

Joe Tesla thrillers set in the tunnels under New York:
The World Beneath
The Tesla Legacy
The Chemistry of Death

Humorous and irreverent mysteries set in the sunny and glamorous world of Malibu (written with Sean Black):
A is for Asshat

Mystery/thrillers in the award-winning Hannah Vogel series set in 1930s Berlin:
A Trace of Smoke
A Night of Long Knives
A Game of Lies
A City of Broken Glass

Gothic thrillers in the Order of the Sanguines series (written with James Rollins) following an order of vampire priests:
The Blood Gospel
Innocent Blood
Blood Infernal

Young adult novels in the iMonster series (as Bekka Black):
iDrakula
iFrankenstein

THE CHEMISTRY OF DEATH

REBECCA CANTRELL

Copyright Information

This book is a work of fiction. All of the characters, organizations, and events portrayed in this novel are either products of the author's imagination or used fictitiously. Any similarity to any real person, alive or dead, is completely coincidental.

THE CHEMISTRY OF DEATH

Copyright © 2015 by Rebecca Cantrell

Cover Design by Kit Foster www.kitfosterdesign.com

All rights reserved.

Dedication

For my husband, my son, and my readers

PROLOGUE

October 27, last year
Tunnel near Platform 6
Under Grand Central Terminal

Ziggy smiled when the woman's designer shoes slipped on the train ties. Those shoes were at home in the expensive club where he'd picked her up, but they were worse than useless down here in the subway tunnels.

He caught her ice-cold arm. He'd made sure she'd forgotten her coat when they left the club, and he knew he must feel warm to her, warm and safe. She would trust him. She let him steady her for a heartbeat before pulling away.

"Watch the third rail." He pointed to the raised metal track that ran along the inside rail. "It's dangerous."

"I want to go back." Her lower lip quivered, and she tucked it between even, white teeth. The drug was already affecting her. He'd given her a high dose because she hated the tunnels more than any other woman he'd brought down here.

"Put on more lipstick." He held his breath, wondering if the drug had kicked in enough for her to comply. "You'll feel better when you look better."

She fumbled in her expensive purse and pulled out a hand mirror. She angled the mirror to catch the faint light. Her movements were clumsy but practiced.

Without looking, she pulled a shiny black tube from her purse. He knew the lipstick's color even before she opened it.

Christian Dior 999. Classic red.

She pulled off the cap and twisted the base. He breathed in the lipstick's heady perfume. The scent took him back to other lipsticks, other women, and how his mother had forced him to wear dresses and Christian Dior 999 lipstick when he was a little boy to punish him. He remembered how he had looked in the mirror in her high heels and long skirts, how the lipstick smelled on his own lips, the soapy taste of it.

He took a deep breath to ground himself back in this moment, this tunnel, this woman. He was in charge here.

With a trembling hand, she slid the lipstick across her full lips. He wanted to touch the gleaming redness, and he clenched the slippery lining of his pockets to keep his hands from reaching for her. These lips weren't for kissing.

She dropped the case back inside her purse and straightened her slim shoulders. Her breasts pushed against the thin fabric of her dress. The sharp tang of vodka from her cosmopolitan obliterated the last traces of the lipstick's delicate fragrance.

"Do you feel better now?" he asked.

Wide eyes stared back into his. "What's wrong with your v-voice?"

"Nothing." He dropped his voice back to its normal register, the one he used everywhere but here. Only in the dark tunnels under New York could he let the other voice go. But not yet.

She pulled her arm out of his grip. He let her. The drug would ensure her compliance. Even without it, she was too afraid of the dark to venture far.

She was so miserable. It was good of him to help her. He wished that someone would help him. He needed someone to be a friend to him like he was to her.

"It's easy to get turned around down here." He pointed to his right. "The platform is that way."

That way was a dead end, but he doubted that she'd remember where he pointed anyway. The alcohol and his drug slowed her thinking. Her eyes darted back and forth, as if she might see something to show her what to do. She'd find no breadcrumbs in this deserted tunnel.

He rumpled his hair with one hand and smiled, showing his dimples. Women always relaxed at his boyish grin. "Come along with me?"

"Is it far?" She sounded like a little girl. Tremulous, uncertain, and trusting.

"Not far." He wrapped an arm around her shoulders, and she leaned into his warmth. He stroked her cold arm, knowing how she would welcome the heat.

Together, they walked along the tracks. Her high heels clacked against the wooden train ties, but his dress shoes were silent. Nobody down here to notice either way, not at this time of night.

They were alone, but then, everyone was always alone. He never felt lonely down here. Aboveground he went to the crowded clubs and worked in a busy office. Surrounded by people, but always alone.

He would have been even more alone had anyone recognized his nature. He should have been cast out, a bad seed. He'd have cast himself out, but he lacked the nerve. So he helped others to do what he could not.

Her scream interrupted his thoughts. A rat stood on the tracks, not giving ground. Its black eyes glinted in the overhead light, and its sharp nose rose to sniff the air. It didn't budge at the noise.

"It's New York," he said. "Rats everywhere."

Humans had done that. They'd built a perverted world that was perfect for rats, better for rats than for men.

She stood rigid with one slender hand clamped across her red lips.

He bent and picked up a stone, but the rat melted into the shadows before he threw it. The rat feared him. In a lot of ways, rats were smarter than people.

They set off down the track. He put his arm around her shoulders again. Her movements were unsteady, her motor coordination compromised. He kept her upright and moving deeper into the tunnels.

"Your last boyfriend never took you on this kind of adventure, I bet." He worked to use his regular voice. "He didn't plan much, did he?"

She shook her head. "Slade was busy."

He cupped her elbow. The skin was surprisingly rough. "You make time for important things. Important people."

"I wasn't important to him." She lurched to a stop and looked up at him. Her pupils had dilated so much he could barely tell what color her eyes were. Maybe blue? "Not ever."

"Why do you think that's true?" He tucked a strand of long, blond hair behind her ear. She'd begun to look messy. That he could not abide.

"Because I wasn't worth anything to him." She saw herself clearly, probably for the first time. Friends and family always tried to talk a person through these moments, teach them lies to give them hope. But these dark moments had a bitter truth to them that was more potent than a thousand moments of false hope.

"Surely you're worth something to others?" He squeezed her against his side. She was so tiny, barely larger than a child.

"To you, maybe?" Her voice quivered.

"It's too soon for that." He loosened his hold on her, but kept her close. "Plenty of other people love you. Your family. Your mother. Your father."

Her face sagged. Her mother had died when she was a teenager, and her father had disowned her when she left their small religious town to seek her fortune in New York. He'd overheard her life story in the club where he'd picked her.

"Just Slade. And I drove him away."

She might have driven him away, but it was Slade who had changed the locks on their shared apartment and left her neatly packed bags with the doorman. She came home from work to the doorman's smirking face and a locked apartment door. So she'd dropped the suitcases in her office, changed, and gone out clubbing.

Ziggy had met her at his third club. She clearly needed someone and was willing to trade sex for a moment's connection. Ziggy had taken over.

"There are more people in the world than Slade," he said.

"Not for me." She looked down at the buckles on her ruined red shoes. "What's wrong with me?"

"Did Slade say anything was wrong with you?"

"We'd still be together if he didn't see something wrong with me. See some giant flaw."

"What did he see?" Ziggy put his hand on the small of her back and guided her forward, faster now. He had a train to catch.

"I don't know," she whispered. "But they all see it. My mother. My father. Now Slade."

"There's nothing wrong with you?" He raised his voice at the end, turning it into a question instead of a reassurance as he pulled her close. She trembled in his arms, scared, cold, and drugged.

"Yes, there is." Tears ran down her cheeks, mixed with mascara. "What am I doing wrong?"

She was a beautiful, broken doll. He hoped her face wouldn't be marred. "Maybe you aren't doing anything wrong."

She twitched at the sound of his voice. It had come out high-pitched again, like an excited child's. He couldn't force it back into its usual register. They were almost there. The voice had to come out.

"I've done something wrong," she whispered. "I must have. Or else why would everyone run away from me? Why am I alone?"

"What's wrong with a life lived alone?" he whispered back.

She dropped her head against his shoulder, and again, he smelled her lipstick. "Everything."

The metal track vibrated against the toe of his Oxford. He didn't have much time.

"You can live alone for years and years. Get old alone. Die alone," he said.

She sagged against him. "I have to find someone."

"How?"

She tipped her head up toward him again and searched his eyes for hope. He didn't give her any. "Won't the next man turn away from you? Like your father? Like Slade?"

The train rattled closer, but she acted as if she didn't hear it.

"He didn't even say good-bye." Ziggy let go of her, knowing how cold she'd feel when he stepped away, the dank tunnel air replacing the warmth where his body had pressed against hers.

He clutched her purse and its valuable contents in one hand.

Goose bumps rose on her chest and neck, and she wrapped her arms around herself in a lonely hug. Her lips moved as she repeated the last words he'd given her. "He didn't even say good-bye."

Ziggy backed into the darkness of the tunnel so he couldn't be seen by anyone but her. So far as the train operator would see, she was alone on the tracks. His heart danced in anticipation. It was like Christmas morning, and he was a young boy looking at the gaudily wrapped boxes, ready to tear open the paper and discover the real treasure underneath.

"Stay," he said, and she nodded her head like the good girl she was.

The headlights of the oncoming train illuminated her fragile form. Her silvery dress sparkled like tinsel, and her golden hair glowed like a halo. Tears glistened on alabaster cheeks. She was radiant.

White showed around her irises when she looked forward into the light, but he knew she would not jump away. Fear would pin her there. At first, he'd thought they feared the train, but now he knew differently.

They feared the light.

Brakes shrieked. Sparks flew from the tracks, skittered over the ground, and winked out. The driver was braking on instinct and prayer, but the car would not stop in time. Physics always trumped faith.

If Ziggy looked, he knew he'd see the driver's face trapped in a rictus of horror. He didn't look. Her death shouldn't be seen as a horrible event. It was liberation.

The car slammed into her bright body and thundered yards down the track. The car took the light with it, and welcome darkness enveloped him. Bliss coursed through his veins. He threw back his head and moaned his ecstasy to the screaming brakes.

The air pulled in the wake of the hard metal cars stroked his cheeks, forced his eyes closed. He swayed back against the hard wall. The stone anchored him, and he didn't fall. He took one shuddering breath and then another.

She'd been everything he'd hoped.

His ears rang in the sudden silence. The car had shuddered to a stop. When he opened his eyes, the red taillight shone on the spot where she'd stood. He had to leave her soon, but first he needed to see her one last time.

He crept from pillar to pillar. His shoes made no sound on the sharp stones.

Her broken body hadn't left the tracks. Sometimes, they were thrown clear, and he could have one last look, but not today. The subway cars hid her from him, but he could smell the rich, coppery scent of her blood.

With a pneumatic whoosh, the door opened. The driver stumbled out and retched next to the tracks. Shakily, he stood again.

Ziggy melted into the darkness before the man's smells could overtake him. He caressed the purse, the leather as smooth as her skin, the lipstick within practically glowing.

999. His favorite.

1

October, present day

Joe Tesla had acquired the best modern and antique maps when the tunnels under New York City became his primary domain. Much information was written down, but when he walked the tunnels, he often found things not marked on the maps: filled-in tunnels, bricked-up doors, a deserted train car, and hidden passages. The tunnel system grew and decayed like a living thing. And like any living thing, it held on to its secrets.

In companionable silence, he and his psychiatric service dog, Edison, walked along at a brisk clip. The dog ranged a little farther ahead, sniffing the ground. Joe checked for the flashlight in his pocket as he walked. He had extra batteries in his backpack, and he might need them. The tunnels he intended to map probably wouldn't be lit.

Joe stifled a sneeze. The tunnels had their own smells—steel dust, engine oil, rocks, and rat urine. The sense of adventure that came from exploring this hidden world buoyed him. It was still early, and nothing ran down these tracks at this time of day.

He kicked a rock, and it pinged against the metal track. Far to his left, a quick patter of tiny feet told him that he'd disturbed a rat. Edison pricked his ears and looked toward the sound, but he stayed close in front of Joe.

Joe slipped on his night vision goggles, and the world appeared in shades of green. The change always made him feel like he was playing a zombie video game.

Eventually, Edison's greenish form stopped. The dog looked over his shoulder at Joe, waiting for instructions. His tail wagged in an electric green blur. Next to him loomed the black maw of an unknown tunnel.

Edison looked into the unexplored tunnel, then back at Joe.

Joe pulled the map out of his backpack, a signal they'd be here for a while. Edison trotted back and sat next to him. Joe handed him a treat.

Night vision goggles weren't ideal for reading maps, so Joe slid the goggles onto his forehead and clicked on his flashlight. He traced their journey with his finger. They'd made good time through their well-known haunts to reach this blank spot on his map.

"You know what they say about the blank spots on maps, don't you, boy?"

Edison didn't.

"Here there be dragons," Joe told him.

Clearly unimpressed, Edison scratched his ear.

Joe took out a compass to get the direction exactly right, then marked the new tunnel in pencil. With precise strokes, he filled in the blank spot. Hopefully that would vanquish the dragons.

He walked to where Edison had first stopped and aimed his light down the new tunnel. Brackets that had once held pipes protruded from the stone, but the pipes were gone, leaving only long streaks of rust that showed where they had leaked. An abandoned steam tunnel.

Probably the building those pipes once serviced had shut off its steam, or maybe the tunnel had been built by a competing steam company long since devoured by Con Edison. Either way, the short tunnel dead-ended at a rusty old door. Barely worth exploring, but he was already here.

The dog pressed against Joe's leg. Ever since being shot in one, the dog didn't like steam tunnels. Joe didn't really blame him.

"It's OK, Ed," he said. "Ain't nobody here but us chickens."

Edison didn't find the reference comforting.

"You're too young to know that song," Joe said. He stroked the dog's back and shoulder, fingers grazing the lump of scar tissue where the bullet had entered. Edison relaxed and cocked his head, ready to go.

Pausing at the tunnel entrance, Joe listened. Faraway, a train clattered, then the underground labyrinth again fell silent. He heard only his own breathing and the light panting of the dog. They were alone.

He aimed his flashlight toward the new adventure. The beam revealed lines of footprints on the dusty floor between him and the door. Someone had walked back and forth several times. Without wind or weather to disturb them, tracks stayed down here for a long time. The walker could have been here last week or last decade. Hell, the tracks might even have belonged to the workers who took away the pipes; they might be older than Joe.

"Just a quick look, Edison," he said, "then we'll head back to the siding by FDR's car and play some fetch before we go to work. How's that sound?"

Edison's tail usually wagged at the word *fetch*, but this time he just stood by Joe's side, looking forward.

Feeling guilty about putting the dog through this trauma to fill in a white spot on his map, Joe walked to the door. Raised letters spelled out *Consolidated Gas*. That company had predated Con Edison, so it was definitely an old door. He pressed down on the cold, metal handle. It didn't budge.

Interesting. Maybe the door was connected to a building above, and that was why it was kept locked. If so, Joe might be able to venture outside of the tunnel system from here. That was definitely worth exploring.

As part of the terms of his lease of a house built in the tunnels, he had keys that pretty much granted him access to all the underground doors he was likely to encounter. He'd gone through a lengthy background check before he was given them, but they'd proven worth the time and expense. He took the massive antique key ring out of his backpack and crossed his fingers.

He sorted through keys, settling on an old one with a top like a clover. Consolidated Gas would have been merged with Con Edison years before, so the key for this door was probably pretty old. The more he thought about it, the more he was sure the merger had taken place before 1936. Joe had synesthesia, and the numbers lit up in his mind (cyan, scarlet, red, orange).

The clover-topped key didn't work. Nor did the next. He resigned himself to going through all the steam tunnel keys in order and found the right one on the seventh (slate) try.

Surprisingly, once he found the key that worked, the lock turned easily. Most of the older doors required lock oil and finesse, but every so often he stumbled across one that seemed to have withstood the depredations of time.

This door swung inward without a creak, and the smell of mildew drifted out. A delicate floral scent threaded through it, and the hair stood up on the back of Joe's neck. That smell did not belong in these tunnels.

Edison growled. He'd only made that particular sound out in the tunnels once before, when they'd discovered the body of a recent murder victim next to FDR's old train car. Joe was tempted to retreat, but he had vowed not to run from anything in the tunnels. He'd withdrawn from the world as far as he was willing to go. He had to take a stand.

Joe tightened his grip on the flashlight. The flashlight was big enough to make a formidable club, and it also contained a Taser. It'd have to be enough to take on whatever or whoever was in there.

He flashed the beam around the Spartan room.

"It's OK, boy," he said.

Still growling, Edison took a stiff-legged step inside.

Joe discovered a light switch to the right of the door. He didn't expect it to work, but he flipped it anyway. Ghostly blue-white light flickered. The overhead fixture buzzed like an angry bee, and Edison gave it a quick glance before stalking forward another step.

The smell of flowers was gone, and Joe wondered if he'd imagined it. The room looked ordinary with walls once painted olive-green now grayed with mold and a hard-packed dirt floor. He examined the only furniture in the room: a gray chair and a battered metal table. Both looked government-issue, maybe World War II era, maybe more recent, but certainly not new. A thick layer of dust shrouded their surfaces.

A doorframe on the far wall showed where the room had probably connected to the building serviced by the steam pipes, but the door had long since been removed and the opening had been bricked closed. Joe walked across and tapped the bricks. Just as solid as they looked.

Edison kept growling. Joe didn't want to shush him. The dog was spooked, and anything that spooked him had to be taken seriously, especially if Joe couldn't figure out what it was.

Edison headed for the northwest corner of the room. Once there, he began to dig. At least the effort stopped the growling.

Joe stood guard over him and waited. Edison was onto something. A dead rat? Edison liked to roll around on dead rats. It was practically his only flaw. But dead rats usually made him excited, not on edge.

Edison ducked his nose into the hole and pulled out a small object. He dropped it next to Joe's foot, and Joe bent to pick it up. Dirt clung to a black, plastic cylinder dripping with dog saliva. It took him a second to recognize the object.

A tube of lipstick.

Edison often dug up things in the tunnels. Usually those things were rotten and smelled terrible. He'd never found scented lipstick before.

"That's a pretty girlie thing to be digging up," Joe told him. "But at least you won't need a bath when we get home."

He pulled out a waste bag he carried around to pick up Edison's poop and dropped the lipstick inside the empty bag. Why had someone or something buried a tube of lipstick here, and why did his dog care?

Edison dragged a small gray purse out of his hole. The surface was dusty but dry. It looked expensive and fairly new. Edison cocked his head and barked.

"You like the purse?" Joe held it out for him.

Edison sniffed it once and growled.

"That seems like a strong fashion statement," Joe said.

Edison turned back to the hole and dug some more. He dropped two (blue) more lipsticks at Joe's feet. Three (red) identical lipstick. Joe's uneasiness grew. Why would someone bury lipstick in this out-of-the-way room, locked behind an antique door? Could a rat have done this?

"Sit." Joe palmed a treat for Edison, and the dog sat.

Joe picked up the next tube using a fresh poop bag like a glove. The top had the letters C and D on it. He dropped each lipstick in a separate bag and put the bags into his backpack next to the purse.

He walked around the room, looking for places where a rat could get in. The brick wall was solid, as were the other walls. But the wall with the door had four (green) holes, round like boreholes and orange with rust. The steam pipes must have gone through here a long time ago. A rat might fit through them carrying lipstick, but not a purse. Even if he rolled the purse up, Joe wouldn't have been able to force it through any of those holes, and he liked to think he was stronger and more enterprising than a rat.

Still, rats collected odd things. In his explorations, he'd come across empty nests containing all kinds of objects: old subway tokens, bones he didn't want to identify, shredded tissue, grass, and once, a half-eaten roll of Rolaids (for the rat with acid reflux). A rat that liked the taste or smell of lipstick couldn't be that unusual. But that didn't explain the purse.

The tunnels had plenty of secrets. Maybe the rat had moved the purse in before the door was locked. Joe wasn't an archaeologist. For all he knew, the purse was twenty years old or more. Or the door might have been locked last week, and the rat wasn't able to get its treasures back out again.

He pictured a gray sewer rat with oily fur and yellow teeth returning to find the door locked, squeezing its burly form through the pipe holes to check on its booty. Maybe it had wanted to build an upscale nest but had been interrupted when the door was closed. No point in second guessing the motivations of a tunnel rat.

Edison looked at the hole he'd dug and barked a question at Joe. He wanted to go back to digging, so there must be more there. Maybe even the corpse of the rat himself. Or herself.

"No," Joe told him. "We leave the rest of it undisturbed. Just in case."

2

Vivian Torres stood in the middle of a Prada store on Fifth Avenue. Ridiculously expensive handbags posed on moodily lit shelves. Tall ceilings, mirrors, and the smell of leather and perfume made the narrow shop feel luxurious.

A salesman in a tailored suit eyed her disapprovingly. Her off-the-rack clothes and scuffed shoes probably told him she wouldn't be leaving with one of the shop's expensive bags. He was right, of course. Even if she could afford it, she'd never buy one, and right now, the only new purse she could afford was a paper bag.

She ignored him and studied the rest of the clientele. Two women in jeans and knee-high leather boots stood in front of a shelf of bags, speaking in the hushed tones usually reserved for church. Vivian's charge, Katrinka Kazakov, wandered past them, expensive boots tapping against the gleaming black-and-white checkerboard floor. The blond teenager wore jeans that looked like they were falling apart and a burnt orange top from some designer Vivian had never heard of. The outfit probably cost more than everything in Vivian's closet.

Katrinka eyed a butterscotch-colored purse. It matched the deeper shades of blond in her hair. She tried to hand Vivian her shopping bags.

"I need to keep my hands free." Vivian stepped back.

"You work for me," Katrinka said. "Hold these bags."

"I work for your father," Vivian corrected. "And I'm a bodyguard, not a butler."

"You're supposed to help me out."

"I'm supposed to keep you safe." So far, Katrinka hadn't needed any real body guarding, but her father was a powerful Russian businessman married to a former model, and they wanted to make certain their daughter was protected. Vivian had quickly figured out her real job wasn't to keep trouble from finding Katrinka, but to keep Katrinka from finding trouble. She had her drivers and the rest of the staff wrapped around her manicured pinky finger.

"Do you have a copy of your contract, the part where it specifies that you aren't supposed to help me carry things?" Katrinka raised one waxed eyebrow.

"You'll have to take it up with your father." Vivian didn't intend to give in to her. It'd make her job tougher if she did. Vivian had a sister the same age as Katrinka, and she knew better than to back down.

Katrinka's brown eyes darkened a shade, but she set the shopping bags on a black tile without any more conversation. Then, she picked up the purse and caressed the golden crocodile skin as if it were some kind of weird pet. Maybe it had been Crocodile Dundee's guard dog.

Three women on a mission came in and headed straight to a display in the far corner. They pointed at a pink bag and launched into a rapid-fire discussion in Chinese. The salesman who'd so quickly dismissed Vivian headed in their direction like a bloodhound on a scent.

Out of the corner of her eye, Vivian saw Katrinka drop the butterscotch-colored purse into the giant Macy's bag at her feet. A slick maneuver. The salesman wouldn't have seen a thing.

"Not happening," Vivian said quietly. "Put it back."

Katrinka widened those brown eyes, mascaraed lashes framing her fake surprise. "I know you aren't going to hold my bags. You don't have to get all bitchy about it."

"Unless you pay for that purse, you're not leaving the store." Vivian raised her voice, and the salesman glanced over at them.

"We've had a long day, and I want to get some coffee. I'll text Mr. Alenin to circle around and pick us up. Maybe we'll go out for dinner after. My treat." Katrinka gave Vivian her sunniest smile and pulled out her phone.

The salesman returned to his Chinese marks.

Vivian couldn't let Katrinka steal, but she couldn't get her arrested for shoplifting either. Her father would buy her out of trouble and fire Vivian, and Vivian needed this job.

What was the best way to protect a girl who was her own worst enemy?

Screw the philosophizing. Vivian blocked the salesman's line of sight, reached into the Macy's bag, and pulled out the yellow purse. She set it on the shelf behind the teenager's head between a green one and a black one.

"It must have fallen in there," Katrinka said.

Vivian didn't bother to acknowledge the lie. She gestured toward the door, and Katrinka flounced out to where a Lincoln Town car idled at the curb.

Vivian ducked down to confirm the chauffeur's identity before she opened the door and let the sulky teen climb inside. Vivian slid into the stuffy car after her, hoping this shopping trip was over.

She missed Joe Tesla. Keeping him out of trouble might be more complicated than babysitting Katrinka, but it was a lot more fun.

3

Ziggy watched his administrative assistant through the glass office door. She was young, twenty-five max with breasts too large to be natural, a mane of platinum-blond hair, flawless skin, and full red lips. She was also good at her job. He gave her more responsibility than others would, and she was up to the task. Usually, they worked well together, but it was fall, and he never worked well with anyone in the fall. Fall was hunting season.

When the leaves started to change and the air got a cold bite to it, he changed into another man. As a child, he would be sent away, full of hope, to a boarding school every fall. Every year a different one and, before he could settle in, his mother would pull him out and bring him home to finish his studies by her side. Fall meant hope and failure and, now, hunting.

For most of the year, he ran the company with ease and humor. He would walk by his name on the door and know he made a difference in the world, that he was remaking nature and man according to his wishes. Everything meshed.

Once the summer temperatures started to drop and the leaves began to die, nothing fit. Every year he vowed to take a vacation in the fall, let things run themselves or run themselves down, and start again in the winter.

But he didn't. He stayed at his desk, knowing he'd probably drive his assistant to quit, and that he would have to work like a demon once the snow fell to catch up on the work left undone. This cycle would continue until the day he died, an event he worried was too far in the future, but inching closer every day.

He went to the window and pulled it open. It wasn't easy to find a building with windows that opened anymore, but he'd insisted on it. Cold air gusted into the room. The air smelled of the chemicals people pumped untrammeled into the atmosphere every day; of cold, high winds; and, he fancied, a faint undertone of dried leaves. He inhaled the mixture, letting it ground him in the poisoned, autumnal world.

Then he sat in his new leather chair and called up his email. He had many things that he should respond to, but he wouldn't, not until the kills were behind him. He had to hunt soon.

He hadn't hunted successfully in almost a year. A few months ago he'd tried to hunt outside of the fall season. But he'd failed. The hunt had been badly planned, the victim different from all his other kills, the setup different, too. It hadn't been a stranger, that was his first mistake. It hadn't been a grief-stricken woman, his second. The victim had been whisked away before the drug had time to work, his third and final mistake. It had been too risky, so Ziggy had let that victim go. Since then, he had vowed to stick to his established hunting season.

Out in the main office his assistant lifted a stack of papers and stood. Today he noticed that, from the back, her ass looked like a peach: round, firm, and begging to be bitten. The deep-green suit clinging to her curves showed him where he wanted to bite first. He shifted in his chair to give his burgeoning erection room to grow.

Just this morning, he'd thought of installing a spy camera behind her desk so he could make a highlights tape of her bending over to get files, walking down the hall, maybe touching up her lipstick. He'd researched it enough to know it was possible, but decided that if he were caught, the political blowback would be too unpleasant. The Internet had plenty of sleazy images. Besides, he was breaking so many big laws that he needed to be careful about the small ones.

She turned around, and her lips tightened. She'd caught him looking, but what could she do? Looking wasn't against any sexual harassment law, and she still enjoyed the vestiges of summer goodwill.

She crossed the ash-gray carpet on her long legs and stood in front of his door. She lifted the papers, a question on her face.

"Come in." He rolled his chair up against his antique mahogany desk and smiled. She smiled back. The expression never made it to her eyes. As far as he was concerned, it didn't need to.

Tight, controlled steps brought her to his desk. She was a master of moving in those high heels. He bet she had ballet training.

Her fragrance enveloped him, musky perfume, a trace of face powder, and a note of lipstick. Not 999, but the lipstick's scent still tickled his nose.

"These are for you to sign." She handed him a sheaf of papers. "I flagged the signature lines with sticky notes."

"Thank you, Miss Evans."

"Mrs. Evans," she corrected.

"Where do I sign?"

She leaned closer, and he breathed in her scent, quietly so she wouldn't notice. One long, crimson nail pointed at a blank signature line next to a yellow arrow. The sticky note.

Without reading, he slowly signed his name. She flipped several pages and pointed to another location. This time, he signed it even more slowly, forcing her to stand next to him and wait. Her warm form tensed with irritation, but he didn't care. He liked having her there.

The phone on his desk rang. Ordinarily, screening his calls was her job, but he reached for the phone himself. She'd have to stand there while he talked or come back to show him where to sign the papers. That'd help him through the day.

"I'll get that." She hurried toward her own desk, although she could have answered the call at his.

Her ass cheeks bounced as she walked, and he waited until she was sitting in her own chair before he looked away. He had to control himself in the office, but each day was more difficult than the last.

He needed to hunt the tunnels soon.

4

Joe sat on the gray planks in his underground front yard and looked around at the carpet of living greenery covering his once bare stone floor. The plants were still too fragile for Joe to walk on, but Edison sniffed around amongst them in a complicated pattern.

A bank of LED spots provided the plants with light. Water from his household pipes trickled down a nearby rock face and fed into an irrigation system originally designed for exactly the opposite environment—a rooftop garden. The system worked down here, too, and it had brought him something he'd sorely missed during these months inside.

He inhaled the smell of rich soil, wet rocks, and the green scent of ground cover. He'd picked out the plants with his garden designer, savoring their evocative names— creeping mazus, brass buttons, and blue star.

Edison looked toward their Victorian house a few yards away. The white door was thrown open onto the newly swept porch. Maeve Wadsworth, his eccentric garden designer, had ordered her crew to pressure wash the yellow boards and red and white gingerbread before starting on the garden. The house sparkled. It probably hadn't been this clean in a century.

Like every day, he felt grateful to the gifted engineer who'd designed the city's underground train system and built this house deep beneath his greatest creation, Grand Central Terminal. Without it, Joe would have been stranded in the modern glass and steel Hyatt where he'd been staying when the agoraphobia struck. Instead, he had a home of his own.

Still tense from work, he rolled his shoulders to relax them. He'd pulled back from Pellucid, the facial recognition software company that had made him his fortune. He only did occasional consulting work for them now, which enabled him to maintain access to their databases without raising suspicion. He didn't miss running Pellucid.

Lucid was his new baby. It was his brain-mapping company. The human brain was already mapped on a large scale, but he intended to penetrate its secrets at a neuronal level. Like his almost-ancestor Nikola Tesla, Joe was convinced the answers to the brain lay in electricity. Not the dramatic electricity that powered Nikola's legendary devices, but in the tiny blasts of electricity that pulsed through the nervous system at the speed of thought.

He measured that electricity using electrodes that recorded the voltage fluctuations in neurons. The tests were called EEGs, and he intended to build up the largest database of EEGs in the world. Once he had enough data, he intended to apply his pattern-matching abilities, the ones that had made Pellucid the most successful company in its field, to map the brain's activities.

With a lot of luck, he might be able to figure out what exactly had gone haywire in his own brain and be able to walk on real grass again. He'd not only cure himself, he'd be able to help millions who suffered from agoraphobia and other anxiety disorders. Or at least that was his goal.

Joe pulled dinner out of his takeaway bag—Greek salad. Edison sniffed the air and gave Joe a painfully embarrassed look. The dog had a deep mistrust of salad.

Edison licked his hand apologetically, then trotted over to the porch, scooted up the stairs and disappeared through the open door. He'd had a long day at Joe's office. He'd earned some decent kibble.

"Abandoning me to salad?" Joe called after him. "The shame of it!"

He laid his meal out on a blanket he'd spread over the boards: salad, beer, and a hunk of bread. This represented his first picnic in the tunnel. Then he phoned the person he most wanted to share it with.

"Celeste," said a breathy voice on the phone. Her picture, taken years before when they'd been lovers in college, smiled from his screen. When they talked, she could see his face in real time, but he could never see hers. She wouldn't allow it. Not anymore.

"Joe here. I'm in my garden!" He moved the phone's camera across the plants. "Welcome to my picnic."

"Mm-hmm."

He let out a contented sigh. "One small step for a Joe, one giant leap for Joe-kind."

Celeste made a breathy exhalation that might have been a laugh.

He wished she could be here to see it, or that he could see the view from her window, but his agoraphobia kept him a prisoner down here just as much as her ALS kept her a prisoner in her expensive penthouse hundreds of feet above the city.

"The LEDs." He pointed the phone at a bank of lights. "They're on a twelve-hour timer to make sure the plants get enough light, and they're motion sensitive. Whenever I come outside, they retract against the walls so I can see the whole lawn. Maeve thought of everything." Maeve was a genius—she had an incredible visual sense, was good with plants, and had designed and built the light setup herself. Truly a steampunk-esque Renaissance woman.

"It looks like it ought to be on a moon base," Celeste said.

Trying to ignore her tone, he kept talking. "It actually ought to be on a pot farm."

"Are you growing something useful, then?"

"This is useful." His buoyant mood settled. "I just meant that indoor gardening is mostly the province of me and a bunch of guys growing marijuana in a closet."

"A select bunch. Your mother would be proud."

She was clearly grouchy about something.

"Did you get my present?"

"It came in with the tide this morning. Like garbage being washed ashore."

Garbage. "You didn't like it?"

"It was a" —she coughed— "wheelchair."

"A state-of-the-art wheelchair. Did you put on the hat and test out the wireless EEG system? You can control it using your thoughts. You need to set up images in your head for directions, like raspberry for right or lemon for left."

"It's a gift you send a cripple, not your girlfriend."

"I didn't mean it like that."

She sighed. She had so little breath it barely sounded like a sigh, but he recognized it anyway. He'd hoped to make her time in the wheelchair easier, but he shouldn't have reminded her that he knew she was stuck in a wheelchair in the first place.

Slowly, he panned the camera across the whitewashed walls and up to the painted ceiling. The ceiling glowed a soft blue, like the real sky. Painted clouds adorned its surface. If he squinted, he could believe he was outside, but without the panic attack that going outside would bring on.

"Is that a seagull?" she asked.

"I put it up there for you." Gulls were her favorite bird, and he'd insisted the artist paint a faraway gull flying close to the artificial sun. Its gray and white wings were angled in eternal flight.

"I like it," she said.

Joe gazed up at the bird, making sure the angle of the phone let her see the same thing. He took another long breath of green-scented air and felt himself relaxing. The phone was a warm rectangle in his hand.

"Tell me about the lighting." She was trying to act interested.

His good mood returned. He could make do with this. "We installed lights behind the painted clouds, and they dim or brighten depending on the weather outside. At twilight, pink and orange lights come on so the ceiling looks like a sunset. Then, at night, the lights dim down, and the paint darkens."

"Really darkens?" Celeste was a former artist, so she was skeptical.

"Yup." He waited for her to figure it out.

She did, of course. "You used thermochromic paint? Like a mood ring?"

"Exactly—it's blue when the lights are high and indigo when they're low. It gives me night and day like everyone else."

"You're a very talented and artistic nerd." He was grateful to hear a smile in her voice.

"Maeve did the real work." She usually worked designing stage sets and museum exhibits, but he'd lured her away to transform the tunnel in front of his house. He had the money to tempt her, and so few other things he could spend it on. Not cars, travel, or partying. He was the most boring rich guy he knew.

"Yes, Maeve." Celeste had recommended her. They'd gone to art school together and stayed friends after. "Lucky Maeve."

The bitterness in her voice was unmistakable. Was she jealous? Maeve was enigmatic and beautiful, but his heart belonged to Celeste. After all this time, she should know that.

"How are you feeling today?" Joe turned the phone around so she could see his face, even if he couldn't see hers. He wanted her to see his concern.

She let out a rattling breath, and he wondered what number she'd say. She rated her days numerically. Low numbers were bad, high ones good.

"Three," she said.

The color for three, red, shone in his head. Three was always red. "Three. Red like love. Red like lipstick."

"Lipstick comes in lots of colors—pinks, oranges, whites."

"Sunset colors," he said. "But I saw some red lipsticks today, when—"

"Out there flirting?"

"Edison dug up some tubes of lipstick in the tunnel. Plus a purse."

"Were you by Herald Square?"

"Under Macys?" He smiled. "Nope. Anyway, it's no big deal. Tell me more about your three. That's not a good number." She didn't sound especially ill. She hadn't struggled for breath during the call. Something else must be wrong.

"It's October," she said. "And, well…"

Her voice trailed off, and Joe remembered what it was about October. Celeste's overbearing and abusive mother had died years before, in October. They hadn't been close, and Celeste had once told him that she and her brother Leandro had a drunken party after the wake, dumping their mother's ashes down a sewer grate. She had died before Joe met Celeste, and he'd never even seen a picture of her. It was as if Celeste and Leandro had been raised as orphans.

"Your mother's death?" he guessed.

"Or mine," she answered.

"What?" His stomach clenched. "What's happened?"

"Six months ago, they gave me six months to live."

Six (orange) months. She'd been living with a six (orange)-month death sentence for half a year, and she'd never told him.

"Stephen Hawking has lived with ALS for over fifty years," he said. Fifty (brown, black), a nice, reassuring number.

Celeste sighed into the phone. "I don't want to die the same month as her. It's bad enough that I look like her, that I have her DNA in my body."

Dread settled in his stomach. He'd been hoping all these months that she had the Stephen Hawking version of ALS, and that she'd be around for a good long time yet. She'd never told him the specifics, and he'd never asked. "Are you that sick right now?"

"Nobody knows," she said. "Nobody fucking knows anything."

"When is Leandro coming over next?" He would know what to do with her. The twins had always been so close that Joe felt left out, but he was grateful she had someone who loved her in her everyday life, even if it wasn't him.

"He leaves tomorrow to go to Key West for Fantasy Fest."

Typical Leandro. Selfish enough to go on a drunken binge and abandon her when she might die at any moment. "But—"

As if she heard his thoughts, she broke in to defend her brother. "It's just for the weekend, and he needs time away from the stress of his crippled sister. He *should* go."

"Fantasy Fest?" Joe backed off. He imagined a festival dedicated to fantasy literature and tried to make her laugh. It was all he could think to do. "People dressed like hobbits?"

"It's a big party, like Mardi Gras."

"Topless hobbits?"

"Maybe," she said heavily.

The thought of topless hobbits hadn't made her laugh. "I could come over there for the weekend and keep you company while Leandro is gone."

He was a poor substitute for her brother, but he had to be better than no one at all. Probably sensing how the conversation was going, Edison poked his head out the front door and looked over at Joe.

"You?" She laughed, but it wasn't a happy sound. "You haven't been outside in months."

"When they took me to the hospital. I was outside then." He shivered at the memory, and Edison walked across the planks to sit next to him.

"You were unconscious. Doesn't count."

"I could get a knockout drug. Vivian could drag me across town. In an hour I could be drooling on your carpet."

She fell silent for so long he worried she'd fallen asleep. Edison cuddled up to him and rested his head on Joe's arm. The dog always knew when Joe needed reassurance. Joe petted his square head, and Edison thumped his tail against the ground in thanks. He and Joe had an uncomplicated relationship.

"I don't want you to come," Celeste said.

"It's not that risky. I could hire a doctor." The thought terrified him. Him, outside and helpless under the sun. His heart raced, and Edison licked his bare arm.

"I wasn't thinking of you," she said. "I was thinking of me."

"But you just have to receive me, like a queen on a throne. We could keep the visit short. I wouldn't want to overtire you."

"I don't want you to come," she repeated.

Edison nudged the phone with his nose. The dog knew the call was upsetting him. Joe lifted up the phone and motioned for the dog to sit back. "Thanks, Celeste."

"I don't want you to see me." She coughed for a long spell, and he waited her out. "Like this."

"You're beautiful." He'd fallen in love with her the moment he saw her, before he'd even known the wonderful, complex mind behind her gorgeous face.

"I look like Stephen Hawking."

"I'm a nerd," he said. "I think Stephen Hawking is kind of hot."

Even that line didn't get a laugh.

"I used to be hot, but I'm not anymore," she said.

Edison licked his cheek and nuzzled his shoulder. Joe took a couple of deep breaths. He focused on the warm dog leaning against him and the sound of water trickling down the wall. Celeste needed him to stay calm. It wasn't about his hurt feelings. She was dying, and he needed to be there for her, however she wanted.

Still, he tried again. "I don't want to remember you from five years ago." The color for five appeared—brown. "I want to make new memories with you."

"We do." He strained to hear her words. "Like this. On the phone. We do."

"I want more," he said.

"This is a lot."

"How can you not know that you will always be beautiful to me?"

"If we stay like this."

"My mother used to say that physical appearance is vanity," Joe said. "That the real truth about anyone is never on the surface."

"Your mother always looks like a model."

"That's not my point." A lifelong performer, his mother always looked ready to step onto a stage. "I'm not going to think less of you if I can look you in the eye. If anything, I'll think more of you because that's the real you."

"This is the real me, too." She was quiet for a long time. "Maybe it would be best if we stopped the calls, too."

"But—"

She'd already broken the connection.

He called her back immediately. His call went straight to voicemail. Their first fight since he'd inadvertently moved to New York, but it was a doozy. She still didn't want him to see her, but now, maybe, didn't even want to speak to him again.

Joe stuffed the phone in his pocket and sat up. The magic of the garden was gone. He was just a guy sitting in a tunnel. Celeste, the woman he'd always known was his one true love, was worried about dying sometime in the next month, and she wouldn't let him go to her, hold her, and comfort her.

Edison climbed into his lap like a giant housecat and leaned against Joe's chest. Joe wrapped his arms around the dog and rested his chin on top of Edison's head. Together, they stared up at the seagull.

For the first time, Joe noticed the bird wasn't flying toward him. It was flying away.

5

Vivian waited to talk to Mr. Kazakov. She had to check out with him personally every time she went home for the day. A pain in her ass since he was always busy, but it meant he knew exactly who was supposed to be protecting him and his family at any given time. Not a sloppy man, Mr. Kazakov. She respected that.

She'd been told to wait in the library and make herself comfortable, so she stood next to a massive white fireplace that looked like it was cleaned daily with a toothbrush. She certainly wouldn't sit down without being invited. Even if she didn't have eyes on Katrinka, she was on duty.

A carved chess set rested on a small table. A game was in progress, but Vivian didn't know enough about chess to know if black or white was winning.

Tall bookshelves reached up to twelve-foot ceilings. Leather-bound books filled each shelf. Some people bought books by the foot to color coordinate them with their furniture. Was Mr. Kazakov one of those?

She walked over to check out the titles. All in Russian. Her respect for her employer kicked up a notch. Maybe he hadn't read these books, but he'd bought them in Russian and probably shipped them here at great expense so he might read them. They weren't just furniture.

Katrinka wandered in and flopped into a white leather chair. She kicked her sock-clad feet against the dark wooden floor. "Why are you still here?"

"I'm waiting to check out with your father. You know the procedure."

Katrinka snorted and looked at the flames. "Are you going to tell him about the purse?"

"He's my employer." In truth, Vivian wasn't sure what she'd do. Katrinka hadn't broken the law, and maybe she hadn't even intended to. She might have returned the purse herself. And monkeys might fly.

Vivian's phone buzzed. Joe Tesla. Hopefully, he had some work that was more interesting than babysitting.

"Is that your boyfriend?" Katrinka grinned.

"Another employer." Vivian took the call, ready to disconnect if Mr. Kazakov arrived.

"Tesla here," he said. "Do you have a minute?"

"I might have to hang up on short notice."

"Fine." He'd called her using Facetime, and he looked off camera at something else.

"Are you in immediate danger?" she asked.

He gave a forced laugh. "No, nothing like that."

Katrinka came and stood behind her. "He looks cute. Like a vampire."

"Who's that?" Tesla asked.

"Katrinka," the teen said. "Vivian works for me."

"I work for her father," Vivian corrected. "And you were saying, Mr. Tesla?"

"Edison dug up some interesting artifacts in the tunnels. It's been bothering me all day." Clearly Tesla didn't want to get involved in her arguments with Katrinka. "Let me show you."

The camera dipped and came to rest on a black tube resting on a green surface. He must be in his billiards room. The camera moved across three identical tubes and settled on a gray clutch.

"Lipsticks and a purse?" Had Tesla lost it? "I see them, sir."

"Can you get closer to the clutch?" Katrinka leaned against Vivian, her head practically obscuring Vivian's view.

"The what?" Tesla sounded puzzled.

"The bag," Katrinka said. "Pan across it slowly."

Tesla did as he was told.

"That's Prada!" Katrinka said. "Can I have it if you don't want it?"

"Why are you showing me these items?" Vivian took control of the conversation.

"Edison found them buried in a locked room a couple of miles south of the house."

"Probably rats," Vivian said. "Rats bury all kinds of things."

"It's a pretty big purse—"

"Clutch," Katrinka corrected.

"Clutch," Tesla said. "It's a pretty big object for a rat to drag all the way down there and bury."

"You have pretty big rats," Vivian answered.

"Can you find out who this stuff might have belonged to?" Tesla asked. "Maybe get some fingerprints off them?"

After they were buried by a rat, dug out by a drooling dog, then handled by Tesla. "I can try."

"You can look up the serial numbers on the bag," Katrinka said. "And then, if you don't want it, you can give it to me."

"You want a bag that was dragged through filthy tunnels by a rat?" Vivian asked.

"It's a fifty thousand dollar clutch." Katrinka tossed her hair behind her shoulder. "I'll get it cleaned."

The camera dropped a bit as if Tesla, too, thought this an unfathomable amount of money to spend on a bag. Vivian's sister could go to college for the price of a scrap of leather that had dangled from a rich girl's wrist.

"Tell me more about the serial numbers," Tesla said.

Katrinka tapped the image on the phone. "Prada puts them in their most expensive bags. And that one looks like a custom bag. Did you see the diamonds along the top?"

Vivian ran her finger across the image of a row of dirt-covered stones. "Those are diamonds?"

"Diamonds and white gold," Katrinka said. "It's a specialty bag. They probably didn't make many of them."

"I'll be by to pick it up as soon as I'm done here, sir," Vivian said.

"Thank you," Tesla answered. "Before I go, when are you going to stop by Lucid to get scanned?"

Vivian stifled a groan. Tesla had been nagging her to get some kind of weird brain scan at his new company. He wanted to use her reactions to provide a control group for soldiers with PTSD. It was a worthy cause, and she'd agreed, but she kept putting it off. "Soon, sir."

"We have an opening on Friday afternoon at four."

"I'll see if I can fit that in." She ended the call.

"Scanned for what?" Katrinka asked.

"Brain scan to see how I react to certain situations. It's a virtual reality simulation thing."

"Is it fun? Can I get scanned, too?"

"Maybe. First, tell me about this bag and why you think it has a serial number."

Katrinka launched into an enthusiastic explanation of how the designer printed its bags with special serial numbers because theft and counterfeiting were common. "If you know what you're looking for, you can break into the right apartment and come out with a hundred grand in bags that'll fit in a backpack."

"And you know this how?" Vivian asked.

"It's happened to my friend's mom," she said. "That's why I'm so careful with my stuff. A bag like that is an investment."

"How do I find out who bought this particular bag?"

"If it was reported stolen, the police probably have the numbers in the police report. Or the owner might have written the numbers down for her insurance company."

"People insure purses?"

"Wouldn't you? Look how much they're worth. Anyway, even if you can't find it like that, Prada has a record. That's a special bag, not one you could buy off the shelf. I bet that cute cop friend of yours can call up Prada and get an answer for you. What's his name?"

"Mr. Norbye?" Dirk worked for Mr. Kazakov in his off hours. A former Army buddy, he'd gotten Vivian this job. Some days she didn't want to thank him for it.

Katrinka laughed. "Dirk Norbye! That's right. The blond god."

Vivian had to smile. "Don't tell him that. He's already got too fine an opinion of himself."

"Are you two together?"

"No."

"Why not?"

No point in lying. "I was engaged to his brother, Nils."

"Was?" Katrinka arched her eyebrows. "That's not the same as *is*, so that doesn't make this particular blond god off limits."

"His brother died." In her arms. Screaming.

Katrinka must have read something in her face because she looked away and went quiet.

A figure appeared in the doorway, and Vivian instinctively stepped in front of the girl.

"It is only I." Mr. Kazakov came into the room and took the seat next to his daughter. "Katrinka. Go."

The teen stood quickly, kissed her father on both cheeks, and headed toward the door. She brushed past Vivian on her way out, tossing her a pleading glance. She didn't want Vivian to mention the attempted shoplifting.

"Katrinka likes you," Mr. Kazakov said. "You were having a spirited discussion when I arrived."

"She's a smart girl."

"Too smart for her own good sometimes."

"Probably an inherited trait, sir." It slipped out before Vivian had a chance to think better of it.

He laughed. "I hope you can keep her in check."

Nobody could keep that girl in check. She needed something to do besides hang around with her shallow, rich friends and talk about purses. A stint in the military would straighten her right out. Vivian knew better than to say any of that. "I do my best to keep her safe, sir."

"And that, as you point out so cleverly, is your job. You may go."

Vivian scooted out of there before he started asking about what Katrinka had got up to that day.

Katrinka waited in the hall by the elevator. "Thank you."

"You used your get out of jail free card," Vivian said. "No more chances."

Katrinka nodded. "Will you tell me what happens with the clutch?"

"Probably somebody mugged the woman who carried it, took out the money, and threw the purse down a tunnel where a rat found it. Most muggers don't have your encyclopedic knowledge of purse pricing."

"It might be more interesting than that," Katrinka said. "But either way, will you tell me if you find out more?"

"So long as it isn't confidential."

Katrinka smiled. Not the manufactured smile Vivian had seen in the store, a genuine one that made her look like a little kid again. "Thanks."

"It's probably nothing," Vivian warned. But she was starting to think Katrinka might be right.

The bag might prove very interesting indeed.

6

Joe hurried through the concourse at Grand Central Terminal with Edison by his side. People eddied and swirled around them, caught in their own currents. They rushed off trains, across platforms, and emptied out through the concourse's vast doors. At this time of day, they were on their way to work. Later, they'd wash back through the terminal onto trains that brought them home.

These days, he had his own regular destination, too. Every morning he went into work at Lucid, and every evening he went home—without ever going outside. Usually, he was thrilled to go to work, but today, his steps faltered. Stalling, he stopped by Starbucks and ordered two (blue) coffees.

Lucid's headquarters weren't far, since the offices were inside Grand Central Terminal. After a bit of convincing, he'd managed to rent a retail space and convert it from a drug store into every geek's dream workspace—a cool lobby, two offices, a few cubicles, a room with an MRI machine, and the best game room ever.

His palms were slippery with sweat when he reached the glass doors. Edison nudged his palm reassuringly. Joe stroked the dog's head and fondled his silky ears. "We'll get through it."

Edison looked forward at the office doors. Joe put one hand next to the word LUCID and pushed open the door.

An anatomically correct glass brain about the size of a sofa sat in the center of the waiting room. Fiber optics ran through the inside of the glass like axons through a flesh-and-blood brain. The optic lines pulsed blues, greens, reds, and yellows, showing electronic responses that matched a real human brain, one taken from scans in the database. Joe could sit and watch the sculpture for hours, wondering what thoughts were laid bare in front of him. What would his own thoughts look like? He was about to find out.

"Good morning, Joe," said Marnie Kay. She was his administrative assistant, come all the way from California to help him start his latest venture. Unflappable, and used to working crushing hours, she was an undeniable asset. To bring her on board, he'd given her better stock options than she could get anywhere else.

He handed her one of the coffees he'd picked up in the terminal. The boss wasn't supposed to get the coffee, but he liked keeping their dynamic informal.

Marnie nodded her thanks. "Frank called in sick. A backup MRI technician is coming in at nine thirty. Your scan can proceed at ten."

Joe's stomach clenched. He wasn't worried about the MRI. He'd had a few and knew what to expect. He'd be lying on his back in a white tube while it sounded like someone was pounding on a metal drum by his head, like a bunch of angry dwarves trying to break in with hammers. He could handle angry dwarves.

"Before you start nagging me, I had my brain scanned and had an EEG done for every scenario on the list last night," Marnie said.

"Do I nag you?"

"Let's just say that if my daughter could nag like you, she'd have a pony."

"I really appreciate you taking the time—"

"You already got your pony. Go find your next victim."

Joe let her get back to work and walked over to the game room. The room was painted forest-green and kept dark to help the subject become fully immersed in the virtual world. The only thing illuminated was a giant screen. A transparent brain, much like the brain in the lobby, rotated slowly onscreen. After his MRI was complete, a see-through version of his own brain would be displayed there at ten (cyan, black) times its actual size. He could project Marnie's up there now if he wanted to.

Instead, he touched the neoprene cap he'd soon be placing on his head. Inset with electrodes, the cap would record his EEG and transmit it to a powerful computer in the corner of the room. As soon as it received the data, the computer would project his brain's electrical activity onto his transparent brain. He called it "the lucid brain" because the model illuminated a subject's brain activity. A short time lag existed between when the EEG registered electrical activity and when it displayed the activity on the giant screen along the wall, but it was the closest man had ever gotten to electronically reading someone else's mind in real time.

Marnie had been scanned as part of the control group—a person without anxiety disorders or PTSD. Joe was part of the experimental group, and soon he'd be subjected to his worst fear—going outside. His brain's reactions to that experience would be stored for study. He would be completely terrified in front of his colleagues, and the moment would be preserved for eternity. His respect for the other study subjects grew. They had to undergo the same scary process since Lucid's initial EEGs would be performed on people with anxiety disorders. He and his team had designed scenarios to simulate post-traumatic stress events in soldiers or survivors of 9/11 (scarlet, slash, cyan, cyan) or moments of extreme anxiety for those with agoraphobia.

He had some time to kill before his scan, and he decided to spend it playing some of the coolest and most immersive video games on the planet. He had the toys right here—a souped-up version of Oculus Rift, a state-of-the-art sound system, and an array of games made just for fun.

He stepped onto the gaming mat, put on his virtual reality helmet, and started to play. He heard Edison lie down in a corner of the room, and he knew the dog's brown eyes were watching his every movement. Edison never stopped looking out for him.

By the time Marnie came to get Joe for his MRI, he was pretty calm, and he stayed calm through that long and uncomfortable procedure. He used the time to work on his strategy for attracting investors to Lucid.

The second he stepped back into the game room, his heart rate went up. The sight of the virtual reality helmet that he'd enjoyed wearing earlier filled him with dread. He wiped his palms on his pants.

"Ready for this?" asked Dr. Gemma Plantec in her clipped British accent. She was probably the best neurobiologist in the world.

He remembered her job interview. He'd spent a little time going over her qualifications, making sure she knew everything her curriculum vitae said she did. She answered his questions easily and with a sly British wit. He'd liked her from the start.

At the end, when he'd asked her what questions she had for him, she'd said, "You've seen my credentials, so you know I'm brilliant. You also know that I'm black and a woman. I want the same opportunities and working conditions as a white male. If I can't get those, let's stop this right now."

He'd been a little taken aback, but he'd seen enough sexism and racism in the tech world to understand where she was coming from. He'd promised her she'd get the same deal as anyone else in that position, and she'd accepted his offer.

Since then, they'd fallen into a tough, no-nonsense working relationship. She was the last woman in the world he wanted to witness his weakness and terror.

She was short, just over five (brown) foot tall, and he bent down so she could get the EEG cap on his head. "I understand this will be traumatic for you."

"That's the whole point, Dr. Plantec," he said.

She adjusted the electrodes. "And here I thought our work had a wider scope than torturing you."

"Not just me," he said. "We'll be torturing lots of other people, too."

"So, I've signed on for science's Guantanamo Bay?" She didn't give Joe time to answer. "Whenever you're ready."

Before he had time to think about it, Joe pulled down the virtual reality helmet. Edison sensed his mood and came over to stand next to him.

"Will the dog skew the results?" Dr. Plantec asked.

"The dog stays." Joe's tone brooked no argument.

He actually heard her teeth click together when she shut her mouth. "I'll start the simulation, Dr. Tesla."

He wondered if she was reminding him that he had a PhD so he'd feel better about himself when he freaked out. "I'm not a medical doctor."

"It still counts," she said.

Bright images appeared in the virtual world around him. He walked down a virtual corridor. The floor was golden oak, the walls painted a soft yellow. To most people, this was bright and soothing. Ahead of him, virtual sunlight spilled through an open door, forming a warm square on the wooden floor.

His stomach tightened at the sunlight, but he moved toward the door. He wanted to remind himself that it wasn't real, but the point of this exercise was to believe it was. Edison's nose bumped Joe's knee.

He didn't slow his virtual steps, walking until he was right next to the door. His heart pounded, and his breath came fast and shallow. He tried not to think of Dr. Plantec watching him. His father had once said that you could look good, or you could learn something, but you couldn't do both at the same time. The time had come for Joe to learn something.

He had to force himself to open his eyes. Waves tumbled over each other and flattened against a sandy beach. Bright sunlight reflected off the water. A lovely day at the seashore. To anyone else, this would have been a scene of great tranquility.

His legs started to tremble, and he tensed. He wouldn't let himself run away from the simulation. He had to stay as long as he could. Every second's data was precious.

Edison bumped his leg harder. The dog whined, and Joe turned away from the ocean view to look down the empty corridor.

"I can take the dog out," Dr. Plantec said.

"He... stays." Joe forced out the words.

"Then Edison's not going anywhere," said Dr. Plantec. Her voice was probably supposed to be soothing. It wasn't soothing enough.

Sweat ran down Joe's forehead and dripped into his eyes. His T-shirt was drenched, too. His whole body wanted him to rip the helmet off and run away.

But he didn't. He counted to ten, each number flashing in his head. One was cyan; two, blue; three, red; four, green; five, brown; six, orange; seven, slate; eight, purple; nine, scarlet; and ten, cyan and black. He used his hard-won breathing techniques, trying to get his heart under control.

Edison fastened his teeth around Joe's jeans and tugged. The dog didn't know where to pull him because he couldn't see the simulation, but he knew something was wrong. He whimpered.

Slowly, Joe reached up and took the cap off his head. His hands shook so hard he dropped it. Dr. Plantec picked it up and put in on the desk.

"I think that's enough for today," she said. "We definitely captured a lot of activity."

Joe forced himself to nod politely. "Excuse me."

He fled the room with Edison. It had been worse than he'd expected. He'd only lasted fifteen (cyan, brown) seconds. At least he hadn't fainted or thrown up. Celebrate the little victories.

When he barged into the lobby, Marnie jumped.

"Is everything all right?" she asked.

Joe dredged up the best approximation of a reassuring smile he could muster. Judging by the expression on her face, it wasn't convincing. He took a deep breath and petted Edison's head, his hand lingering on the dog's velvety ears.

Marnie held a black tube in her hand. She'd been behind her desk, touching up her lipstick. The tube reminded him of the ones he'd handed off to Vivian the day before. "What kind of lipstick is that?"

Marnie's eyebrows rose. "Christian Dior 999."

The colors strobed in his head (scarlet, scarlet, scarlet—very apt for red lipstick). "Is it easy to come by?"

"Pretty much," she said. "Though it's fairly expensive."

"How much does it cost?"

"Around fifty dollars a tube," she said. "If you're birthday shopping."

Joe stared at the black tube in her hand, thinking of the ones Edison had found. A woman would be careful with lipstick that cost fifty dollars (brown, black).

"Dr. Tesla?" she asked.

"I'm going to my office for a minute." He had to change his shirt. It was soaked with sweat. But he wasn't frightened anymore. He was thinking about the lipstick.

7

Vivian petted the warm nose of a draft horse named Hercules. The horse and carriage were waiting at the Fifth Avenue entrance to Central Park for tourists who would pay for a ride through its leafy precincts. If she'd had the money, she'd have done it herself.

It was a fantastic day—blue sky, bright sun, the bite of autumn in the air, and the leaves had started to turn yellow and orange. Fall was her favorite time of year, and New York was her favorite place to be.

She nodded to Mac, the carriage driver. He'd retired from the post office about ten years before and turned to driving carriages so he could stay outside all day. She'd seen him about once a week since she got kicked out of the Army and moved home.

"May I give Hercules a carrot?" she asked.

"Like I could stop you, girlie."

The horse grabbed the proffered carrot with his warm lips and tucked it into his mouth. The carrot crunched as he chewed. Vivian stroked the horse's neck, then checked her phone.

"Off for a run?" Mac asked.

"Almost late, too." She tossed him a wave and jogged north into the park. She'd be at the reservoir in five minutes or so. Sun warmed her shoulders, cool wind fresh against her cheeks. She could run all day in these conditions.

A man in blue sweatpants and a gray hoodie caught up to her. Dirk. They jogged along together.

"You're the last jogger under fifty who wears sweatpants." She tapped her sleek, black leg. "It's all about spandex."

"I couldn't fight off the women if I wore spandex on these fine legs," he said. "I'm wearing this for your protection."

"Always the altruist." She grinned. "And always deluded."

Dirk was actually a pretty good-looking guy—light-blond hair, blue eyes, and a chiseled chin. And he would look fine in spandex, but she'd never let him know that. He was unbearable enough already.

"Denial," he said. "Want to bet I can beat you in the first loop?"

"How about an easy loop to warm up?" she asked. One loop around Jacqueline Kennedy Onassis Reservoir was a little over a mile and a half. "I want to talk."

She and Dirk settled into an easy rhythm. They'd been running together since their Army days. They'd probably logged a thousand miles in Afghanistan and New York. She preferred running next to the calm blue lake here than out in the hot deserts where she had to worry that the ground might explode, or a sniper might drop her.

"Mr. Kazakov likes you," Dirk said. "Says you're steady."

Light glinted off the blue surface of the pond. "Katrinka says you're a blond god."

"Smart kid."

"Maybe Hephaestus." He was the ugly god. She wondered if Dirk knew that.

"A god's a god," he said. "Immortal and badass."

"Remember that purse I told you about?"

"Prada. Expensive. Dug up by a dog."

Dirk sounded out of breath. She slowed. "Not just expensive, really expensive, even for Prada. That arm ornament could put Lucy through college."

"She still waiting to hear about her student loans?"

Vivian didn't want to get into that. "I called Prada and found out who bought the bag."

"Yeah?"

"An investment banker named Sandra Haines." She wondered if Sandra had run this very path. Lots of people did.

"Bet she was glad to hear from you."

"She might have been." Vivian skirted an uneven patch in the trail. "Except she's dead."

She practically saw his ears prick up. Dirk was a cop, and he had cop instincts. "Natural causes?"

"Not unless you count being hit by a train as natural."

"Can be," he said. "Depending on the circumstances."

"About a year ago, she allegedly jumped in front of a subway train." Vivian looked out across the shining water at the sky and the gray trees dazzling in their autumn finery. So sad to think of people throwing away any chance to be part of the good things in life. A tragedy to instead choose to die alone underground. She sighed at the thought that Tesla was making that choice every day.

"Guess Prada bags don't buy happiness," Dirk said.

"I dug a little deeper—"

"Course you did." He kicked his running up a notch, as if he wanted to run away from her findings.

"A lot of folks jump in front of trains in New York. About one a week."

He whistled. "That many?"

"New York's a big place. Lots of sad people and trains." The leaves floating on the water looked like tiny gold boats.

"Why do I think you didn't invite me out here to talk about what a big, sad place New York is?" he asked.

"How'd her purse get buried in a tunnel over two miles from where she was hit?"

"Rats? Cats? Crazy homeless trannies?"

"Maybe," she said. "Maybe not."

They finished the rest of the lap in silence. Both sped up at the end because they were too competitive not to. Dirk won by half a length and settled back into a comfortable jog for the second lap.

He flashed a victor's grin. "You're losing your touch, Viv."

"Distracted," she said.

"Sure," he said. "Sun was in your eyes. Perfectly understandable."

She punched him in the shoulder. "If it were just this purse, maybe I'd buy your theory, but the lipsticks, too?"

Dirk's blue eyes looked thoughtful. He had a damn adorable thoughtful look. Part of his blond god persona. It kept his private life too complicated for Vivian to follow. "Rats collect things. So do people. Maybe someone or something liked the smell."

"The items were behind a locked door." Of course, if Tesla had a key, who knew who else did.

"A locked door might deter your average homeless person, but rats can find a way into just about any place. Like your toilet."

"I'm trying to pretend that rats in the toilet is an urban legend," she said. "But you're right. The purse and lipsticks are probably nothing."

Dirk laughed. "Yeah. You let me win the first lap for nothing."

"You won fair and square," she said.

"Like I didn't notice your fake zombie-girl stumble at the end?"

Vivian laughed. She hadn't stumbled on purpose, at least not consciously, but maybe he was on to something. "I'm going to look into it more. If it turns into something, be ready for me to dump it in your lap."

"Don't be surprised if you don't find anything but a sad jumper," he said. "Sometimes, we're our own worst enemies."

Vivian had found pictures of Sandra Haines online. She hadn't looked sad. She'd looked young, rich, pretty, and blond. A lot like Katrinka actually. What did someone like that have to worry about? Plenty, she guessed. Dirk was right. Prada bags really didn't buy happiness.

Dirk kicked into higher gear and started a flat-out run. Vivian stopped worrying and took off after him. The second lap went a lot faster than the first and, at the end, she didn't stumble.

8

Ziggy finished his quick circuit of the office and returned to his desk. Everyone was out to lunch. He had the place to himself.

He settled in his chair and placed both palms flat against the top of his antique desk. He'd paid a fortune for it during the recent move, but it was worth it for times like these. He giggled in anticipation, then pressed an unassuming rosette on the left side of the desk, above the drawers.

With a small click, the rosette swung open like a tiny door to reveal a hidden compartment. This wasn't the only secret hidden away in this antique desk, but it was his favorite. He took a long, trembling breath to draw out the moment.

Then he slipped his index and middle fingers inside the tiny slot. It was a little compartment, barely large enough to hold a pen or a single well-folded document. Or a tube of lipstick.

His questing fingers found the object and stroked it in the dark. He pulled it out into the light, cradling the slick tube in his palms. He imagined he could smell the red lipstick, but he knew he couldn't, not until he opened it. The cool, black surface warmed in his palm as he held it, and he savored its slight weight.

She'd held it. She'd stroked it against her lips for the last time when they were alone together in the tunnel. Her full lips had gleamed with a velvety sheen.

Fingers trembling with excitement, he drew off the slick top. Sunlight winked against the silver shaft that encased the precious red lipstick. The light dazzled his eyes.

With excruciating slowness, he turned the bottom until brilliant red lipstick crested the silver tube. The distinctive smell of 999 exploded into the air. He drew the scent deep inside himself, letting it pull him back to her last luscious moments.

Delicate hands cupping her elbows, she'd stood in front of him as balanced as a dancer. The silver dress skimmed her shivering form. The headlights of the oncoming train shone on her slender body like a spotlight. She was a star, but she performed only for him.

Her giant, dark eyes looked helplessly into his. Even now he couldn't see their color. Blue? Brown? It didn't matter. They were black pools of despair. She stood motionless in the light. She didn't shy from her fate. She almost begged for it.

He'd done that. He'd made her yearn for the train to end her misery. He'd brought her to the explosive release she needed. He had freed her.

He breathed harder. The sound reminded him of the sighing wheeze of the train's door, the last moment he'd be alone with her before the driver came out, before the passengers would know what had happened. It was the last moment of their shared secret before she would be swept away from the world, and he'd be left alone with his bliss.

A faint vibration trilled up through the soles of his shoes and yanked him back into the sunlit office. Someone was in the building. Someone was walking toward him. His eyes snapped open.

He capped the lipstick, almost dropping it on the carpet in his frantic hurry. Somehow, he managed to toss it back into its hidey hole. He barely had time to close the rosette before Miss Evans appeared in the hallway. She knocked on his door.

He tapped the computer mouse with his elbow so the screensaver would disappear.

"I brought you a sandwich," she called.

"Thank you," he said through gritted teeth. Sandra's moment was ruined. He'd have to go back down into the tunnels and get another lipstick.

Miss Evans walked into his office hesitantly, graceful legs stuttering like a fawn's, not sure if the bright world was safe.

She was right to be afraid. He was a wolf, and her world was dangerous. He imagined a wolf tearing out her trembling throat. But the thought cheered him only a little.

"A Reuben, like you asked for." She stopped a few paces from his desk, stretched her graceful arm out as far as she could, and dropped the sandwich on the edge.

With a quick nod, she turned and hurried out of the room as if she were barely holding back her panic. She carried another lunch bag. She had probably intended to eat at her desk, but she didn't even pause, instead rushing straight for the elevator. She was afraid, but she didn't know why. The cold winds of fall had changed him, and she couldn't understand.

He bit savagely into the sandwich, barely tasting the pastrami and sauerkraut of her peace offering. He hadn't wanted the food. He'd wanted the moment. Sandra, staring at him from the tracks, gleaming red lips practically thanking him. Her last words "good-bye." Words now ruined.

He probably had another half hour of alone time, but it didn't matter. He closed his eyes and ran through his catalogue of women. Sandra was useless. But what about Rita? She was the first in the pair, Sandra the second.

Rita had worn a siren red dress and black shoes. Her blond hair was spiked and threaded with orange highlights like a cockatoo. She hadn't been as classy as Sandra, nor as rich, but she'd been at her own crossroads of doubt and despair. And she'd been rich enough to afford Christian Dior lipstick.

He'd go down into the tunnels after work and switch out the lipsticks before bed time. He drummed his fingers on the desk. He could evade any other person in the tunnels. No one knew the twists and turns and hidden rooms better than he. But Tesla had brought a dog down there, and he couldn't hide from the dog. A dog could track him by smell.

Months had passed since he'd let the man and his dog move down below. He could no longer let them get in his way. He took another bite of the sandwich, rolling the meat around on his tongue. He had to take back his tunnels.

Starting tonight. With Rita.

9

Joe stared at his onscreen brain. Colors flashed through the axons so quickly he could barely track them. Watching his recorded fear replayed in slow motion was surprisingly disturbing.

As expected, his amygdala pulsed with activity, shooting out electrical panic to the rest of his brain. The scans from his control group showed that their amygdalas didn't react to the sunny day and the beach that he'd glimpsed through the open door. He'd expected that—the simulation was designed to terrify him, the Joe of today, not the Joe who had gone through life unafraid of the light and beauty of the outside world. This thing that calmed everyone else submerged him in an ocean of fear.

Even on the frightening simulations, where their amygdalas were engaged, the control group fared better than he did. Even though they were initially frightened, the other parts of their brains immediately got busy filtering the signals and calming things down. Within seconds, everyone in the control group seemed to recognize that the stimuli weren't worrisome, shake it off, and move on.

But he had lost his calm switch. His brain panicked at the sight of the bright outside world, and it didn't calm down until he got away from it. His calming breaths didn't stop his amygdala from firing, nor did Edison's soothing presence. Only removing the threat worked.

His own brain overloaded itself and couldn't recover.

Edison snored under his desk, content after a long romp in the park with his dog walker, Andres Peterson. Edison had come back smelling of cold and fall leaves. Joe had untangled an orange leaf from his furry belly and set it on the edge of his desk—a bit of the outside world.

His mailbox dinged, and he switched over to it.

Mr. Tesla,

I'm attaching a picture and short report on the woman who owned that purse you found. According to Prada, her name was Sandra Haines. About a year ago, she died. The police ruled it suicide by train.

I'm not certain that I agree. She was hit at 72nd Street. That's more than two miles from where you found the purse, which is a long way for a rat to carry something that large, although I suppose it's possible. To me, it seems more likely that a person took the purse and buried it in the room where you found it. Also, those three lipsticks concern me—are they all from Sandra Haines or might they belong to other women?

Should I look into this further?

Vivian

Joe opened the first attachment. Sandra Haines had been twenty-six (blue, orange) when she died. She'd worked in the accounting branch of KPMG. No known living relatives. The police had ruled her death an accident or a potential suicide. An autopsy had been performed, although Vivian didn't include it. She did mention that Sandra's blood alcohol level was 0.16 (black, decimal point, cyan, orange), more than twice the legal limit. At that level, she'd have been staggering, but probably still walking, maybe throwing up. But she wouldn't have been completely incapacitated.

Because she'd been found near 72nd (slate, blue) Street, the theory was that she'd stumbled or fallen off the platform and wandered down the tracks until the train hit her. That scenario happened far too often, although usually people were hit trying to get back onto the platform. Most people, even drunk, didn't head off into the dark and threatening tunnels.

The second attachment was a picture. Sandra had delicate features and wide blue eyes. Her hair was butterscotch blond, the same as Celeste's, but her smile looked uncertain, not like the almost manic smile he always associated with Celeste, although he hadn't seen her smile in years. For all he knew, she couldn't smile anymore. The women looked similar enough that it caught at Joe's heart to think of Celeste alone in his tunnels, depressed, perhaps seeking to end her own life as Sandra had.

He called Celeste to tell her he wanted to talk. She didn't answer so he left a message saying that he'd follow her wishes, that he didn't need to see her in person, and that he just needed her. By the time he finished, he felt like a fool, but he didn't delete the message.

Celeste had cause for despair. She'd lost so much—her art, her mobility, and, if she was to be believed, her beauty. He corrected himself. She was still beautiful, no matter what the disease might have done to her, and he wished she could understand that as well as he could.

But he didn't want to fight about it with her. Her life was fading away. If she could go down into the tunnels and jump in front of a train, would she? No, not Celeste. She'd fight till she drew her last shallow breath. He was sure of it.

He had lived through dark times after he was struck by agoraphobia. Since the day he'd expected to come into his millions, the day that Pellucid had gone public, he'd been unable to go outside. From that day on, he'd never felt sun on his skin, never felt clean wind against his cheeks. He'd worked hard and attained an unimaginable level of success, only to find that he was forever trapped inside. But he hadn't given in to self-pity. He hadn't stepped in front of a train. He hadn't grabbed the third rail. He'd kept going, making a life for himself in the place that he'd been given.

What had driven Sandra to make the opposite decision?

He hid his IP address, stepped through a few machines to hide his trail, then logged into Facebook. He kept a fake account there, mostly to download pictures he used for test images for Pellucid's facial recognition software. No point in limiting himself to government databases when Facebook had a far larger array of pictures.

He searched Facebook for a Sandra Haines in New York. Like just about everyone else, she'd had an account. Her timeline was topped by condolences and pictures of flowers. Many people had come to this space in a uniquely modern ritual of public grieving.

He skimmed through their sentiments, but didn't find anything unique. Her friends would miss her smile, her ability to find good shoe sales, and the way she could knock back cosmopolitans. The generic nature of their one-line comments made him feel tired and sad.

No one had a single specific anecdote, a moment that illuminated who she might have been, how she was different from the seven billion (slate and a long row of black) other people on Earth. He wondered if his own Facebook page, had he created a real one, would have been as remote in the event of his death, if anyone really knew anything about him either.

He reined in his self-indulgent gloom and scrolled back to the top of her profile to look at her pictures. She was a beautiful woman who photographed well. Even in candid shots, she stood out. She wore an array of black and silver dresses, and high-heeled shoes. Her carefully made-up face was almost always smiling. She was photographed most often with a pair of women, Iris and Antonia, and a man named Slade.

Iris stood to her left in pictures, an Asian girl with a round face and alert eyes. Iris usually wore red, her dresses often matching Sandra's lipstick. They were photographed in a lot of clubs—people dancing behind them, a bar behind their heads. Iris wasn't in Sandra's league beauty-wise, and she seemed to know it, often turning away from the camera, her face half hidden, her smile uncertain. Antonia was taller than the others, always scrunching down to fit into the shot. She wasn't in the most recent pictures, having moved back to Iowa.

Slade hadn't been on his Facebook account since soon after Sandra's death. It seemed that Iris, in particular, didn't like him. He'd dumped Sandra the morning of the day she died, and Iris had posted vitriolic rants against him on his timeline. He'd never responded, even when Antonia had posted the information about Sandra's funeral. Joe wondered if Slade had attended. Had he written Sandra off completely when he dumped her, or had he blamed himself for her death? It was hard to imagine that he could drop her cold like that, but people were often that cruel.

If Celeste were to die tomorrow, he wouldn't be able to attend her funeral either. He'd have to send Vivian, as he'd sent her to his own father's funeral. If he'd had a Facebook page, would Leandro and Celeste's friends blame him for her death? Would he blame himself? He was useless as a boyfriend. He couldn't even talk to her, let alone hold her and comfort her.

He went back to Sandra's page to see what she liked. Musicians. Films. Books. Nothing unusual. Wait. She'd liked an Urban Beekeeping page. Joe went over to the page and found a picture of her there, wearing a heavy beekeeper's suit, the hood half on. She looked so different she was almost unrecognizable. He'd spotted the wide set eyes, the three (red) faint freckles on her left cheekbone, and the curve of her hairline. She'd been an active member, and the beekeepers had named a memorial hive for her.

He went back to his email and typed out a quick message to Vivian.

Stay on it. See if you can get the police to run more extensive tests on her tissue samples and see if there was anything in her system besides alcohol.

If the cops won't do it, send the lipsticks out to a private DNA lab on my dime, and ask for expedited results. Did all the lipsticks belong to Sandra? If not, then who? If those lipsticks belong to other women, I want to know what happened to them, too. And I want to know why.

He imagined Sandra working during the day, partying at night, and still spending every weekend husbanding bees on rooftops throughout the city. That was the incongruous detail he would have put on her timeline. A woman obsessed with flowers and honey and the furry yellow insects that pollinated most of our foods. She had been vivid and connected to life. A surprising suicide.

10

Vivian glanced up and down Park Avenue. It was busy this time of morning. Yellow taxis and black town cars moved like a seemingly endless conveyor belt to deliver office workers to the towering glass building in front of her.

Tesla had suggested she speak to an Iris Wu, a friend of Sandra Haines. He'd sent her the woman's work phone number. Vivian had tried to find that information on the Internet herself, to see if that was how he did it, but she'd come up empty-handed. He probably had access, legal or illegal, to databases she'd never see.

However he got it, the number worked. Iris Wu had agreed to meet Vivian for fifteen minutes at 10:15 precisely. Vivian guessed that a lot of tasks had been juggled to carve out that much time. Iris Wu, the short phone call told her, was a busy woman.

Vivian gave her name to the round-faced security guard on the ground floor at 10:05, figuring it would take her a good ten minutes to get through the layers of bureaucracy and security surrounding Iris Wu. Turned out Vivian was a good guesser, because at exactly 10:15, she was admitted to a sterile, modern waiting room where she checked in with a receptionist who looked like a model—emaciated and blond, with an asymmetrical haircut that Vivian was still trying to figure out when Iris Wu arrived a few minutes later.

Wu wore a black business suit with a purple silk top that made her look like an expensive plum, but her handshake was as strong as your average Marine's. "I apologize for the delay, Miss Torres."

Vivian didn't need to check the time on her phone to know the woman was less than two minutes late. "I appreciate you taking the time to speak to me, Miss Wu."

Wu swiveled around and marched down a hallway, moving at a pretty good clip for someone her height, in high heels that looked like they cost more than Vivian made in a week. "We can speak in the conference room."

A few seconds later, they were seated across from each other at a wide table made out of a grayish wood. Eight empty chairs ranged around the table waiting for a more important meeting to start. A triangle that was probably a phone sat in the center of the table.

"I understand you were friends with Sandra Haines." Vivian didn't think Wu needed any preliminaries.

Something flickered in Wu's eyes, but it was gone almost instantly. "I was."

"I'm investigating her death—"

"You mean her murder?" Wu said.

Vivian leaned forward. "What makes you think she was murdered?"

"I don't think he pushed her in front of that train, but that bastard Slade is as responsible for her death as if he had."

Legally, not true. Vivian didn't see the point of parsing the distinction with Wu. "Slade?"

"Slade Masterson. Sandra's boyfriend. I guess you'd have to call him her ex-boyfriend since he dumped her the day she died."

"Why?"

"He found someone richer, that's why. Slade was sponging off Sandra, and he found a better source of cash, so he cut her loose." Wu's nostrils flared. "After three years of whatever the hell their relationship was, he sent her a text message saying it was over, he'd changed the locks, and she could get her stuff from the doorman."

That was pretty cold. "How do you know this?"

Wu tugged one purple sleeve, adjusting how much of it peeked out of her suit jacket. "Because she came into the office and told me."

Which fit with Tesla saying they were friends. "What happened after that?"

"We went out. After a couple of clubs, Sandra's goal was to have some fantastic revenge sex and move on. She met some guy and ditched me." Wu's bitter tone was clear.

"Who was the guy?" Seemed like he was a better suspect than Slade.

Wu shrugged. "Some random guy. I think he was blond? Tall. Nice suit. Anyway, the guy she left the club with might not even have been the guy she ended up with. She said she was going hunting and didn't need me around."

More bitterness. Sounded as if Iris wasn't happy to have been left for some cute stranger. Or maybe she felt responsible for leaving her friend alone on the night she died. "Did the guy have a name?"

"Why would he need one?"

"Because he might have been the last person to see your friend alive."

A muscle worked in Wu's jaw. "I thought she jumped in front of the A train at 72nd Street. The train driver said Sandra was alone in the tunnel. So that makes the train driver the last one to see her alive."

"How did you find that out?"

"After I identified Sandra's body." Wu swallowed back tears. She was tough. "I asked."

"I'm sorry you had to see your friend like that."

"What would you know about it?" Wu glared at her.

"I served in Afghanistan and Iraq. I've identified friends' bodies."

"I'm sorry." Wu looked down at the table. "I still can't believe she would do something like that. Sandra was brilliant. She was funny, even if she worried too much."

"Did you follow her out of the bar?" Vivian didn't want to ask her straight out about her alibi.

"I left before she did. As soon as she said she was going hunting, I went home."

"Alone?"

"I had to work the next day, and I was in a relationship anyway. We're getting married in June."

"Congratulations," Vivian said automatically. She could double check that alibi later, but Wu didn't strike her as someone who had murdered her best friend.

"Plenty of fish in the sea." Wu sighed. "She could have found someone else easy. Instead, she threw it all away because some asshole changed the locks. She could have replaced him with another asshole in a week."

Maybe she was through with assholes. "Was she generally depressed?"

"She had dark moments, sure. She always came out the other side. I would have called her a mostly hopeful person. Until Slade."

"Do you have his contact information?"

"I've been waiting a long time to give it to someone who might use it to nail the bastard." Wu took a yellow sticky note out of her pocket. A man's name and address were written on it in a feminine hand, one much more elegant than Vivian would have expected from Wu's no-nonsense manner.

It sure sounded like Sandra had committed suicide—dark moments, recently dumped, drunk, and out on the tracks. A lot of things had conspired to end Sandra's life.

"Of all the ways to go, I never thought she'd jump in front of a train," Wu said.

"Why is that?" Vivian had never really thought about what methods her friends might use to commit suicide.

"She never took the subway. We always took cabs or walked."

That was one thing out of place. "Why?"

Wu shrugged. "She never said, but I always thought it was weird."

Had Sandra been afraid of the subway? What would Tesla do if he were afraid of subways? Considering all his other mental problems, it was a damn good thing that one wasn't on the list. "Do you have anything more to add?"

"Did they ever find her bag?" Wu asked.

Vivian went on alert. "What bag?"

"She had this custom Prada clutch. Worth a fortune. A guy gave it to her, some coke dealer she dated for five minutes. Anyway, I always thought it was weird that it wasn't with her when she died. She watched that thing like a baby. Never let it out of her sight. I always wondered if someone pushed her in front of the train to get it."

Clearly Katrinka wasn't the only one who knew how much that bag had cost. "Did you tell the police?"

"I told the guy at the morgue, and he said he'd pass it along."

Vivian had read the files. The purse hadn't been mentioned, but evidence had pointed to a suicide, which is how it had been labeled, and that made the missing purse irrelevant. The transit authorities and the police had been fairly thorough. Sandra's death looked like a tragic accident, nothing more.

Except that her bag, along with several lipsticks, had turned up miles from where she died.

"Do you know what kind of lipstick Sandra might have been carrying?"

Wu's eyebrows rose. "Christian Dior 999. It was her favorite, since Natalie Portman modeled it. She was crazy about Natalie Portman. The red was too dark for Sandra, but she wore it anyway. Why?"

"Just a line of inquiry," Vivian said. "It probably doesn't mean anything."

Her mind jumped to three smooth black tubes laid out on Tesla's pool table. That lipstick meant something.

THE CHEMISTRY OF DEATH

11

Joe checked again, but the files were gone. He'd hacked into the Grand Central Terminal surveillance video database for nothing. It looked like they wiped it every three (red) months, and Sandra Haines had died almost a year ago. He heaved a frustrated sigh. He should've known.

He'd already clicked through her friends and their friends and the people they were tagged in photos with. He assembled pictures of a group of young people in designer clothes with practiced smiles eating carefully arranged food and drinking liquids of various colors. He'd hoped it would be touching, but Sandra's life was mostly banal.

What he didn't find was as interesting as what he did. She had no family members on Facebook—no parents or grandparents or siblings. She didn't even have friends from junior high or high school. For a woman in her early twenties (blue, black), that was practically unthinkable these days. It seemed she'd appeared at New York University out of nowhere. She was either a spy, in witness protection, or homeschooled. He was leaning toward homeschooled. If she were a spy, the government would have made her an identity that went back more than seven (slate) years, and if she were in witness protection, she would have been told to keep off the Internet.

Regardless of her life before New York, she hadn't been linked with anyone suspicious after she appeared online.

None of her friends had committed suicide, been murdered, or been accused of crimes more serious than drunk and disorderly. If any of them were killers, they were playing a long, careful game.

Edison nudged his knee, reminding him that everything was fine, and that he probably ought to do some work. Or maybe he was reading a little too much into the nudge.

He pulled up five (brown) scans of his brain. The first (cyan) was him playing an innocuous video game. His axons fired, but it looked pretty calm. The second (blue) was him walking down that damn virtual hallway and looking out the door at the ocean. His heart beat a little faster thinking about it, and Edison nudged him again.

"Right you are," Joe said. "Look at the data instead of freaking myself out."

Edison flopped down in the doggie bed that Joe kept next to his desk. The crisp smell of cedar chips drifted up from the bed's stuffing.

The data said that Joe's amygdala had gone nuts when he looked out that door. It had started firing before he even got to the door, when he first saw the light falling through onto the floor, and it got worse all the way up until the moment he'd turned away. Outside scared the hell out of his brain.

His pre-frontal cortex was firing back, but it had clearly lost the battle. The pre-frontal cortex was supposed to control emotional impulses, and had apparently been trying to tell his amygdala to chill out. The message wasn't getting through.

It was exactly the same pattern he'd seen in a patient with post-traumatic stress syndrome when he was confronted with images from his nightmares—the view from the dusty window of a Hummer, a shadow, an explosion, and blood and shrapnel everywhere. That made sense. That poor man had watched his friend die and lost his own legs in that environment. Those experiences were enough to terrify anyone.

Joe had never been traumatized by light on the ocean or the breeze on his face. So why did his brain act as if he had?

He'd spent a lot of time trying to figure that out, consulting doctors, psychiatrists, and others with agoraphobia. Initially, he'd been told to settle for the reality that most adult onset agoraphobia had no specific cause, but he'd dug deeper. After extensive blood tests, doctors had found a substance similar to scopolamine in his blood, a substance that he had never knowingly consumed. No one knew how this particular substance worked or how it came to be in his body, but the drug might have flipped a switch in his brain and caused all his troubles.

All he had to do was flip that switch back, and he and Edison would be jogging in Central Park. But he hadn't yet found that switch.

Still, he and Edison could still get across town to see Celeste. She'd have to forgive him once she met Edison—Edison had that effect on people. Celeste didn't like animals, hadn't had pets since childhood. But Edison would probably win her over anyway.

Joe glanced at his cell phone. He'd placed it next to his keyboard, out of its Faraday bag, so he could pick it up the second it rang. It had stayed stubbornly silent all day.

His apology roses should have arrived hours ago. He'd sent yellow ones, because Celeste had always loved bright yellow things. Bright yellow set Joe's teeth on edge. He wasn't sure why, but he was glad that no number in his lexicon corresponded to that shade.

On a whim, he looked up Celeste on Facebook. She hadn't posted anything in over a year, although she'd been a frequent poster before that. If she died, would Leandro post an announcement on her page and trigger a wave of condolence messages like those for Sandra?

Joe found Leandro's page. Unlike his sister, Leandro posted all the time. His latest posts were from Key West— Leandro dressed as a pirate in a bar full of pirates, standing next to women wearing bizarre bikinis, a sunny beach. He was certainly enjoying Fantasy Fest, but Joe couldn't begrudge him that. It wasn't Leandro's fault that Joe was stuck inside.

He tabbed back to the window displaying his brain. The colored lines flashing across his onscreen brain kept him from Celeste. He had seen a beach similar to the one on Leandro's Facebook page, and his brain had gone nuts. Had Sandra's brain looked like that before the train hit her— frantic with terror? Or had she sought out the train and the oblivion it would bring? Had that moment been like looking out at a calm, starry night?

12

Ziggy crept down the empty tunnel like a rat. He darted between shadows, ears pricked for danger. Once, he was alone down here. Once, he strode through these tunnels like a man, knowing no one of consequence would ever see him. The occasional homeless people he encountered weren't a threat. They didn't care what he did. No one did. Everything changed when Tesla moved into his tunnels.

Ziggy hissed an expletive. That man thought *he* owned the tunnels. He walked around at all hours of the day or night with that animal of his. His actions had brought police down here. On one occasion, they'd occupied the tunnels for days, and Ziggy had been denied access to his trophies. That's why he had to keep one at the office. He needed something to tide him over in case he was cut off again.

He should have killed him before he came down here. Since his arrival the man had been too well-protected by his dog and his friends. Ziggy had been forced to declare an uneasy truce.

His pace didn't slacken when he entered the darkest tunnel. His excellent night vision allowed him to see things the women never did—tunnel openings, distant switching stations, and the silhouette of others moving about in the darkness. He'd been this way so many times that he could find his way with his eyes closed. Years before, he'd unscrewed the bulbs, separating them from their power source. No one had ever bothered to fix them, and darkness became a permanent presence here. No one could see him.

He stepped onto a rusty track and walked it like a balance beam. Rust made whispering sounds under his shoes, a noise he'd never be able to hear in the clamor of the city above. Down here he'd found true peace.

He spun around and walked backward, moonwalking like Michael Jackson along the track. He was confident on the balance beam. Long ago, his mother had enrolled him in gymnastics, and he'd been surprisingly deft at it. He had the coordination and strength of a feral animal. He never used his strength, even down here. He preferred to stalk and conquer his prey using only his insight into their natures. Once he showed them their innermost selves, the women were grateful when he helped them do the one thing he could not yet do himself.

His feet advanced along the metal until the old track ended. He knew to step off right before it ended. His front foot landed lightly on sharp rocks covered with dust. He took seven medium-sized steps, then reached for the door handle.

The door was open.

His heart jackhammered in his chest. He touched the edge of the door one more time, hoping he'd been wrong, that it was closed the way he'd left it. His fingers ran down the edge of the cold metal, slipped off the door, and touched the frame a finger's length behind it.

"How could they?" his childish voice wailed.

He clapped his hand over his mouth. He must be quiet. He must be cunning. He turned in a slow circle, eyes probing the inky blackness, listening, smelling. Minutes passed before he was satisfied that he was alone. Someone had come, but was now gone.

With two fingers, he swung open the door. As always, the well-oiled hinges didn't make a sound. He stepped over the threshold and closed the door behind him. Back against the door, again, he listened. All was still. His breath came out in a whoosh. He was alone in the room.

He reached to the side and flicked on the light switch. Milky light flooded the empty room. He blinked in the brightness. He saw the damage at once. Someone had dug up his special spot.

He rushed to the corner and fell to his knees in the cold dirt. Claws had gouged the soft earth and torn out what lay below. A dog. Not just any dog. It must have been Tesla's yellow mutt. The beast must have smelled his treasures and taken them. Why would a dog want his prettiest things? A dog didn't need them.

With a howl, Ziggy dug as the animal had. He should have found nine lipstick cases. The tenth he carried in his pocket. His collection contained ten lipsticks, divided into five pairs. The sets had to be used in pairs.

The hole was very deep before he gave up. He laid all the lipsticks he found in a line on the floor. Seven remained. The man had taken away three. Even worse, those three were part of three different pairs. Ziggy would have to throw the singletons away. That left him with only two intact pairs—four precious lipsticks.

He cradled one in his palms. Mud streaked its shiny black surface. He polished it against his pant leg until it gleamed again. He remembered the woman who'd stroked this lipstick across her thin, expressive lips. Rita.

He dug frantically, throwing dirt around the tiny room, but it was no use.

Ziggy repeated the ten names in his head, each tragic face appearing before him. Without the lipsticks to anchor him, he'd start to forget them. Each woman was irreplaceable—Brittany with her warm brown eyes and her sexy despair, and opposite her, Inga with eyes like chips of ice that masked a deep, cold sorrow; Gretchen with the spray of freckles across her cheekbones and a nose like the beak of a stork, and Nan with her sensible shoes; Heather with her tilted nose, Irish accent, and hands like a lumberjack, and Monique's waist-length hair that shimmered like a curtain of gold when she moved; Paulina had short hair like a GI and wore a flowered dress and smoked two packs that evening, paired with Angela whose hair was too red to consider until he saw it was dyed. Rita with her red dress and spiky hair and Sandra sparkling in silver. Only two pairs remained: Brittany and Inga, Sandra and Rita.

His treasures had been dug up like bones, their elegance defiled by mud and dog spit.

The child inside grieved the loss of his treasures and the years of work, but the man worried that the objects had been found. It would take an extraordinary turn of events for the lipsticks to be tracked to their erstwhile owners or to him, but it'd already taken an extraordinary turn of events for that man and his dog to find his hiding place. He could leave nothing to chance.

He'd allowed the man to live unmolested down here.

But the truce was over.

13

Joe nodded to the fresh-faced young man behind the counter at the Vanderbilt Tennis and Fitness Club. The fitness center was on the second floor of Grand Central Terminal, so it had become Joe's gym. He'd liked the guy who had the job before, but after he was stabbed to death by a killer who mistook him for Joe, Joe had been careful not to strike up a friendship with anyone at the club.

He grabbed a towel and headed for the courts. Edison was off for his daily walk, probably soaking up the last remnants of fall sunshine. Joe glanced at the arched windows that looked out onto the street. If he were outside, he knew he would look above those windows to admire Grand Central's famous clock with the statue of a winged Hermes. He'd seen it when he'd arrived in New York, back when he was still an outside person. Since then, he'd only glimpsed the statue in photographs or surveillance footage from the building across the street.

Steeling himself, he stepped closer to the windows. These windows, like all windows, made him nervous, but they had thick panes separated by metal bars. Their solidity reassured him.

Alan Wright came over. He wore all black, a tennis-playing Johnny Cash. His shirt had a Nike swoosh on it. Just Do It. Alan was the founder and CEO of Wright Industries, an environmental company that made its money off green technologies. Alan was saving the world, and Joe knew he should like him for it, but he didn't. He suspected Alan's real goal was an Earth without humans. Alan hated most people.

"Ready to lose?" Alan called.

"I won last time," Joe said. "I'm ready to start a streak."

Alan lunged to the side, stretching. He looked pale and drawn. He hadn't shaved for a couple days. Joe had never seen him like that.

"That last ball was out," Alan said.

"Independently verified." Joe bounced the end of his racket against his toe.

"You probably paid him off."

"Seems like you could have topped whatever offer I might have made." Alan was one of the few people Joe knew who was wealthier than he.

"Beneath my dignity." Alan jogged across the court, taking the first serve. "Ready?"

Joe positioned himself near the back of the court. "Always."

Alan slammed the ball across full force, and Joe backhanded it back at him, aiming the ball short so Alan would have to run a bit. Joe had more endurance than Alan. Alan might be quicker, but in a long match, Joe always won.

"How's the brain lab?" Alan knocked the ball back.

Joe sprinted across the baseline to return it. "You should come, get scanned."

"And let you inside my head?" Alan didn't get a good piece of the ball, and it went into the net. "My head's private."

"We anonymize the data, so it would stay private." Joe loosened his grip on his racket. "You'd be a great test subject. Not a lot of people with IQs in your range out there to scan."

Alan laughed and served again. "Flattery won't get you there."

Joe returned the ball deep and low to Alan's right. It was his weakest shot. Alan swung and missed.

Joe smiled.

Alan flipped him off. He hated to lose even a single point. Was that coded in his brain? What parts would light up when he played? Would they be different from an average player's? Would they be different from Sandra's? Had sadness left a mark on her brain? Long-term depression shrank the dorsolateral prefrontal cortex. Would he have seen that if he'd been able to scan her?

They rallied in silence, until Alan missed again. His game was off.

Joe's thoughts wandered to Sandra. If he could see her brain, or scans of it, he might know if she was chronically depressed or not, but she'd been cremated long ago. Plus, what difference did it make? She'd been depressed when it mattered.

"Good God!" Alan yelled when he missed an easy one.

Joe kept playing. By the end, he'd won again, easily. Something was wrong with Alan.

"Barely worth kicking your ass today." Joe swiped at his face with a towel. "You OK?"

Alan shrugged. "I despise this time of year. In the fall, everything's cold and dying."

"Going into hibernation, not dying. It'll all come back in the spring." Joe had liked the fall, back when he could experience seasons outside.

"Not all of it comes back. Winter kills the weak. But I don't mind winter. At least it's honest." Alan glanced toward the window. "How about you? You don't seem like your usual self, either."

Joe hesitated, then told him about the woman who'd died in the tunnels.

"Maybe she's better off dead. Put out of her misery." Alan never minced words.

"Like a horse with a broken leg?" Joe asked.

"Like a person with a broken life, lucky to be rid of it." Alan pulled his wet shirt away from his chest. "She was depressed, probably would have killed herself someplace else soon enough."

"Suicide's just as often an impulsive act as it is a long-planned event, despite what movies of the week say," Joe said. "If she'd live past that moment, she might never have tried again."

"Sounds like liberal horseshit to me." Alan bounced the tennis ball against the floor and caught it. "Not even as useful as real horseshit."

"Almost half of those who try suicide and live to talk about it say they made the attempt after fewer than five minutes of thought. That's why they put up suicide nets—turns out most people won't even walk a few blocks to find a different bridge to jump off." Joe didn't know why he was defending this woman to Alan. "Maybe this woman had one really bad day, got hammered, and made a mistake. She doesn't have to have been depressed for years."

The logic was sound, but the way Edison had growled, the sight of those lipsticks gathered together behind a previously locked door, and the thought of a rat dragging that purse for miles told him otherwise. She hadn't committed suicide. She'd been murdered.

"Maybe this act saved her and everyone around her from a lifetime of misery. Maybe it was a gift." Alan tucked the ball into his pocket. "Like it would be for Rosa."

Rosa was Alan's ex-wife. The one time Joe had met her, Rosa had seemed fragile. Everyone seemed fragile next to Alan. "That's harsh."

"If she killed herself, I wouldn't cry. I'd thank her for leaving the world a better place." Alan strode off toward the locker room. The conversation was clearly over.

That kind of breathtaking cold-heartedness reminded Joe why he and Alan couldn't really be friends, no matter how much they had in common. If Alan were in charge of the world, he'd sweep it with a big broom, sweeping away overpopulation and people with broken brains (like his own ex-wife and daughter and Joe himself). Hell, he'd probably eliminate everyone who didn't recycle.

Joe smiled at the thought, but he couldn't shake the feeling of dread that rose up in him after. Someone like Alan could kill those women without a second thought. Someone like Alan could dress the part, turn on the charm, and convince others to do exactly what he wanted.

14

Vivian's stomach rumbled. She hadn't eaten all day. At this rate, she'd starve before she penetrated the bureaucracy far enough to get the subway accident reports. Nodding knowingly, future supplicants would walk by her dried husk stretched out on nondescript gray carpet. Death by referral. The fact that it was Friday only made things worse—everyone was already gone.

She'd tried to find the right department by calling ahead, but she'd still been shunted from room to room at the Metropolitan Transit Agency. The most boring game of tag ever—nobody was ever *it*. She kicked her feet against the bland carpet and knocked on another door.

"Yo!" called out a young-sounding male voice.

That was new. Everyone else Vivian had talked to was her mother's age. Maybe she'd meet someone who still thought customer service was more fun than customer obstruction. A girl could hope.

She went inside. The back of a giant computer monitor confronted her. Otherwise, the room looked empty. She peered around the edge of the monitor to see a young man sitting in an orange ergonomic chair. His bright red hair had a wave in front like a cartoon character. His hair clashed with the crushed velvet purple jacket he wore over a green shirt. He vibrated against the background of steel-gray carpet, dark-gray desk, and a black and white picture of a whale on the wall.

Vivian introduced herself and explained she was there to look through the MTA accident reports.

"I'm Mortimer," he said. "And you have to file a Freedom of Information Act request."

"That takes weeks to process." Six to eight, she'd heard.

Mortimer ran his hand across the sides of his hair. It was lacquered with hairspray and made a rustling sound. "Better start now."

"What if we pretend that I filed one of those weeks ago, and I'm picking it up?"

"What if we pretend that you didn't ask me that?" He already sounded like a bureaucratic lifer. So young to be so obstructionist.

"I'm interested in suicides," she said. "Or accidents that might have been suicides."

"You a reporter?" He rested his elbows on this desk. "The subways are practically the safest places in New York. You're more likely to die in a McDonalds. Eating that crap is a slow suicide. Do a piece on that."

"Do you have the statistics?" she asked.

"On red meat?"

"On the number of suicides and accidents in the New York subway system, say in the past ten years?"

"Why ten years? Why not twenty?"

She shrugged. "Twenty then. I think there's been a murder, maybe more than one."

"Someone pushing people in front of trains?" Mortimer's hair bobbed when he shook his head. "We'd know. The stations have surveillance cameras."

"What about the tunnels between stations?" she asked.

"Why would anyone be between stations?"

"Maybe to push young women in front of subway trains." Although she had no evidence, there was no point in telling him that.

"Why would the women go? This is New York. They're smarter than that."

"Why not look and see? I won't take any notes if you don't want me to. And I won't tell anyone where I got the information."

He folded his arms. "Are you really a reporter?"

"Why?"

"As a reporter, you have to protect your sources, so you would be bound not to rat me out if you printed a story."

"Then let's say I'm a reporter."

"That doesn't mean you are." He fidgeted with his purple lapel. "Do you have a recording device?"

She gave him her friendliest smile. "It's illegal to record a conversation without consent in New York. Any reporter knows that."

He studied her face, then shook his head. "I'm not allowed to show you any files without the correct forms."

"If I'm right," she said, "lots of women died and more might die in the time it takes to wait on those forms. Do you want that on your conscience: 'I let women die because the paperwork wasn't in order?'"

"How about: 'I lost my job because I illegally released documents?'"

"Do you know that most people who are hit by subway trains don't die right away?" She was winging it. "They lie there in terrible pain with broken bones poking through their skin, their insides jumbled into a milkshake."

He tightened his lips.

"What if there's someone out there who gets off on that? Someone who lures women into the tunnels, pushes them in front of trains where there are no cameras, then watches them die? I have evidence that this has happened to at least three women." If the lipsticks were evidence of any such thing.

"Why don't you go to the police, not to me?"

"I tried them first," she said. "And I have to prove there's been foul play, that there's been a pattern. If we can't find a pattern, maybe I'm wrong. If we can, you can save lives, right here from your desk."

He didn't say anything for a minute. She let him think. He looked like he'd make the right decision. Eventually, he stood, walked past her, and closed the door. "I'm on break."

She wasn't sure where he was going with that. "Are you?"

"I can look things up on my breaks, so long as they're not confidential, which this isn't really. I can't give you print outs."

Vivian hefted her phone. "I'll take pictures."

"Let's start with accidents with fatalities." He clicked away. "It says five hundred and seventy-two people have died since 2000. Let's use that as a range."

"Women?" she asked.

"Why just women?"

"A purse and lipstick have been found, and the victim who started me down this path was a woman."

"Right." He tapped away. "About three hundred and eighty-seven of those were women."

Vivian groaned inwardly. "That's a lot. Let's see if he's got a type. Eliminate women over fifty and under eighteen."

He did. "We've got three hundred and sixty-two."

Vivian did the math in her head. "That's about twenty-four a year."

He scanned the headers. "I'll eliminate women who died in well-documented accidents, like retrieving a dropped object off the tracks. We can leave those out, right?"

"Right." She peered around the edge of the monitor. His long, white fingers flew across the keyboard, and his blue eyes darted back and forth as he read. He reminded her a little of Tesla.

"Eighty-five." He started bringing up reports, one after another on his screen. "At Penn Station. At Fulton Street."

"Let's get rid of those that happened at a station, and see what's left."

A few minutes later, they were down to ten victims, all in the last five years. The latest one was Sandra Haines.

"How's that?" Mortimer asked.

Vivian searched for the woman who had died before Haines—Rita Blaskowitz. She was in her mid-twenties and blond. With her wide-blue eyes and even features, she looked eerily similar to Sandra Haines.

Mortimer was already searching for the others. He tiled his monitor into ten squares and overlapped the pictures under the names. The women were blond, young, and pretty. Vivian felt nauseous.

"They look like sisters." Mortimer's pale face whitened another shade. "That's your pattern."

Vivian had hoped Tesla was wrong, that a rat with a lipstick fetish had buried those lipsticks, and Sandra Haines's death was a tragic accident. She no longer had that hope.

Mortimer maximized each window so she could get a good picture, with details about the date and location of death, names and addresses of next of kin. She snapped a picture of each woman's face before taking a picture of the report detailing how she'd died.

"What will you do with this?" he asked.

"Take it to the police," she said. "It'll be a tough sell."

"It sure looks like someone prefers blondes," he said. "The fact that they all look so much alike has to mean something."

"None of these women were listed as murdered, and the reports say they were alone when the train hit them."

"Bullshit." Mortimer tapped picture after picture. "You mean to tell me there isn't a link?"

"I don't mean to tell you anything," Vivian said. "Except thank you for getting me this information."

"I feel like a jerk for not helping you right away," he said. "I mean, wow."

He stood and gestured to his chair. She sat and read through the Blaskowitz file. The woman had died less than a week before Sandra Haines. On a hunch, Vivian checked the other dates of death. Two women died every October, like clockwork. Each of the women in the pair died within a week of each other.

"He kills them in pairs," she whispered. "Every October. Like turkeys."

"Turkeys?"

"Doesn't mean anything," she said. "October is turkey hunting season in New York."

Mortimer leaned over her and pressed a complicated set of keys.

"What's that for?"

"I'm printing you the reports," he said. "You can send the police back to me if you want."

"Won't you get in trouble?"

"Not as much trouble as these women did."

15

Ziggy ran down the track, swift and silent as the wind that followed the trains through the close tunnels. Meeting Tesla was not a worry. Dog and man were at work for the day. The man had a company in Grand Central Terminal, and he'd be up there all day. For now, the tunnels belonged to Ziggy.

Owning the tunnels during the day was useless. The trains ran so often a man couldn't hear himself think, let alone have a sustained conversation with someone else. Track workers and the occasional homeless person wandered around, so there was no real privacy. Most importantly, during the day the women didn't have the feeling of despair Ziggy craved. He needed the tunnels at night.

His legs burned, and his backpack thumped against his back, but he didn't slacken his pace. He liked running in the semi-darkness. He moved between gray walls of Manhattan schist like a ghost, shoes quiet against train ties and stones. No one could catch him down here.

He was wild and free, and his new mission was driving that man and his dog out. But the man had to choose. Though an outsider would dispute it, Ziggy hadn't killed those women. He'd held a mirror up to their pitiful lives and, gazing into its depths, they had chosen their fates. He'd not pushed one, never even touched one in her final moment. Every single one could have stepped off the tracks and walked away unharmed.

None had.

He'd always found women who sought death. Even if they didn't know it themselves, he did. Despair hung around each woman like a black miasma. He drew the darkness around her like a cape, showed her how the blackness had reached inside of her, and let her decide how to save herself from her misery.

He envied them. They had courage so few possessed, including him. They always reached peace; he never did. His doom was to keep searching for them, set them free, but remain trapped himself.

It wasn't fair.

Tesla was trapped, too. He couldn't leave the tunnels. He, too, despaired. Ziggy felt it. He only had to show the man his own well of darkness. Then Tesla would make the same choice the women had, the choice he should have made all those months before. Then he would be dead.

And Ziggy would be alone again.

Tonight, he'd find a woman. He'd draw his game out over the next few nights, taking her only when the man was neutralized. He hadn't ever stalked a woman for more than a single night before. It would be fun to draw it out, to play with her again and again before freeing her from her despair. He'd have more moments to look back on when he held the new lipstick in his hands.

Breathing hard, he stopped in front of a metal door. Next to it an electronic keypad glowed green. They guarded the tunnel to the man's house. Behind that door, the man and his dog had built a comfortable life together. They had settled too easily into his underground world. He must change that.

He took a small object from his pocket. Still in a protective bag, the plastic crinkled in his hand. He'd bought the device at a shop downtown, paying cash instead of using a credit card, although he didn't see how the device could ever be traced back to him. But it was always better to be careful.

The device was the kind of thing that made him happy to be living in the twenty-first century. It was a tiny spy camera that fit easily in his palm and weighed very little. According to the package, the camera was activated by body heat and could record hours of video on a single charge. It even had night-vision capabilities. All that for less than the price of dinner at a high-end restaurant.

He shrugged off his backpack and set it on the stone floor. Metal clanked inside. With one quick unzip, he revealed a tactical portable ladder designed for military operations. It was lightweight and folded down small. He'd bought it at a military supply store, also using cash.

Working quickly, he donned gloves and positioned the ladder against the wall next to the door that blocked his way into that man's domain. He climbed up, calculated the angle, and stuck the camera to the ceiling with a piece of double-sided tape. He aimed the camera's gaze directly at the keypad. The next time Tesla came in through this door, Ziggy's hidden eye would see his password.

Excitement bubbled up in him. By tomorrow, he'd be in Tesla's house, able to show him the darkness that choked his life. Ziggy would use his drugs and his wits, and the man would realize he had nothing to live for.

That's when he'd make his choice, the same as the others.

16

Joe paused in his garden for another breath of green air. It wasn't actually green, of course, but it smelled greener than anything he'd encountered in months. He'd installed a whole-house air filter in the Victorian soon after he moved in, and it helped with the musty, dusty smell, but the air down here still smelled like an old library, like books, stone, dry wood, old paint, and wool. He hadn't minded the smell, but being able to step out into the green was intoxicating.

Something smelled like flowers, which was odd because Maeve had explained that the groundcover would probably never flower under his makeshift lighting conditions. Sniffing, he turned in a slow circle. Edison looked at him like he was crazy, and Joe couldn't really blame him. By the time he completed the circle, the floral smell was gone. He'd probably imagined it.

He held up a glow-in-the-dark tennis ball, and Edison dashed to the door that led to the outside tunnels. Joe shrugged his stained hoodie on, hefted his grubby backpack, and followed. The hoodie and backpack helped him blend in with the occasional homeless person he encountered so they didn't challenge him or mug him. He had ID to show any track workers or transit police he met, and they left him alone, too.

Edison's tail waggled as he waited for Joe to punch in the numbers to let them out. He'd take the dog for an extra-long walk to burn off that surplus energy.

Edison walked through the door next to him, but instead of waiting while Joe closed the door, the dog went to a nearby wall and peed on it. Odd. Edison had various places where he marked his territory. None were so close to home.

Joe sprayed the liquid with a bottle of odor remover he carried in his backpack. The product claimed to destroy odor using bacteria. He wasn't sure if that was marketing hype, but the tunnels had started smelling better since he'd begun using it.

"This is a one-time pee, right, buddy?" he asked.

Edison was too busy sniffing the ground to glance up. He made a thorough circuit of the ground around the door and the electronic keypad in front of it. Probably a rat had wandered by. Edison was fascinated by the comings and goings of rats.

Joe's phone rang. He'd accidentally put it in the wrong pocket, the one without a Faraday cage. He didn't get reception many places in the tunnels, but he'd installed a leaky coaxial cable at his house to give him a signal when he was close to home. Vivian's picture popped onto his screen.

"Tesla," he answered. He and Edison weren't going anywhere fast anyway since the dog was still busy sniffing. He might as well take the call.

"Bad news or worse news?" Vivian never bothered to sugarcoat anything.

"Let's start with bad."

"I think it's not just a single death. I think ten women have been murdered in the subway tunnels over the course of the past five years. Every October, within a week of each other, two women die."

Colors flashed through Joe's head ten (cyan, black) women, five (brown) years, and two (blue) at a time. "Why do you think it's murder?"

"Check your email."

Joe switched over to his email and skimmed the attached report. Vivian had been thorough. All the women had died in October, in pairs about a week apart; they'd all been hit by trains between stations; and they'd all been depressed before their deaths. "What did the police say?"

Vivian made a noise that sounded like a growl. "That's the worse news. They said it's probably a coincidence. Probably some weird moon cycle or something."

"So, the autumn moon causes blondes to jump in front of trains?" Edison stopped sniffing and trotted over to Joe, alerted by his tone.

"Yes." Vivian's answer was one syllable of tightly contained anger. "The accident reports show that no one has ever seen anyone else in the tunnels where the women were struck, so how could they be being pushed onto the tracks? Or at least that's the theory."

Joe threw the tennis ball. Edison cocked his head as if to ask for permission, and Joe nodded. The dog leapt after the ball.

"Depending on where you are, it wouldn't be that difficult to push someone in front of a train and then escape down a side tunnel." He'd visit the locations where the victims died and see if he could find a place where an assailant could slip away. "It's like a maze down here."

"There's one more thing." She paused. "The reports say the women were standing still and facing the train when it hit them, as if they stepped in front of the train of their own volition, not as if they were pushed."

Joe looked at the ten (cyan, black) sad faces of the dead women. They looked so much alike. "Even so, it feels wrong."

"Does that mean I have your permission to follow up, talk to the family and friends of the women who died? Look for connections between the women?"

"And see if you can get a thorough toxicology screen on their bodies, if the coroner kept samples. Maybe they were drugged. Also see if you can match them up to those lipsticks."

Vivian ended the connection, and Joe whistled to Edison. They started off at a jog. They'd take the tunnel for the seven (slate) line west, get through the Times Square tunnel, and then head north on the A. Joe'd already mapped the locations in his head. Every woman in Vivian's report had died on the A line.

Unfortunately for Joe, it was the longest line in the system—thirty-one (red, cyan) miles. They'd check out the Manhattan tunnels tonight, north to the 207th (blue, black, slate) Street train yards. That was about ten (cyan, black) miles one way, but they could take the subway back. Tomorrow they'd go south and east, into Brooklyn, to check out the rest of the line. He wanted to see where each woman had died. Maybe he could figure out the escape route a killer might have used. Maybe even find evidence.

Edison fell in behind him. The dog seemed to sense his determination. Together, they loped along in silence, legs eating up the distance. After a mile and a half, they reached their first destination: the tunnel between the 59th (brown, scarlet) Street/Columbus Circle Station and the 72nd (slate, blue) Street Station.

The tunnel was dimly lit but bright enough for him to see without a flashlight. Trains thundered past every few minutes, breaking his concentration and forcing him and Edison back against the tunnel wall. Steam tunnels branched off around the main tunnel, their mouths a darker shade of black. It would be easy to push someone in front of a train here and then fade into the background. The train driver would be more concerned about the woman he'd hit than about looking for other people lurking in the tunnels.

Joe stepped into a steam tunnel and checked the ground for tracks. Lots of people had been here before him. It'd take someone with more forensic experience than he had to puzzle it out, and there was no telling if this was the right tunnel. He counted two (blue) other tunnels that would provide useful escape routes.

Edison sniffed and peed on the wall.

"Another rat, boy? Or do you smell something else?"

Edison looked at him.

Joe sprayed the spot. Edison couldn't smell the killer. Sandra Haines had died at this spot almost a year before. No scent trail could last that long. He'd have that problem with most of the evidence. If any traces had been left, they would probably have dried up and blown away by now.

Almost a year before. Joe's mind snagged on the phrase. It was October already. If Vivian's data was correct, two (blue) women were going to die somewhere along this line in the next two (blue) weeks. He'd see if he could get the transit police to step up patrols and walk the tunnels with Edison himself.

He wasn't going to let the killer end one more life in his backyard.

17

Vivian approached the dilapidated building, a coffee in one hand, her phone in the other. She positioned herself across the street and fiddled with her phone. She had some time to kill and standing around staring at a phone screen was the best cover there ever was. Everyone did it.

Today, she intended to talk to the elusive Slade. She'd called a few times, but he hadn't answered, and he hadn't responded to the messages she'd left. After that, she'd looked for his address, but he'd moved since Sandra's death, and nobody knew where. If Iris was right, probably in with his new rich mark.

Vivian had created a fake account on twitter and used it to follow his account. His handle was @sladethemaster, and his profile picture showed a blond man with curly shoulder-length hair and a rugged face. He looked the part of struggling actor or gigolo.

Last night he'd tweeted: *auditioning for mercutio send positive vibes*

It hadn't taken much searching on the Internet to find the audition notice for *Romeo and Juliet*. She'd decided to come and use her negative vibes to get some information out of him.

The call time was for ten on Saturday morning, and men and women with nervous walks showed up about a half hour after Vivian did. They wore a lot of black, a higher than average number of them smoked, and they had very good hair. Actors.

She paced in front of the building across the street. Her coffee cup was long empty, but she held onto it anyway, using it as the prop of an actress too nervous to go inside for her audition. She'd worn black herself—leggings, an oversized black T-shirt, and a battered leather jacket that she'd found at a flea market as a teenager. Her hair wasn't coiffed up to actress standards, but nobody seemed suspicious. A few women cast pitying glances in her direction, so she reckoned that her disguise was working well enough.

Most everyone was there by 10:30. Still no sign of Slade. Maybe he'd decided to skip the audition after all. His three hundred fifty-seven twitter followers would be so disappointed.

She'd give him until 11:00 and then try to figure out another way to meet him. At one o'clock she needed to be in front of Katrinka's school. It was a half day, some kind of teacher development.

At 10:49, she spotted him half a block away. He strode along with the graceful swagger of Mercutio, probably already in character. He wore tight brown pants, a blousy white shirt, and a brown leather jacket that hung mid-thigh. Not a bad choice. He'd stand out amongst the other men in black.

Since she knew where he was going, she fell in ahead of him. She reached the building before him, but waited until he was through the doors before pressing the button for the elevator. She got lucky, and they entered an empty elevator together.

He pushed the button for the eighth floor. That didn't give her much time. She positioned herself with her back to the buttons.

"Here for the audition?" she asked.

He stood straighter. "I am."

"Let me guess," she said. "Not effeminate enough to be Romeo. A certain swagger. Mercutio?"

His chest swelled like a courting robin's. "Who are you going for?"

Vivian's mind drew a blank. Juliet's mother? The nurse? Instead of lying, she reached behind her back and pressed the STOP button. The elevator lurched to a halt.

"What the hell?" Slade glared at her as if it was her fault. Which it was.

Vivian waved up toward the ceiling.

"What are you doing?"

"Getting the attention of whoever is watching that camera." She wasn't sure there was a camera, but it would make things easier if Slade thought that there was.

Slade smiled up at the camera with practiced charm.

Vivian stifled a smile at his vanity. She spread her legs a little, shook out her shoulders, and dropped her hands to her sides. Slade might not like the next few minutes, and she needed to be on guard. "You're a hard man to find, Slade."

His eyes narrowed. "How do you know my name?"

"Iris Wu mentioned you."

He looked up at the ceiling, squinting. Probably too vain to wear glasses. "Who the hell is that?"

Either he didn't remember Wu, or he was a better actor than she'd given him credit for. "She was a friend of Sandra Haines."

His muscles bunched under his silly white shirt. "She always had it in for me."

"Iris Wu or Sandra Haines?"

"Iris. I always thought she was a lesbian and was crushing on Sandy. Sandy thought I was nuts."

"Where were you the night Sandy died?" She didn't have long before he figured out she'd stopped the elevator.

He glared at her.

"If you don't tell me, you'll have to deal with the police," she said. "They said to report back to them if I turned up anything suspicious, like an ex-boyfriend without an alibi."

"I have an alibi." He didn't offer it up.

"Something legal?"

He growled. "I was on stage."

"That should be easy enough to verify," she said. "Where?"

"I was playing Nick in *Who's Afraid of Virginia Woolf?* The company still has photos on their web site. Applebaum Theater."

That was a big role in a big play. It shouldn't have been so hard to get out of him. "You're sure that will check out?"

His shoulders tensed, and Vivian kicked her readiness up a notch. He didn't look like he had much experience fighting, but you never knew. "Do you think I killed her?"

"Do you think anyone killed her?"

"She didn't jump in front of that train on her own. Not Sandy. She wasn't that kind of person." He glowered down at her.

"Wasn't *what* kind of person?" Vivian kept her hands loose, ready to go.

"The kind who goes down into the subway and jumps in front of a train."

"Why not?"

He clenched and unclenched his jaw like he was chewing a piece of invisible gum while he thought that one over. "She had a freaky childhood. They used to lock her in a root cellar when she was a kid. She couldn't stand to be confined. Wouldn't go underground in the subway. Wouldn't even go into a club that was in the basement. She always had to be on top during sex. You're probably that way, too."

That matched up with what Iris Wu had said about her dislike of the subway, although it was sad to think that Sandra had revealed this weakness to Slade, who didn't seem to care, and kept it from Wu, who did.

Vivian tried a new tack. "I understand that she was upset that night."

"Iris would say it's because I dumped her." He waved up at the camera again. "Sandy was a big girl."

"Big girl or no, nobody likes having their stuff left with the doorman."

"It saved me a lot of drama." He craned his head to see the buttons. "Saved her a lot of drama, too."

Vivian leaned back against the STOP button. "Why would someone push her in front of a train?"

"Maybe she got drunk and fell in," he said. "Maybe someone wanted her stuff. She had a nice phone, jewelry, and that handbag that cost more than a car."

"You think she was mugged."

"I think you need to get this elevator moving again." He took a step toward her. "Or else."

Her first instinct was to accept his challenge and kick his ass. She hated being told what to do, and she hated bullies. On the other hand, she didn't really have any more questions for him, and it was always best to avoid a fight.

Reason won out, but barely. She pressed the STOP button again, and the elevator resumed its upward course. Slade smiled a mean little smile, very different from the actor smile he'd put on for the camera. Vivian could see why Iris Wu didn't like him.

Slade swaggered off on his floor, his hand on the hilt of an imaginary sword.

"Good luck!" she called after him, knowing the theater superstition that wishing someone good luck would give them the opposite.

He lifted one hand to shoulder height and flipped her off without turning around. She felt a little better as she punched the button for the lobby. Hopefully, he wouldn't get the part.

She stared at her reflection in the mirrored metal that surrounded the elevator buttons. What had she learned? Iris Wu and Slade didn't agree on much, but both of them didn't believe Sandra Haines had gone into those tunnels on her own. That was significant.

Sandra Haines had gone down into the subway, off the platform, and into the tunnels. That was clear. It wouldn't have been easy to drag a panicking woman through a subway station without someone noticing. Or even to carry an unconscious one. Maybe no one would have intervened, but someone would have called the cops, maybe filmed it. Despite what the media would have you believe, New Yorkers cared.

If her journey through the station didn't cause any alarm, that meant someone must have given her so much alcohol or drugs that she didn't know what she was doing. Maybe she'd been under the influence of something, and someone, when she went into those tunnels and stood in front of the train. No matter what the cops thought, in Vivian's book, that meant murder.

18

Ziggy set the glass beaker on his kitchen stove and turned on the fan. When he'd done the remodel, he'd installed a stovetop fan that vented to the outside instead of filtering and recirculating the air back into the apartment. Expensive, but necessary for his purposes. And money was never an object. He had more than he could possibly spend.

He set up four Plexiglas panels around the stovetop and taped the edges together so they were airtight. Next, he ran a line of tape around the bottom to seal the panels to the countertop and another line around the top to seal the panels to the fan hood. The front panel had a round cutout big enough for him to insert one hand. It wasn't a perfect smoke hood, but it was good enough.

He assembled the ingredients on his granite countertop before he put on his thick rubber gloves. Whistling, he measured the liquids with a graduated pipette and dropped them into the beaker on the back burner of his stove. He'd made this concoction many times before, and today he was making a double batch.

He loved chemistry. Everyone forgot that he'd majored in it in college. He'd been expected to major in math or biology or even ecology. Not something where he got his hands dirty, where he worked with substances that didn't occur in nature, or at least not without human intervention.

Chemistry was alchemy, and alchemy required practice. He loved how he could combine two ingredients to produce a mixture much different than a sum of its parts. A harmless substance could turn into something deadly when mixed with the right partner; a deadly substance like sodium could be turned into something as harmless as table salt.

Chemistry governed the world. On a macro scale, chemistry could be used to pollute or clean the earth and water of the world. It could poison ecosystems, and it could save them. On a micro scale, every emotion anyone felt, every disease, and every thought started with a tiny chemical reaction. The man who controlled chemistry controlled the world.

For years he'd tinkered with this mixture, perfecting his designer drug in lab after lab. He'd come up with the idea for the drug during a summer internship. He'd scorned internships with large pharmaceutical companies and chosen instead to spend his time with a legendary chemist: Dr. Bilous. The man was responsible for creating more mind-altering substances than anyone on Earth. The internship wasn't for college credit, but Ziggy learned far more in those three months than he ever did in the classroom.

Most of his mentor's creations were eventually declared illegal, but the chemist experimented with them before they were. He wrote entire books about his homemade hallucinogens. The Drug Enforcement Agency sent agents to learn from him about the latest drugs on the street.

It had been a mind-blowing summer for Ziggy. He'd learned how the tiniest amount of certain chemical compounds could radically affect the brain. In the end the hallucinogens frightened him away.

Unlike some of the other acolytes, he hadn't really been interested in expanding his own mind. He'd been more interested in changing the behavior of others. And he found chemicals for that, too.

He'd learned all he could in those few short months, then slaved away in the university lab after he went back to school that fall. After a bit of tweaking, he'd created a drug he'd named Algea after the Greek goddesses of sorrow and grief. The Greeks called them the bringers of weeping and tears.

Scientifically, he'd say the drug deepened the effects of depression, causing the subject to dwell on the saddest moments of her life. Since it also intensified existing guilt and remorse, the subject was caught in a loop of regret and despair. As an added benefit, the drug made most subjects docile and compliant. Algea was perfect.

It also caused a fear of light and intense agoraphobia. He didn't know if those effects would wear off given enough time, and he didn't care. The women he used it on weren't alive long enough for it to matter. Once they recognized the despair underlying their lives, they couldn't go on. He envied them the clarity they found, but he was too afraid to take the drug himself. He suspected he could make a fortune selling Algea, but he needed to keep the drug for himself.

The mixture started to boil, and he turned down the flame until it formed a thin blue ring. He loved cooking with gas. Gas gave him the precision needed for his hobby. He'd bought the best stove he could, ignoring the kitchen designer who'd gone on and on about the wonderful meals he'd be able to cook. He cooked all right, but never anything he'd eat.

He checked his watch. The mixture needed to simmer for thirty seconds, then to cool. He busied himself putting the stoppers back onto the tiny glass bottles that held his ingredients, wiping each bottle down carefully before returning it to the padded wooden box where his chemicals lived when not in use.

Soon only three empty vials were left, lined up parallel to the stove. They were tiny and would hold a milliliter of Algea—a single dose.

He drew out the stoppers and set them on the counter. Carefully, he filled a pipette from the beaker and moved those precious drops to an empty vial. The liquid was a translucent blue. It didn't have much of a taste, or at least not enough that a woman would notice after a couple of drinks.

He inserted the tiny stoppers, then dropped one vial into his pants pocket. It felt warm against his thigh. The other vials went into the wooden box. Algea broke down quickly. If he didn't use it within a week, he'd have to throw it away and make another batch.

While he disassembled his makeshift smoke hood and meticulously washed down the surfaces, he was conscious of the warm vial in his pocket. The vial touched his thigh when he bent his leg, swung away when he straightened it. This vial was special, because it wasn't for one of his women.

It was for Joe Tesla.

19

Joe turned on the fire in his parlor. The electric flames were artificial, but warm all the same. Their orange glow fell on Victorian-era bookcases full of leather-bound books, an antique Persian rug, and a happy dog. Edison turned in a circle before lying down close to the fireplace.

"You're hogging all the heat," Joe told him.

Edison thumped his tail once (cyan) as if in apology, but didn't move.

Joe petted the dog's shoulder and sank into a nearby leather wingback chair. He was exhausted. He'd spent a good part of his day trying to convince the police to step up patrols in the A line tunnel based on the ten (cyan, black) deaths. They hadn't believed him and had said it was too much money and time to commit to a rich boy's hunch. They hadn't said it in so many words, but he'd got the message.

That meant he had to come up with a high-tech solution of his own. He'd decided to hack all surveillance cameras on the A line and run their footage through an app that would detect when someone left the platform and send him an alarm. He'd know right away if anyone entered the tunnels. Then he could call up the appropriate footage and see if the intruder was someone who had a reason to be there, like a track worker, or someone who might need help, like a beautiful blonde and a companion with evil intentions. If so, he'd send help right away. Hopefully, he could save her life and catch the man responsible for the murdered women. Not as good as regular patrols, perhaps, but better than nothing.

He'd already pulled the footage, so it was a matter of defining the areas that would trigger alarms. Since he'd done similar work at Pellucid, he had tools he could use to streamline the process and chunks of code he could reuse.

He was hard at work when a bell chimed in his front hall. That particular bell rang when the elevator moved. Someone had called the elevator up to the Grand Central concourse.

Edison lifted his head and looked at Joe as if trying to assess how worried he should be. Joe wasn't sure either. Legally, only a few people had access to the elevator—Joe himself, Celeste and Leandro Gallo because they owned the house, and guests who could be put on a list for temporary access. He knew all those guests. That list included only his mother, Mr. Rossi the lawyer, Vivian, Marnie, and Maeve.

Joe blamed himself for not securing the lever when he arrived in the elevator. He usually pulled the lever out and used a small weight to hold it down so no one could call the elevator up again. He'd been distracted by creating his application to protect the A line and must have forgotten to set the lever.

He carried his laptop out into the hall so he could be ready if someone unexpected came out of the elevator. He took the flashlight out of his backpack. He was reminded that he'd never actually used its Taser function before.

"Do you think this Taser even works?" he asked Edison.

Edison fixed his brown eyes on the fancy front door. The door had stained glass panes—lovely to look at, but a security disadvantage. Holding his breath, Joe studied footage from the camera pointed at the elevator.

Whatever happened, he wasn't going to run. This was his home, and he would defend it. Still, he pulled out his cell phone, ready to call Vivian for backup. He might want to defend his house, but he didn't have to go all Wild West solitary gunfighter about it.

The doors slid open, and a short figure emerged. She wore pants with black-and-brown vertical stripes and a tight black T-shirt. A long necklace with a heart covered in tiny gears hung from her neck. Her kelly-green hair fell in locks to her shoulders. Maeve.

Joe blew out his breath with a whoosh and put the Taser back in his backpack. Then he closed the laptop, set it on the coat stand, and went out to meet her.

"Hello, the house!" She waved a black-clad arm at him and hurried over.

Joe smiled at her greeting and opened the door.

"I came down to check on my handiwork," she said.

That's right, she came every Saturday. In all the excitement, he'd forgotten.

She knelt at the edge of the garden then ran the back of her hand across the plants with a tender, almost erotic, gesture. Her sleeves rode up, and a delicate white wrist flashed into view. A dragonfly was tattooed on the soft skin on the inside of her wrist. It looked so realistic that he wanted to touch it to see if it would fly away.

His cell phone rang. He'd put it into his pants pocket in case he needed to make a call. Leandro's tanned face appeared on screen. Behind him a gang of bodies undulated to loud Calypso music.

"Hey, Leandro. Looks like Florida suits you," Joe said. "Are we still on for Monday?"

"Monday?" Leandro asked.

"For your brain scan." Joe was always working to recruit control brains for his projects.

Maeve laughed. "No brain shall be left unscanned?"

Joe grinned at her. "Exactly."

"Save yourself!" Maeve stood and dusted off her hands. "The mad scientist runs amok!"

"Where are you?" Leandro asked. "And who is that in the background?"

"It's Maeve, and I'm in my new garden." Joe spun in a slow circle, letting the phone's camera display her handiwork to Leandro. "Isn't it amazing?"

"It looks like Disneyland." Leandro sounded horrified.

"Happiest place on Earth," Maeve called.

"For the mouse maybe," Leandro said.

Maeve extended her middle finger at the phone and went to the box that determined the amount of water dispensed to his plants. She was forever tinkering with it.

Joe wasn't sure what to say. He'd expected Leandro to be happy with the improvements he'd made. He was bringing life to the house and the tunnels. How could Leandro be angry about that?

"That stuff isn't damaging the floor, is it?" Leandro asked.

"The floor can be returned to its former state of bleakness in a matter of days." Joe took him off speaker phone to spare Maeve's feelings.

As if she guessed his intentions, she gave Joe a thumbs-up before heading back toward the elevator. She'd only met Leandro once, but had taken a violent dislike to him, and clearly didn't want to be part of the conversation.

Edison dropped his tail and leaned against Joe's leg. Joe stroked his head. "She'll be back next week. No worries, buddy."

"I'm worried." Leandro maneuvered away from a dancer who might have been topless, but she was gone before Joe could be sure.

"Worried about what?"

"Celeste."

Joe's heart sped up. "Is she getting worse?"

"She's not getting better." Leandro had found a quiet corner and leaned against dark blue wallpaper.

"Can I see her? I can get out." If drugging himself and being transported unconscious counted as getting out.

"Why don't you rent the apartment under Celeste's? It's open." Leandro took a long drink of something that looked like a mojito but Joe couldn't be sure because the image was too pixelated.

Celeste's apartment wasn't connected to the steam tunnels. If he moved there, he'd be trapped in the apartment building. He'd have to be dragged around like a corpse to leave. Not a long term solution. Edison bumped his knee. "I don't think that'll help."

"Leave your stupid hole in the ground." Leandro rolled his eyes. "Don't dress it up. It's like you're re-arranging deck chairs on the Titanic when you should get off the damn ship. It's sinking, man."

"Thanks for calling." Joe was ready to hang up.

"At least think about it. If you're stuck inside, does it really matter where?"

"Enjoy Florida." Joe hung up, and the festive music cut off. His stone chamber sounded too quiet without it.

Leandro's underlying belief was right. Joe should get over himself and go outside. If it were possible, he'd have done it already. His agoraphobia wasn't something he could wish away, despite what Leandro thought, and he'd much rather live down here where he had his house, Grand Central Terminal, the Hyatt, miles of tunnels, and access to buildings connected to the underground via steam tunnels. It wasn't the whole world, but it was bigger than a single apartment in Celeste's building. He couldn't let himself be tranquilized and dragged around every time he needed to leave the house.

Joe went over to the elevator and pressed the button to call the elevator back from the terminal. Once it arrived, he stepped inside and weighted the lever down. Nobody else would be using it tonight. He and Edison wouldn't be disturbed again.

He went back to the house and ordered fifty (brown, black) sunflowers for Celeste. He dictated a card:

Celeste,

Have you ever heard of the Greek myth of Clytie and Apollo? She was a water nymph who turned herself into a sunflower to grieve the loss of her lover, the sun god. To this day, all sunflowers track Apollo's position as he drives his solar chariot across the sky. That's me, looking for you.

Joe

P.S. Just ignore the fact that I'm doing some god-like gender bending.

The woman on the phone didn't seem to be impressed, but he hoped Celeste would like it. She liked mythology. She liked sunflowers. Maybe it didn't have to be more complicated than that.

He left another apologetic voice mail. If he didn't hear back from her soon, he'd have Vivian tranquilize him and drag him to Celeste's apartment so he could apologize in person, even if that seemed to be the opposite of what she wanted. Maybe he could stay there for a while, if she'd have him.

He wanted to see her before she died. He thought of the funeral she would have that he wouldn't be able to attend. His lonely evenings without her calls. The paintings she would never finish. Dust gathering on the canvases in her bright apartment. The world would be darker when she died. His mind veered away from that thought. She couldn't die. She just couldn't.

He had to do something or he'd drive himself crazy. He should do something useful: finish his A line surveillance program and go out on his first nightly patrol. That was concrete, specific, useful, and attainable.

He returned to his parlor and went back to programming. Hours flew by as he lost himself in the magical world of computer code and numbers and colors. It was almost midnight when he finished. The system was rudimentary and clunky. The different bits were hacked together without any finesse, but it was a start. He could clean it up tomorrow. For now, it gave him what he needed.

Turned out a lot of people went off the platforms and onto the tracks: track workers in reflective vests and boots, signal tower monitors in regular business casual clothes and reflective vests, and drug addicts looking for a quiet place to smoke or shoot up. He'd be getting a lot of false positives, but at least it was something.

Edison slept in front of the electric fire. His legs twitched as he chased an imaginary ball, and his tail wagged in his sleep. What Joe wouldn't give for dog dreams.

Not wanting to wake the dog, Joe tiptoed out of the parlor and wandered into the modernized kitchen. He needed to pack himself some food for his patrol. He and Edison would be out for about four (green) hours. He filled up a water bottle and picked up a handful of fitness bars. They tasted awful, but they were supposed to have the perfect balance of protein and carbs. He opened the Victorian ice box. He'd had a custom refrigerator built inside shortly after he moved in, but he still called it the ice box. It contained half of a cheesesteak sub left over from lunch. He'd split it with Edison. That was better than a power bar.

His fingers closed on the white paper wrapping surrounding the sandwich. The paper crackled, and he wondered if the sound would wake the dog.

Then the room went dark.

Joe's heart started to race. He ordered himself to calm down, tried to talk himself through it. A warm nose pushed against the hand holding the sandwich. Edison.

"Hey, boy!" His voice boomed out. "Just a power outage."

He'd never had a power outage down here before. The lights hadn't even flickered in all the months he'd lived here. If they had, he would have had the common sense to install emergency lighting, which he hadn't. An item for a future to-do list.

"Glad we weren't in the elevator," he said.

Edison nosed the ice box door shut and grabbed Joe's shirt sleeve in his mouth. Did the dog have training for blackouts? Of course he did. Edison was trained for every emergency. He was the Navy SEAL of dogs.

"What's the plan, Edison?"

As if he understood, Edison tugged on Joe's sleeve. Joe took a step forward, and Edison pulled again. Joe let the dog lead him, although he didn't think Edison could see any better than he could in total darkness. Maybe Edison was following a scent trail or his memory.

The dog led him out of the kitchen with its tile floor and down the wooden planks in the hall toward the front door. He stopped, and Joe stopped, too. Did Edison want them to go outside? Joe would need a key for the door that led to the tunnels as the elevator was probably knocked out, too.

Edison released Joe's sleeve, then got another grip. He guided Joe's hand to something that felt like canvas. His backpack.

"Flashlight and keys are in there," Joe said. "Good boy."

He unzipped the backpack, dropped in the sandwich, and pulled out the flashlight. When he clicked it on, the hall looked spooky. Oversized shadows shivered on the walls. The doors to the other rooms in the house were as dark as the tunnels outside. He'd never seen the house in total darkness before. He always left a nightlight burning in the hall so he could find his way around if he woke up in the middle of the night.

The house wasn't just dark. It was dead silent. No hum from the air filter, no murmur from the refrigerator, no quiet thrumming of the computer fans. The only sound was his and Edison's breathing—his nervous and quick, Edison's relaxed. Edison wasn't afraid of the dark.

Joe wondered what to do next. The house didn't have a fuse box. The power supply was connected to one of the lines used for the subway trains, and he didn't see how he could have overloaded it with his lights and laptop. Maybe something had happened with one of the trains. If so, MTA was probably already working on it, and he just had to wait it out.

Sitting in the dark reminded him that he was vulnerable in a way he hadn't imagined, dependent on others for something as simple as light and warmth. Everyone was to some extent, but everyone else had sunlight and moonlight and the headlights of cars. He just had flashlights. He'd have to set up a backup power system.

He pulled on his shoes and his hoodie. He might as well go out into the tunnels, do his patrol of the A line, and hope the power outage would pass by tomorrow morning. He opened his front door, glad he still had an old-fashioned key to lock it with. He'd lock the tunnel doors, too. It wasn't nearly as secure as his electronic system, but it would still keep out most intruders.

When his foot touched the first wooden step, all the lights came on, inside and out. He threw up an arm to block out the light, but it wasn't enough. The light reminded him of being thrust all at once into a sunny day.

Brightness scalded his eyes. He couldn't see his house, his garden, his place of safety. Terrifying light engulfed him. His heart raced so quickly he couldn't differentiate the beats. His breathing came loud and fast.

He felt like he might throw up or die or both. Dizziness threatened to knock him off his feet. Sweat ran down his back. He started to shake.

He wanted to talk himself through it, to slow his breathing, to remind himself again that he wasn't really going to die. Nothing came. Bright light seared his eyelids, and panic filled him.

Edison barked again and again. He should comfort the dog, but he couldn't. He was frozen.

20

Ziggy adjusted the brightness on his laptop so he could better enjoy the scene in front of him. He giggled and touched the screen with one finger. "Gotcha."

Tesla stood on his porch. His eyes were big and round. Round as saucers, Ziggy's mother would have said. She liked to throw saucers and had clipped him on the back of the head more than once.

But Ziggy had never frozen, like the man on the screen. He always had the presence of mind to duck and run. The man on the monitor stared up at the light surrounding him and stood rooted to the spot. He would have been brained by the flying saucers.

His dog stood next to him. Its mouth opened and closed, but the camera Ziggy had installed had no audio. He imagined the animal barking, trying to get the man's attention. If so, it didn't work, and the dog seemed to know it.

He wished he could zoom in. He'd love to study the expression on that man's face. He'd seen terror before, but he'd never filmed it, never been able to watch it in such safety and calm. Maybe he could set up a camera for the next woman.

For now he must concentrate on the delightful images in front of him. The man was brought low. He had taken and taken and taken from Ziggy. He thought that he could keep Ziggy from hunting again. He thought he owned the tunnels.

Well, he was wrong.

Tesla was made of fear and nothing else. He hadn't moved from the spot he'd been in when the lights went on. They always feared the light—it was a result of the Algea. Tesla had consumed the drug when Ziggy dosed him months before, but until now Ziggy hadn't known how long the effects would linger. It was an interesting case study.

The man held up an arm to shield himself from the light. It was a good instinct, but it blocked Ziggy's view. He frowned. "Face the light like a man."

Ziggy had been watching Tesla from the time he had arrived on the front stoop with his pathetic little flashlight. He'd waited until the man was ready to step onto the green grass, then he'd brought back the lights. He'd suspected that would be the most terrifying time, when the man was out of the cocoon of his house. He'd been proven right beyond his wildest hopes.

It hadn't been easy figuring out how to cut and restore the power, but it had been worth it. Ziggy knew of an old junction box halfway up a subway line. It had long ago been automated, and Ziggy had traced it back to an empty electrician's room. He had a key. He didn't have all the keys, like that man did, but he had enough. Money and time were all that was needed, and he had enough of both.

He had looked around the dusty room. It held a panel of circuit breakers with an elaborate diagram identifying what each switch controlled. One was marked "Gallo house" in faint pencil. He had simply switched it off, then on. The best part was that the man himself couldn't control the light and darkness in his own home. Only Ziggy could.

An MTA electrician might come by soon. The system might have registered the power outage, and they might try to find the source. But they might not. The outage hadn't affected any critical systems, such as the subway lines themselves. Even if they did decide to come, he had a few more minutes to watch the scene unfolding in front of him.

He thought of cutting the lights again and then turning them back on, but decided that would give the man a second to collect himself. He might come back to himself given the chance. Better to let him suffer as long as possible.

The man's eyelids were torn open as wide as they could go. His eyes darted from side to side as if they sought to escape his panicked body, his pupils pinpoints of black. The man himself didn't move. He was frozen, like a woman in front of a train.

He was a rabbit cowering in a hole. As soon as he pulled himself together, he'd scuttle inside, climb into bed, and pull the covers over his head. He wouldn't be out in the tunnels tonight.

Which left Ziggy's playground free.

He'd spotted the perfect woman at the club. Emilia. If she was the one, she'd be there when he got back. Fate would make her wait for him.

21

Edison jumped on him, paws striking Joe square in the chest. Joe stumbled back a pace, lost his balance, and fell onto the wooden boards. He smelled fresh paint. He was on his own front porch. Safe.

Edison licked his face. His wet tongue came for Joe's eyes, and Joe closed them. Edison's tongue felt warm against his eyelids, his cheeks, his forehead. It was darker here on the floor with his eyes closed, safer.

The dog's heavy, furry body rested on Joe's chest. Warm weight pressed down. Joe couldn't take a deep breath because Edison was so heavy. The reassuring smell of dog filled his nostrils.

Joe took a single shallow breath, then struggled for another. Without trying, his breaths slowed. He wasn't hyperventilating anymore. The light wasn't blinding him. He was going to be OK.

Joe wrapped both arms around Edison's furry body. "We got this."

Edison's tail wagged against Joe's stomach, and he snuffled into Joe's ear.

"You're the best dog in the world," Joe said. "You know that, right?"

Edison rested his head against Joe's cheek. He knew.

"I'm totally giving you the whole sandwich now."

It felt like Edison nodded.

Joe lay still for a long time, hugging his dog. Eventually, he gently pushed Edison off and sat. He took the sandwich out of his backpack, unwrapped it, and gave it to the dog as promised.

"That was a doozy," he said. "I need to change my shirt, maybe get some tea to calm down. But then we'll head out, OK?"

Edison was too busy wolfing down the bread and meat to respond.

Joe pulled himself to his feet. His legs felt shaky, and he grabbed the railing to steady himself. It had been a long time since he'd had such a bad panic attack. He took a couple of deep breaths. See, body? he told himself. You didn't die from that. Stop freaking out.

His body never listened to him, but that didn't stop him from talking to it. Maybe one of these days he'd make a breakthrough. Maybe one of these days he'd be a billionaire making a difference in the outside world, like Alan. Of course, maybe that'd turn him into a complete asshole like Alan. That thought made him smile, which got a tentative tail wag from Edison.

A faint beeping sounded from the parlor. Was it the electric fireplace? Maybe it needed to be reset after a power failure. Or maybe he had the direction wrong, and the sound was coming from some electronic device upstairs.

He went through the open door and headed into the parlor. The parlor looked as it always did. Wall sconces bathed the room in warm, comforting light, but he kept one hand on the wall and the other on his flashlight. He wasn't going to be caught without it if the lights went out again.

His laptop rested on the ottoman, the screen facing the door. Since it had a battery, it hadn't been affected by the power outage. It was beeping. His A line surveillance app must have spotted something.

Joe sat in his leather chair and picked up the laptop. Probably another stoner sneaking off the platform to find bliss a few feet from the station or a couple of workers headed down to replace a recalcitrant piece of track. He would do a quick check, then change his sweat-soaked shirt, grab a couple of those damn nutrition bars for dinner, and head out. He wasn't going to let a panic attack keep him from patrolling the tunnels. His fear must not be allowed to own him any more than it already did.

The real-time laptop camera showed nothing amiss. He rewound the footage. It took a few extra seconds to get everything working because he had the shakes from the adrenalin he'd pumped out during his panic attack. A jog in the tunnels would clear the rest of the adrenalin out of his system. He'd be OK.

Edison was already beside him, resting his head next to Joe's lap and looking up at him with worried eyes.

"We got this," Joe said. "Everything is fine."

He glanced past the dog's head at the computer screen. Surveillance footage showed a transit employee approaching the end of the platform. He wore a reflective vest and had a paper cup of coffee in one hand, a toolbox in the other. He was alone. Nothing to worry about there.

A few minutes later, Joe was dressed and ready to head out. He had a lot of tunnel to patrol, and it was already late.

He stood on his porch, studying the bright green plants, the whitewashed ceiling, and the seagull. The room calmed him. He was home. He was safe here. That sense of safety would give him strength in the tunnels.

A tiny spark of light caught his eye. Had one of the ceiling LEDs fallen? He hadn't had any trouble with them before, but tonight seemed like the night for glitches. He walked toward the light, careful not to step on the young plants.

The object was tiny, smaller than his thumb. As he got closer, he saw it was painted white except for a tiny stripe around the edges. Light reflecting off that stripe had revealed it. It must have slipped out of position.

The object dangled a couple of feet above his head. It must be part of the LED system Maeve had installed to keep the plants alive, although he didn't recall seeing anything quite like it when they were setting things up. He'd had to work most of the time, so he must have missed it. He hadn't tracked every detail.

He looked up at the object. He couldn't reach it. He thought of going back into the house for a stepladder, but decided to jump for it. He jumped and missed, jumped again and grabbed at it. The object came off the wall with a tearing sound. Maeve wasn't going to be happy about that.

He opened his fist and examined a small plastic object with a round opening at one end. He recognized its purpose at once. It wasn't a fallen LED. It was a spy camera.

22

Vivian breathed in the smell of horse manure and hay. The chauffeur had taken them to the edge of the city to a small riding stable.

"I need to change into my riding clothes." Katrinka frowned as Vivian moved next to her. "It's not dangerous. I can go alone."

"You're probably right, but this is my job." Vivian opened the door to the tiny room and checked it out. A toilet, sink, and garbage can. A tiny open window high on the wall. Katrinka would have a hell of a time getting to the window, and she probably wouldn't fit through it.

Vivian stepped back and let the huffy teen go in. She hadn't wanted to take the girl riding at all, but it was on her weekly schedule, so Vivian had to go. To make matters worse, she'd have to ride with her, and Vivian didn't know how to ride.

When Katrinka came out, Vivian almost didn't recognize her. She'd pulled her hair back into a ponytail, changed into a white cotton shirt and a black jacket, riding pants and high boots. She'd also removed her makeup. She looked fresh-faced and happy.

"Do you have any riding clothes?" Katrinka asked.

"I can ride in what I'm wearing."

Katrinka didn't agree. She nodded to the woman in charge of the stables, and in a few minutes, Vivian was kitted out like some kind of English riding doll. She hated it. At least her clothes wouldn't smell like horse after.

Katrinka waited for her by the horses. She held the reins of a reddish horse with a white streak on his nose. "Meet Blaze."

Vivian looked at the other horse. It was black and looked tall.

"That's Missus Jenkins," Katrinka said. "I thought you might want a beginner horse."

"I want a motorcycle."

Katrinka grinned. "Maybe tomorrow."

Soon they were on the animals, loping along. Ahead of her, Katrinka and her chestnut-colored horse moved as a single unit. Vivian wondered if her own spine would survive the drubbing.

"You have to relax into the horse's rhythm." Katrinka slowed down to ride next to her.

Vivian tried, and it seemed to go a little better, but she still felt like she might fall off at any second. "How long have you been riding?"

"Every summer since I was little. My Aunt Billie in Montana has horses, and I spend my summers there while my parents are in Russia."

"Sounds nice."

"It is." Katrinka's eyes went soft. "If I could, I'd live there all the time."

"Is it a big ranch?"

Katrinka laughed. "It's not a ranch at all. Just a rundown farmhouse with a couple of horses, some chickens, and beehives. Aunt Billie makes her living as a nurse. I help out with the animals when I'm there."

They rode for an hour before they had to get Katrinka home in time for dinner. Her father had business colleagues coming by, and he'd told her that she had to be cleaned up and on time.

Vivian dropped her off, watching all the carefree joy fade away from the girl's face in the elevator. Not that it was any of her business.

She hobbled home. Her butt and thighs hurt from the riding, but walking helped. Once home, she popped two ibuprofen from the big bottle her mother kept in the kitchen. Her mother had gone to bed early, and Lucy was out with her friends, probably getting into trouble. Vivian wished her sister had more direction. Vivian had direction at her age and look where that got her—dishonorably discharged, living with her mother, and babysitting rich kids. Maybe Lucy was better off flitting around aimlessly like Katrinka. Vivian sure as hell didn't have the answers.

With a sigh, she kicked off black leather boots more suited for motorcycle riding than horseback riding. She settled at the scuffed kitchen table with a cup of coffee from the Keurig she'd given her mother for Christmas as a not entirely unselfish gift. She should go straight to bed, but she had some work to do. Hence the caffeine.

She picked up her boots and took them to their spot by the front door, aligning them carefully so no one would trip over them, then went off to hunt up her laptop. She tiptoed around the tiny living room in her stocking feet, glancing at the doily-covered chair, the doily-covered couch, and the neat coffee table. No laptop. She headed for the bedroom she shared with Lucy.

Vivian's half of the room was Spartan and spotless. The top of her dresser was clear, her bed made so tightly that a quarter could bounce off it, and the floor was free of clutter. Lucy said it looked like a barracks, which wasn't far from the truth. But it let Vivian see at a glance that the laptop wasn't on her desk where it was supposed to be.

She ventured into Lucy's territory, stepping over landmines of crumpled clothing before leaning down to check underneath the unmade bed. Bingo. The laptop lay at an odd angle, propped up by a balled-up sock. She hauled the computer out with one hand, glad that Lucy hadn't left it in the middle of the floor to get stepped on.

Tesla had given her one of his old laptops, and it was the nicest computer she'd ever owned. Lucy had glommed onto it right away and was constantly borrowing it for homework. Vivian couldn't blame her. She was probably the only kid in her class who didn't have her own computer.

Vivian carried the device back to the kitchen, set it down, and took a long sip of coffee. She leaned against the ladder-back chair and rubbed her temples. The headache wasn't going away.

A car honked on the street below, and someone shouted. Even this late at night, traffic was noisy. The refrigerator kicked in. These days it made a disconcerting sound, like some kind of appliance death rattle, and she worried that it would soon have to be replaced. Her mother couldn't afford that. She could only afford the rent on her apartment because Vivian pitched in. This was the real reason Vivian didn't find her own place—she'd be kicking her mother out into the street.

Plus, she told herself, the old place suited her. With what she was billing working for Tesla in her off hours, she'd be able to put aside enough for a new fridge. Maybe something that shot ice out of a dispenser on the door. Her mother would get a kick out of that. Meantime, they'd run the fridge until its death rattle overcame it.

Vivian took another sip of coffee and opened up her reports on the victims. Sandra Haines was the most recent one, and Vivian typed in notes about her conversation with that ass, Slade Masterson. Hard to believe that anyone would kill herself over that guy.

Vivian opened a browser and did a quick search on his name paired with *Who's Afraid of Virginia Woolf?* to check out his alibi on the night of Sandra's death. It was pretty unlikely that he'd killed all ten women, but he might still have killed Sandra.

The first entry in her search results pointed to a review on a New York theater web site. She clicked on it, wondering what kind of actor Slade was. The article was dated the day after Sandra's death. Vivian skimmed the piece, establishing that the reviewer had seen the play the night before. Apparently, *Virginia Woolf* was damned long, because it had run from 10 pm to 1:30 am. She hoped they had two intermissions. Regardless, it was being performed when Sandra was hit by the train. If Slade was on stage that night, he wouldn't have been able to sneak across town, drag his screaming ex-girlfriend down into a tunnel, push her in front of a train and be back for curtain. Not enough time.

One line verified that Slade Masterson had been on stage as he'd said. He'd made an impression on the writer of the article. The woman had written: "this reviewer had no trouble believing that Slade Masterson, who played the role of Nick, couldn't perform in the bedroom."

Vivian laughed out loud, imagining the look on his rugged face when he read that review. Sure, it established his alibi, but it didn't do him any other favors. Now she knew why he'd been so reluctant to tell her about the play in the elevator. With a grin, she copied the URL and that snippet from the review into her report, noting that Slade Masterson was no longer a suspect.

That left all the rest of New York.

Her butt felt better. Either the ibuprofen or seeing Slade Masterson get his was helping.

She started researching Rita Blaskowitz. Rita had died a week before Sandra Haines. Unlike Sandra, Rita had a blog. At the top someone had posted the sad news of Rita's death, and the comments underneath showed that she'd been well-liked. No one mentioned her death had been a suicide.

Vivian brought up Rita's earlier blog posts. Apparently, the poor woman had been diagnosed with pancreatic cancer a few months before her death and had started the blog to talk to the world about it. Her early posts brimmed with fight and determination. The later ones tapered off into resignation. In the last one she talked about the despair of realizing that she'd been given a death sentence although, in the end, the cancer hadn't killed her.

Again, the transit authorities had quickly ruled her death a suicide. She'd been diagnosed with a fatal disease and was clearly depressed. It was hard to argue with their findings.

Except for the peculiar fact that she looked so much like Sandra Haines. And both of them looked like the other eight victims. That couldn't be a coincidence, could it?

Vivian wondered what she would find when she'd researched the others. Probably eight more women struggling with difficult burdens, eight women who could easily have chosen to end their lives in front of a train.

But had they?

If they hadn't, what did that mean? Could there be a killer out there who found these women, brought them down to the tunnels, and convinced them to jump? Was that technically murder?

Sadly, it wasn't. It was only considered murder if the women were pushed, and there was no evidence they had been. None of the train operators had seen anyone else in the tunnels. Standing next to a depressed woman and talking her into jumping in front of a train might be despicable, but it wasn't illegal. Vivian had checked. If there was a perpetrator, and she found him, there was likely nothing the police could do. She'd cross that bridge when she came to it.

She shifted in her seat and winced. Her butt hurt, and she wished the kitchen chair had some padding. She was pretty fit for most activities, but horseback riding wasn't one of them.

She sighed. It was late, and she ought to get to bed. This stuff was too depressing to be thinking about at night, alone in a darkened kitchen.

She ignored her sensible impulse and re-read the accident reports, looking for patterns. Different operators, different train numbers, different women. She was so tired her eyes were having trouble focusing, and she still hadn't found anything that linked the women.

Then, she did.

A name kept popping up again and again. Salvatore Blue. He was part of the cleanup crew, and he'd cleaned the front cars of the trains that had hit four of the women. She tried searching for him online, but didn't have any luck, even though it was a weird name.

She forwarded the name to Tesla, knowing he had access to databases she didn't.

Then she went to bed. The faces of the dead women brightened and darkened in her dreams.

23

Joe had a camera detector. He'd ordered it online when he first moved in and had swept the house for cameras and bugs. His work at the time had been so confidential that he hadn't been able to run any risk of being overheard. Back then, he hadn't found anything.

This must be new. Maeve and her people had been all over that wall, cleaning and painting. They would have found the camera during their work. Perhaps one of them had put it there, and it had nothing to do with the dead women in the tunnels. Maeve and her employees had been vetted pretty thoroughly before they were given access to his house, but that didn't mean one of them hadn't left the camera. He was surprised by how much he hoped that the camera hadn't been left by Maeve.

He went back to work. Even though the camera detector was a little bigger than a pack of cards, it scanned all available frequencies for video transmissions. He discounted the surveillance feeds he was currently monitoring himself—namely all the subway platforms on the A line—and didn't find anything else. That just meant that, if there were cameras out there, they weren't using radio frequencies to transmit right now. Maybe the person who set up the cameras had turned them off remotely after they saw him find the first camera.

He had a bug detector that worked the same way for audio signals, and it didn't turn up anything either. That didn't mean everything was clear, but he didn't know what else to do.

For now, he'd have to try a low-tech solution. He pulled the camera out of his pocket and held it at knee height. "Smell it, Edison."

The dog dipped his nose into Joe's palm and sniffed obediently. He growled. Interesting.

"Can you find more of these?" Joe asked.

Edison dropped his nose to the ground and sniffed. He sniffed in seemingly random patterns across the ground. He wasn't trained in any kind of tracking, but he was a smart dog, so hopefully he was looking for things that smelled like the camera and not tracking all the places his own tennis ball had been.

Joe let the dog wander while he tried to sort out his own muddled thoughts. If it wasn't Maeve or her people, then someone else had come into Joe's sanctuary and left a camera. Who? And how? There were only three entrances to Joe's underground house. First was the elevator, but that was manned at the top by the staff at Grand Central Terminal during the day. There was no way someone could open the door to the round information booth under the clock, walk past the people sitting there, and unlock the door that led to the elevator without being noticed. The booth was so small they'd practically bump into the workers stationed there, workers who never left their posts all at once. That entrance was secure.

Maybe they could have done it at night if they managed to hide in Grand Central until the building was closed, but even then there were cleaners around, and Joe usually disabled the elevator so it couldn't be called up to the concourse at night. He'd forgotten to do that when Maeve visited earlier that evening: who was to say that he hadn't forgotten it on another occasion? Joe tried to think back, but he couldn't be sure.

Edison nosed the front door. He hadn't found anything outside. Joe followed him inside, camera and bug detectors out and sweeping. An hour later, neither of them had found anything inside, either.

Joe disabled his security and went out the second exit to his house: the main tunnel exit. Edison sniffed the ground and growled. If the dog was saying what Joe thought he was saying, the man had been here, too. But to come in via this entrance, he needed Joe's security code. Only two people knew that code: Joe and Celeste. It couldn't have been her—she didn't leave the house, and she never would have told anyone. So how else could an intruder find the code?

His phone beeped. It had come out of its Faraday pocket again. He pulled it out.

It was a text from Alan. *Must cancel tennis. Things heating up. Maybe a quick drink next week instead?*

Alan had never cancelled tennis before, not when he was in town. There must be more going on with him than the season. Joe didn't like him, but he texted him back anyway. *Meet at Campbell instead of the club.* The Campbell Apartment was trendy enough for Alan, and it was inside Grand Central so Joe could get there.

I want to come down to your house, Alan answered.

That was weird, too. Alan had never had any interest in Joe's living space, had never wanted to visit him there. Edison scratched against the door, reminding Joe that they were supposed to be looking for traces of a man who had broken into Joe's sanctum.

Meet at the clock, Joe told him. He didn't like the idea of being down in his house with Alan, alone, but he pushed the thought away. He'd known Alan for years. The man wasn't exactly harmless, but he wasn't a psycho killer either.

Before he forgot, he texted his lawyer, Mr. Rossi, to get Alan Wright added to the list of approved visitors. Given his high visibility, the security checks would fly right by.

Matter decided, Joe punched in the code and opened the door. He stepped out quickly with Edison, so they wouldn't be silhouetted against the light from his chamber. After his eyes had adjusted to the light outside, he looked around.

"You smell anyone?" he asked Edison. He could tell by the dog's relaxed manner that no one was there.

Joe examined the dusty ground, searching for footprints. It was hard to see if anyone had walked through the dust because he and Edison walked this way every day, sometimes a couple of times a day, and their footprints had disturbed the ground.

Edison sniffed the ground around the door, ending up at the wall. He barked. Joe shone his flashlight where Edison was looking. Two neat rectangles had been pressed into the dust. The rectangles were parallel to each other a few feet apart, and about a foot from the wall.

He swept his flashlight up at the ceiling and stopped at a small square of clean rock. That was odd. His best guess was that something had been taped up there, and when the tape had been peeled away, it had taken dust and soot with it.

The camera inside had been taped up against the wall with double-sided tape, so it made sense that one out here would have been, too, but he didn't have any proof. It was just an empty square. Still, it was the right place to record Joe entering his code in the security system when he came home.

This probably cleared Maeve and her crew, and he breathed a sigh of relief on that score. He liked Maeve and wanted to trust her.

He reset the system, choosing new random numbers, colors floating in his head as he entered them. He leaned low over the device, so that, if there were another camera out there, it couldn't see what he was typing in.

"I think he came in here, Edison," Joe said. "He got my security code with that camera and came in through the tunnel door. What do you think? Do you smell anything?"

Edison cocked his head and wagged his tail.

"This would be a lot easier if you could talk," Joe told him.

Edison licked his hand.

"Yeah, you're pretty good at the nonverbal communication thing," Joe said. "Because you are a great dog!"

He gave Edison another treat, then looked around the rest of the tunnel. He found nothing else out of place.

He returned to his parlor and ran through the footage from his own surveillance cameras. He had one by the elevator and one by the inside of the tunnel entrance. He'd need to install one outside, too.

Most of the footage was boring, and he fast forwarded through it until two (blue) o'clock. At that point, both cameras blacked out. Someone must have cut the power. The cameras had backup batteries, so they kept filming.

At first it was all black, then a thread of light leaked in from the tunnel entrance as someone opened the door. Proof in black and white that someone had broken into his sanctuary. All this time he'd thought he was invulnerable here, but he wasn't.

A figure dressed in black entered holding a tiny flashlight with a red bulb, like the ones used by astronomers. The red light illuminated such a tiny scrap of darkness that Joe couldn't see a face or determine a gait, but the size and shape told him it was a man. He crossed the ground quickly, as if he knew where he was going.

The man stopped and set his backpack on the ground near where Joe had found the camera. He pulled a square object out of his backpack and extended it to about six (orange) feet. A ladder. He scampered up. His movements were hard to see, but he must have been fastening his camera to the ceiling. He climbed down, folded up his ladder, and turned off the light. Several minutes passed before the door to the tunnel entrance closed. He could have done anything during that time.

Joe played and replayed the footage. He could tell little about the man. He was about Joe's height, six (orange) foot tall. He seemed bulky, but that could have been his clothing or the shadows. Joe couldn't see his face. He might have been wearing a ski mask, but Joe couldn't even be sure of that. The light was too poor. He could tell that the guy was wearing gloves, which meant that he wouldn't find any fingerprints.

He ran the footage through some filters to lighten and enhance it. Nothing worked.

His laptop beeped. Probably that track worker ending his shift. Still, Joe tabbed over to the surveillance window to make sure. Nothing to see now, but he rewound a few minutes.

A light-haired woman stumbled down the empty platform at 23rd (blue, red) Street. She wore a dark-colored outfit with expensive-looking high heels. She wove from side to side as if she were drunk.

A man in a light-colored fedora held her elbow. As if he knew right where the camera was, the man adjusted his hat so its shadow fell across his face. Joe couldn't see his features. The man walked with a slight limp. There was something familiar about his gait, but Joe couldn't pinpoint it. Athletic, long stride length. The limp was awkward, almost artificial.

The man pointed to the end of the platform, and the woman nodded. Blond hair hung halfway down her back. She leaned against the man, resting her head against his dark shoulder. It looked as if she were crying. Her shoulders shook. The couple reached the end of the platform, climbed over the gate, and walked off into the tunnel.

Joe took his phone out of his pocket. He'd call Vivian and have her alert the transit cops on the way. They might make it in time.

If they didn't, he had to get to that woman before she died in front of a train.

He ran.

24

Ziggy practically bounced with elation. His enemy was contained, and Emilia had been waiting for him to come back and take her home just as he'd hoped. She was full of despair. She'd discovered that her boyfriend had made a sex tape of them and posted it to a revenge porn website when they broke up. Users on the site had rated her sexual prowess as poor—attractive but unenthusiastic was the most common comment. She'd repeated this part to Ziggy several times.

"I lost my job," she said. "I loved my job."

He led her deeper into the tunnel, away from cameras and prying eyes. "Can you get another one?"

"I was a preschool teacher," she said. "This is a permanent black mark."

"Maybe the next employer won't notice. It's not like everyone researches candidates on the Internet."

"They do! Of course they do!" She wiped at her eyes with the back of her hand. "I love the children, and I didn't even get a chance to say good-bye."

Why did all of them think that saying good-bye somehow made things all right? It didn't change anything. Life rolled along whether you said good-bye or not. "The children probably won't notice."

She looked stricken. "They'll notice. Of course they will. They need me. I spend more time with them than their parents do."

Lucky kids, being able to get away from their parents like that. "The school will hire someone else. The children will be fine. In a few months, they probably won't even remember you."

"I let them down." She sniffed and stared at the track. "Nobody will remember me. Except maybe you."

"I have a bad memory." He'd remember her. Emilia with the red shirt that matched the color of her lipstick.

"Thanks." She tottered to a halt. The drugs were kicking in. Her eyes overflowed with tears, and she grabbed onto his arm like a drowning man to a life preserver.

"Put on some lipstick," he said. "You'll feel better if you look better."

"Attractive, but unenthusiastic." She sighed, but she got out her lipstick and smoothed it across her too-thin lips.

The smell bloomed in the tunnel. His excitement grew with each breath. It had been such a long time since Sandra. "What does unenthusiastic mean?"

"Bellows like a cow," she replied. "According to *anonymous73*."

Light shone against her lips. Her hair ran down her back like a golden river. A woman who looked like that could bellow all she wanted. "Nothing wrong with cows."

"What will I tell my father?" she asked. "Why I got fired?"

"You could tell him the truth. He might already know if he has Internet."

Her eyes widened. "He might have seen it."

"You said that someone tagged it on your Facebook page," he said. She'd said no such thing.

"I did?" She reached out a white hand to touch the wall.

"All your friends know by now."

"I can't face them. I can't go back to Indianapolis. I'd rather die."

He didn't say anything.

"Blake will never let up," she said. "He still has the tape. He can post it anywhere."

"Lots of sites to choose from. And the Internet is forever."

"The Internet is forever," she repeated.

"Maybe no one in Indianapolis knows. Maybe you could get a job back there."

"They're all my Facebook friends," she said. "They know."

"That's unfortunate." It would probably all blow over in a few months, but she couldn't see that now, and he didn't want her to.

"I had a chastity ring in high school. Did I tell you?"

"What's that?" Let her explain, get her invested in that memory.

"It means that I was saving myself for marriage. I was the only girl in my high school with a ring like that." She touched her bare ring finger as if she felt the weight of the missing metal.

"How did you get the ring?"

"My father gave it to me," she said. "Everyone made fun of me for it. They called me a stuck-up bitch. Frigid. A prude."

"They won't call you those names now."

She closed her eyes as if picturing all the things that they would call her. He let her think. "They'll call me worse."

"What about a different job?"

"Teaching is all I ever wanted to do. From the time I was a little girl, I knew I wanted to take care of little kids and babies. What's left for me?"

"New York is expensive," he said. "You can't stay here without a job."

"I'll have to go back?" Her eyes stared into his. Tears trickled down her cheeks.

"It sure sounds like it."

"My father is a minister. He'd never forgive me for something like this."

"You don't know that." But she did. She'd already told him.

"He beat my mother once for wearing a dress that he said was too low cut. And he left her when he caught her talking to the gas man. He called her a whore."

"What happened to her?" He struggled to keep his voice deep and even. The high voice wanted to come out to sing.

"She took sleeping pills."

"How do you know?"

"I found her," she whispered. "I was five years old and I came into her bedroom to wake her up, and she was still and white and had foamy vomit leaking out of her mouth."

"Why did she do it?"

"Because she couldn't live with the shame."

He stepped away from her.

"Shame eats away at you," she said. "It consumes you like hot waves of acid until there's nothing left but bleached bones."

That was the most poetic thing any of them had ever said. "Bones?"

"Bones so smooth and polished and white that there's nothing left to be ashamed of."

He took another step back. The track shuddered to life. Soon now. So soon.

"Is that what you want?"

She turned her head toward the sound of the approaching train. "I do."

He stepped behind a pillar and watched her. Like the others, she was luminous. The light shone against hair like beaten gold, alabaster skin with a scattering of tan freckles, trembling red lips, and those shoes. They were royal purple, fit for a queen.

She turned to face the distant train and reached her arms toward it as if embracing her fate.

25

Joe huddled against the side of the tunnel. A train raced by, hot and bright. Edison pressed himself against the wall, and Joe held his hands over the dog's ears. This could be the train that would kill the woman on the video, and there was nothing he could do.

A knife stabbed his side with each breath. His mother would have called it a stitch. "*Slow down*," she would have said. "*Collect your breath and collect yourself.*" He waited for the train to pass so he could run again.

After the last car passed, he jumped onto the tracks behind it and ran. Edison's solid form loped next to him, unfaltering. The train's red taillight receded.

He settled into his rhythm. Each stride covered three train ties, his foot landing on the solid wood surface and pushing off to the next one. His pace felt slow, but long practice had taught him this was the fastest way to run along the tracks. He couldn't sprint pell mell. It would be too easy to trip and fall onto the third rail. He couldn't help anyone if he electrocuted himself.

Another train rumbled behind him, and he pushed himself to move even faster. If the last train hadn't already killed her, this one might.

Then he saw her. A tall blonde standing in the middle of the tracks. Hair fell to her waist, and it glowed golden in the weak light. Like the others, she had come here to die.

He screamed a warning, but his voice must have been drowned out by the approaching train, because she didn't even look at him. She stood still as a statue. Her unblinking eyes were black holes in a pale face.

A dark figure stood a few feet away from her, half obscured by a pillar. The man. Joe had known he would be there, but the sight still shocked him. These women had not come down here by accident and alone. This man had brought them here.

Rage coursed through Joe. The man had brought her here to watch her die.

Joe's shadow loomed in front of him. The train was close.

An alcove beckoned a yard away. He and Edison could hole up there safely until the train passed, but if they did, the train would kill the woman.

He didn't slow as he approached the pocket of safety. He had to get to the woman. She would die if he didn't.

He pointed toward the alcove and shouted, "Go!"

Hopefully, Edison would heed his command and leap to safety.

The train's brakes screeched in his ears. It would never stop in time for him, or for her.

26

Ziggy held his breath and watched her. But then Tesla appeared. Ziggy couldn't believe his eyes. That man should have been home, cowering in fear. He was stronger than Ziggy had given him credit for. The man waved his arms like a monkey.

The train operator saw him, and the screech of metal on metal tore at Ziggy's ears. The operator was braking too soon. Tesla might ruin everything.

Ziggy turned his attention back to Emilia. His hold on her might break in the extra seconds it took for the train to reach her. Or the impact might not kill her. She didn't know his name, but she could describe him, tell the police what had happened to her, maybe lead them to wonder if there had been others. If they looked for it, they might even find his drug in her system. He needed her to want to die, and to die.

She never wavered. She set her purple shoes on the train ties and held her hands out from her sides like a crucified Christ. A dreamy smile crossed her shining face.

Then the train took her.

He didn't dare stay to see what happened after. If he'd survived the train, Tesla would come for him. He would bring his nasty dog, and there would be no escaping them.

He would have to miss Emilia's death, the most satisfying part of his ritual. Tesla had taken her from him. First the lipsticks in his special room, and now this.

Clutching Emilia's lipstick tightly in his fist, he turned away. He had that, at least, and he had the memory of her standing there with her arms out, crucifying herself because that was how a minister's daughter should die. She'd been so beautiful and brave. An angel.

His steps turned to an escape route he'd never thought he would need. He always planned his escape route. Sometimes, in life as well as in chemistry, reactions were too energetic, and the energy needed a safe place to vent. He sprinted down a side tunnel.

27

A heavy weight struck Joe at waist-level. The impact knocked him off his feet and threw him sideways. He landed hard in the protected alcove, his ankle bending sharply beneath him. A furry body pinned him to the ground. Edison.

The train thundered by. Joe saw the face of a man in a suit inside as he tumbled forward. The train car passed in the blink of an eye. Then the next car and the next. The train was slowing, but it would never stop in time.

The high-pitched sound of metal grinding against metal drilled into his head. He screamed to drown it out. With both hands, he reached around and covered Edison's ears. The dog had saved his life, again. He had driven Joe into the only safe spot in the tunnel, forced him to take cover. He had known what Joe wouldn't admit, that he wouldn't have reached her in time. That the train would have cut him down like wheat. As it had probably done to the woman.

Maybe she had left the tracks. Maybe the train had been able to stop in time. The operator had braked to avoid Joe, and maybe that extra time was enough to have saved her life.

As soon as the train had passed, Joe lifted Edison off him.

"Good dog," he said.

Edison licked his face.

Joe hauled himself to his feet and limped after the slowing train. His foot throbbed, and blood trickled from his nose. He'd landed hard, but there was nothing wrong with him that wouldn't heal.

The train jerked to a stop. Its taillights bathed the tunnel in an eerie red light.

Edison's mouth moved, but Joe couldn't hear the bark. He heard only the ringing in his ears. He hoped that Edison's hearing hadn't been affected. The dog shouldn't have to suffer because the master was a fool.

Joe crossed behind the train, away from the third rail, and turned sideways. If he flattened himself against the wall, he fit between the edge of the train and the tunnel wall. He sidestepped as quickly as he could, pain driving up from his injured foot each time it came down on a train tie. Just a sprain, he told himself, but he could tell it was something worse.

Light from the cars above fell across his face. Through one window, Joe saw a man in a suit with a cut on his forehead. Blood poured down the side of his face. He leaned against the window as a gray-haired woman in a housecoat lifted what looked like a tea towel up to his wound. Joe passed their car and moved to the next, hurrying toward the front of the train.

Headlights illuminated the train operator. Joe recognized his profile. He was a new driver, and they sometimes had coffee together after his shifts.

"Martel," Joe called.

Martel turned to look at him. Shaggy black hair framed a shocked face.

Joe stumbled over. His ears still rang.

"I tried to stop, Joe," Martel said. "You heard the brakes."

"I know you did."

Joe looked down at the woman he had failed to save. Her arms were thrown into unnatural angles, the bones clearly broken between the wrist and the elbow. Her legs were under the train. Joe imagined they looked worse than her arms. Blood leaked out of her mouth and drenched the golden hair that lay across the dirty ties.

"Stay with her," Martel said. "I have to call it in."

Joe knelt beside the woman. He was afraid to touch her, couldn't imagine where he could touch her that wouldn't hurt her. Her chest rose slowly. She was still alive.

He took her hand gently in his. Her hand was wet with blood, and a palm tree was tattooed on the inside of her wrist, like Maeve's dragonfly.

"I'm sorry," he whispered. "I came too late."

Her eyes searched for his. Tears leaked out of the corners of her eyes and ran down her temples. Joe wiped the tears away with his thumb and laid his the back of his hand against her cold cheek.

Her garish red lips twitched as if she wanted to say something.

He leaned down toward her pale face.

"Remember me," she said.

"I will," he said. "Always."

The edges of her lips rose in the tiniest of smiles, then her face went limp.

Her breath rattled out, and her chest didn't rise again. Her eyes stared sightlessly at his.

She was gone.

28

Ziggy ran hard, ducking from one tunnel to another, changing directions like a fox chased by hounds. It would be easy to get lost down here, but he knew where he was going. The path in front of him was as familiar as his daily commute in the world above. He had walked these underground rooms many times, thinking even then that this knowledge might one day save his life.

He skidded to a stop next to a rusty ladder bolted to the stone wall. He dropped the lipstick into the pocket of his long coat and began to climb. The metal felt cold under his leather gloves, and his thin dress shoes slipped against the rungs with every step. The shoes were probably ruined by the stones he'd run across.

He struggled upward. His shoulders trembled from exertion, and his calves screamed in protest. He hadn't climbed this ladder in ages, had forgotten how long it was. He concentrated on each rung, pulling himself ever farther from the darkness below.

Dim light fell through a square grate above his head. Not far. He would reach that light before his arms gave out, but what if his package was gone?

A small grate, barely large enough for his shoulders to fit through, covered the stone at the end of the ladder. He supposed this shaft was for ventilation, but he'd never bothered to find out. He didn't need to know. All he needed was to get out.

Hooking one arm over the nearest rung, he felt the back of the rung above. His questing fingers found a dirty plastic bag wedged into the space between the top two rungs. He smiled. Still right where he'd left it.

Before he could get it down, he needed to make sure he wouldn't drop it. His hands felt like claws, and he opened and closed his right hand to drive the blood back into it. His left hand kept its hold on the metal rung. If he let go, he wouldn't survive.

Sure that his right hand wouldn't betray him, he reached for a black object he'd left here a long time ago. Water spattered his face as he tore the plastic bag away from the object underneath. The air smelled of dirt and oil and urine, and he kept his mouth tightly closed.

He balled up the tattered plastic and stuffed it into his pocket. He'd take it with him and throw it away when he was far enough to be safe.

Mud-encrusted zip ties secured a long object to the top rung. He took a pocket knife from his pants pocket and cut each plastic tie, careful to keep hold of them, and dropped them, too, into his pocket. If that man found something at the base of the ladder, it might lead him up here. Not that it should matter that the man knew where he'd exited the subway, but it might. He couldn't give Tesla a single clue. He was too smart.

The metal object was still wedged in tightly. Slowly, he worked it free. Dim light from streetlights above shone on long handles and sharp jaws. It was still serviceable, and he congratulated himself for having stored a bolt cutter here all those months ago.

The thick lock that the MTA had installed on the inside of the grate dangled in front of him like ripe fruit. This simple bit of metal was the only thing standing between him and freedom.

After a few false starts, he sheared through the metal hasp and put the lock into his pocket with everything else. He lifted the grate and climbed out onto the deserted street.

He was alone as he closed the grate and headed into the night. A block away, he abandoned the filthy garbage bag against the side of a building. By morning the wind would have carried it halfway around the city.

The zip ties he dropped into an overstuffed green trash can a block later. The bolt cutters he set under a parked VW a few blocks after that. The cutters had served him well, and he felt a pang at their loss.

The broken lock went into another garbage can, far from the first.

He had nothing, except for her lipstick tube. The lipstick was almost meaningless because he hadn't held it while watching her die. He hadn't seen the life leave her eyes while he smelled the floral scent of 999.

He didn't even know if she was dead.

This must never happen again.

29

Vivian didn't need a doctor to tell her that the woman was dead. Vivian touched Joe's shoulder gently. "They have to move her, Mr. Tesla."

He flinched as if she'd struck him, then looked up at her. He'd been crying, his nose was bleeding, and he held one hand against the woman's cheek as if to wipe away her tears.

He moved his hand, and his palm gleamed in the headlights. It was slick with blood. Vivian stood on one side of him and looked over at Dirk. He was already on Tesla's other side. Together, they lifted the man to his feet, careful to pull him away from the body so he wouldn't disturb anything. This wasn't a rescue site. It was a crime scene.

She'd called Dirk in the cab on the way to the station, and he'd met her there. They'd jogged through the tunnels together, but when the tinny voice over the speaker at 23rd Street Station had said that service was interrupted, she'd already known what they'd find.

"I was too late." Tesla's shoulders slumped, and he kept glancing back at the woman on the tracks. He stood awkwardly on one leg, as if he'd injured the other.

"*We* were too late," she told him. "All of us."

Tesla shouldn't have to bear the blame for this alone, but he shook his head at her words. Whatever she said, he held himself solely responsible.

The train operator, a young black man in a blue uniform, turned to her. "Who are you?"

Dirk flashed his badge, but the man looked unimpressed. "Are you with the transit division?"

"I don't need to be," Dirk said.

"I saw someone," Joe said. "A man standing next to the tracks."

"Did you see anyone?" Dirk asked the train operator.

"I only saw Joe running down the tracks, and I put on the brakes and his dog knocked him off the tracks and then I saw her and I knew that I wasn't going to be able to stop before—" The man gestured toward the woman's lifeless body, but he didn't look at her.

"What did the man look like?" Vivian asked.

Dirk shot her a look that made it clear he was supposed to be the one asking the questions.

"He was about my height." Tesla closed his eyes. "He was wearing a fedora, and it shielded his face. I didn't get a close look at him."

Edison licked Joe's hand. The dog's coat was streaked with black. He looked as if he'd been rolling around on the tracks, but otherwise he seemed fine.

"Are you certain you saw someone?" Dirk asked.

"Of course," Tesla snapped.

"Where was he standing?" Vivian got another look from Dirk, but she ignored it. If he didn't ask the right questions, she had no choice but to pick up the slack.

Tesla limped over to a metal pillar, and Vivian followed. Behind the pillar a tunnel stretched off into blackness.

"His escape route," Tesla said. "He's way ahead of us."

"Maybe this time," Vivian said.

Tesla pointed his flashlight down at the ground. His light showed only rocks. They wouldn't find tracks there.

Four people jogged down the tunnel from 23rd Street Station: two policemen and a man and a woman wearing uniforms and carrying an empty stretcher. Paramedics, but there wouldn't be much for them to do.

Tesla shone his flashlight down the empty tunnel. Two more tunnels branched off, both on the right hand side. "He could be anywhere by now."

If the man knew the tunnels, and he must, he'd be nearly impossible to track.

The paramedics had reached the woman's body. The female paramedic shook her head and looked at her watch. Establishing the time of death, Vivian knew. Off by a few minutes, but close enough, unlike the rescue.

The paramedics worked together to pull the woman out from under the train. Vivian looked away. She'd seen too many broken bodies during the war to ever want to see another.

Tesla limped toward them, barely able to put weight on his leg.

"Stop!" he shouted.

Both paramedics froze and looked over at him.

"I beg your pardon, sir." One of the transit cops peeled away from the paramedics and walked over toward Tesla. He had a pointy nose, pale close-set eyes, and gray hair trimmed into a buzz cut. He reminded Vivian of a hedgehog. "Who are you?"

"I'm Joe Tesla." Tesla pointed at the body. "This is a crime scene. You can't disturb it."

"Looks to me like the woman was hit by a train, and there's nothing more we can do for her," Officer Hedgehog said. "We need to get the train moving again, provided it's not damaged."

Not the most sensitive thing to say, but he did have a point. The woman was dead and, even if it was a crime scene, they needed to get the train moving. She had seen a guy bleeding in the car who probably needed to get to a station, and there might be others injured as well. She'd once read that a suicide by train delays the train by half an hour on average. They were coming up on that soon.

A gray-haired woman pounded on the train window and pointed at the paramedics, then back inside the car. The train operator went over to see what was going on.

Tesla stood between the policeman and the body. "You can't move her yet."

"That's not your jurisdiction, sir." Officer Hedgehog was getting louder. He looked tired and crabby. Nobody was having a good night.

"One of the passengers is injured," the train operator called. "We need to get him to a station."

The policeman nodded at the paramedics. "Move her, but be careful."

Tesla reached for the paramedics, but Vivian got to him first.

"You're not going to win this battle, sir," she told him quietly. "Your best course of action is to get photographs before she's gone. At least then you'll have something."

Tesla scowled, but he pulled out his phone and started taking pictures. He lifted his injured foot off the ground completely and photographed while standing on one leg, like a stork. Edison stood close as if he were ready to catch Tesla should he fall.

Vivian looked around for the woman's purse, but didn't find it. She noticed an unusual tattoo on the woman's wrist—a palm tree bent into a crescent shape. If the woman didn't have any identification, hopefully the tattoo would give them something to go on.

Officer Hedgehog started toward Tesla, but Dirk stepped up next to him.

"I'm Detective Norbye," he said. "We got a tip that this might be a homicide."

"What kind of a tip?"

Dirk glanced at Vivian. "An anonymous one."

The paramedics had already loaded the body onto the stretcher. They draped a blanket over her face and body and trotted back toward 23rd Street Station. Tesla looked between them and the tunnels.

The train conductor climbed under the train, probably checking the bottom for damage. Vivian knew from her recent research that a person hit by a train could do a lot of damage to the bottom of a car—ripping out lines as they were dragged along.

The transit policeman shook his head and called out to his compatriot, "Officer Spangler."

The other officer hurried over.

"I'd like you to detain Mr. Tesla here, take him down to the station for questioning," Officer Hedgehog said.

Edison nudged Tesla's hand, which he'd clenched into a fist. He wouldn't go outside without a fight.

"That won't be necessary," Dirk intervened. "I'll take it from here."

Officer Hedgehog looked like he wanted to argue about it, but Dirk outranked him. It probably helped that the officer was coming up on the end of his shift and probably didn't want the hassle. After a bit of thought, he shrugged and stepped back.

"This way, Mr. Tesla." Dirk pointed back down the tracks toward where the paramedics had taken the stretcher.

Tesla limped in the direction Dirk had pointed, with Vivian and Edison trailing behind. As soon as they were out of earshot, Tesla turned to Dirk.

"I want to take you to where I found the lipsticks. Did Vivian tell you about those?"

"She did." Dirk had on his cop face, and she couldn't read him. "Do you have proof that you saw a man back there before the accident?"

"Surveillance video from the station will show her leaving the platform with a man. He was holding onto her elbow. He didn't just disappear."

"When the train came, did he push her or touch her in any way?" Dirk asked.

Tesla hesitated. "Not that I saw. I wasn't looking just before the train hit."

"At that point the train operator would've seen something," Dirk said.

"Maybe." Tesla headed for an access tunnel.

"Is your foot OK?" Vivian asked.

"I'm fine." Tesla kept limping along, looking anything but fine. He'd wiped the blood off his face and hand, but he was still filthy and looked pretty banged up—his foot or leg was wounded, he winced when he moved his shoulder, and he had a bruise on the side of his face.

"Where are we headed?" Vivian asked. His house was in the opposite direction.

"To the room where we found the lipsticks. It's not far."

Vivian fell in behind Tesla, and Dirk walked next to her. At least they were leaving the tunnel where the trains ran. She didn't like flattening herself against the wall and hoping she wasn't going to be smashed, especially after seeing the dead woman on the tracks. She trudged along silently, flashlights lighting the way.

Tesla could barely put weight on his foot, and his forehead shone with sweat. He must be in a lot of pain, but he didn't slacken his pace. Edison threw him worried glances that Tesla didn't seem to notice.

Eventually, he turned into an old steam tunnel. A few paces in, he stopped in front of a rusty door. Vivian shone her light on the lock. No evidence that it had been picked or forced. Dirk ran his light around the door's metal edges. No sign of forced entry. Whoever came in and out of here probably had a key.

Tesla fiddled with his giant key ring. His face was paler than usual underneath the mask of grime, and his hands shook, probably with a combination of shock and exhaustion. He ought to get off that leg, too, but pointing that out wasn't going to convince him. She was impressed that he was still standing.

He found the right key and inserted it. "Usually these old locks take patience to get open, but this one's been well maintained."

She'd have to take his word for that.

The lock clicked, and Tesla reached for the door handle.

"Careful," she said. "Fingerprints."

He pulled his sweatshirt cuff over his hand and turned the door handle. An unexpected smell billowed out. Bleach.

Her gun was in her hand before she realized it. A quick glance to the side showed that Dirk's gun was up and ready, too. She pushed Tesla quickly away from the doorway, and raised a finger to her lips.

Dirk caught her eye, then went in, holding his flashlight over his gun. She quickly followed, breaking left as Dirk broke right. Their flashlights did a quick scan of the room.

"Clear!" she called out.

A light flickered on overhead. Tesla stood by the door next to a light switch.

The walls were a pale gray with the shadow of mold near the bottom. The linoleum floor was free of dirt and dust. Even the light fixture had been recently wiped down. Based on the smell, if there had been evidence in this room, it had been recently destroyed.

Tesla hobbled across to the far corner. Vivian followed. He pointed to a hole. The hole was almost perfectly square and about a foot deep. No sign of the dirt that had been removed. Either Tesla had found the wrong room, which she doubted, or the cleaner must have carted off the dirt. Thorough.

"He was here," Tesla said. "He cleaned up."

"Are you sure this is the right room?" Dirk asked. Better him than Vivian.

Tesla gave him a look that could freeze water. "I'm sure."

"I'll bring a forensics team down," Dirk said. "I don't think we'll find much."

"It didn't look like this a few days ago." Tesla sounded angry, and she couldn't blame him. If they'd come here sooner, they might've been able to find something that could've saved the woman's life. "Not one bit."

"I believe that." Dirk looked around the room again. "I can't see why the MTA would do a cleanup like this, but I'll double check. My guess is that somebody else came down here and removed something, and he must have had a reason to work this hard."

"I have a name you might want to check out," Vivian said.

With twin expressions of surprise, Dirk and Tesla turned to her.

"His name is Salvatore Blue. He works for MTA, and he was on cleanup detail for a couple of the incidents."

"They all happened on the same line," Dirk said. "Probably only so many cleaning crew per line."

"His is the only name that keeps coming up," she said. "So the other cleaners are pretty good at dodging nasty work."

"I'll look into him," Dirk said. "Blue like the color."

Tesla didn't say anything, but she could practically see the wheels turning in his head. He'd look into Blue, too.

Vivian took out her phone and started filming, starting with the door, the lock, and the ground outside. After that, she came into the room and worked in a neat grid pattern. Once Dirk brought people down here, she and Tesla would be denied access to this site. Not that there was much to see anymore.

Dirk didn't get in her way. "Please send me that surveillance video you mentioned earlier, Mr. Tesla. And you, Viv, email me any other notes you've made. We'll get on this."

"Good," she said. "Because he always kills in pairs."

30

Joe stumbled down the tunnels. Hot pain shot up his leg with each step. He'd struggled to ignore it on the way to the lipstick room, but he was tired now, and the anger and hope that had driven him to the room were gone. He was one step behind this killer, and a woman had died on the tracks because of it. If he didn't figure this out soon, another innocent would die, and the only lead he had was the name of a janitor who was probably not involved.

"Do you need a hand, Mr. Tesla?" Vivian asked.

"I got it." He tried to limp a little faster. The pain made him nauseous, and he hoped he wouldn't throw up in front of her.

Vivian didn't say anything, but when they passed an underground scrap pile, she rooted around in it. He leaned against the wall, not asking what she was doing, just grateful to have a short break. Edison leaned against him. Joe's foot throbbed with each heartbeat.

Vivian seemed to have found what she was looking for, and came over carrying a long broom. She handed it to him. "Crutch."

A woman of few words, but always practical.

"Thanks." Joe fitted the wood under his armpit. It was too long, but it helped to bear some of his weight, and it made the going easier.

They pushed on until they reached his security door. He entered the old code first, remembered that he'd changed it, and entered the new one. He looked up to where the camera had been installed. Just bare rock, so the bastard hadn't come back yet. Good.

The security system disarmed, he unlocked the door, and they went inside.

The chamber was barely lit. The ceiling glowed dark indigo to mimic the night sky above. The air smelled of plants and clean water, so much better than what he'd been smelling for the past few hours—rat urine, mold, engine oil, bleach, and blood.

He drew in a deep breath of home. He was tempted to throw himself down on the green plants and not move for a long time, but he kept moving. Once he sat down, he wasn't going to stand up for a while.

"Nice plants," said Vivian.

"They're new," he told her.

He trudged across to the stairs, unlocked his front door, and gestured for her to go in first.

"Where to?" she asked.

"Kitchen," he answered. He was too dirty to sit in the parlor, and too tired to go upstairs.

She went in ahead of him, checking each room in the downstairs to make sure it was empty. He didn't expect her to find anyone. The man had killed tonight. He was probably at home, gloating.

Joe used the surge of anger to propel him to the kitchen. He collapsed on a chair. Edison put his head in Joe's lap.

"You're a good dog," Joe said. Though Edison hadn't been limping during their walk back, Joe felt his silky legs and checked the pads of his feet. Luckily, Edison was unharmed. But filthy. Joe usually washed the dog himself, but he didn't think his foot would allow it.

"Andres can take you to a groomer tomorrow. Get you a bath."

Edison's tail stopped wagging. He'd recognized the word. He didn't like baths.

"You'll feel better after," Joe told him.

Edison looked unconvinced.

Vivian headed upstairs, and he heard her moving from room to room. She was making sure the house was empty. Admirable thoroughness.

Joe took out the last treat in his pocket and gave it to Edison. "Tough day, huh, buddy?"

Edison gulped it down and put his head back in Joe's lap.

Joe stroked the dog's warm ears and closed his eyes, immediately seeing the woman on the tracks, her blue eyes looking into his, her voice pleading that he remember her. As if he could ever forget.

"A doctor should look at that foot." Vivian spoke from near his shoulder.

He jumped. She could move like a ghost when she wanted to. She crossed the kitchen, plugged in his copper tea kettle, and rummaged in his cupboards for cups and tea. She'd been here often enough that she assembled everything with no trouble.

"A man broke in yesterday," Joe said.

"You should file a police report." She poured hot water over the tea. "But there's no one here now. I checked."

Edison would have warned them if someone else was in the house. Joe eased his shoe off, biting his lips so he wouldn't make a sound. She already knew he was injured, no point in being a baby about it. He took off his sock and examined his injury.

His ankle was swollen to twice its normal size, the skin dark with bruises, and it throbbed all the way to his toes. The ankle hurt like hell when he tried to rotate it.

"See a doctor about that," Vivian repeated.

"If it were broken, I couldn't have walked as far as I did," he said. "It's just a sprain."

Vivian looked skeptical, and he didn't blame her.

"How about I get the office tech to do an MRI on it tomorrow instead?" he asked.

"That'll do." She dragged over another kitchen chair and put it next to him. "Elevation."

He propped the foot on the chair. Better late than never.

She opened the ice box and pulled out his ice cube tray. It was geeky, and the ice cubes looked like Tetris blocks. She put the shapes into a tea towel and smashed it against the sink. She handed him the makeshift ice pack.

When he held the pack to his foot, he drew in a quick breath. His foot hurt worse than ever, but he couldn't wimp out in front of Vivian.

She set his tea on the old scarred table. "Do you have any pain killers? Ace bandages?"

"Upstairs bathroom," he said between clenched teeth. Sure, icing was supposed to help a sprain, but right now, it was making it hurt more, which he hadn't thought possible.

Half an hour later, the pain had retreated a little. He'd taken a handful of the ibuprofen Vivian gave him, and she'd wrapped the foot and ankle with an elastic bandage. She'd raided Leandro's liquor cabinet, and he'd drunk a couple shots of whiskey, changed into clean clothes, and transitioned to the parlor. Even with the whiskey, he was too keyed up to consider sleep.

Vivian was drinking tea, not whiskey, and re-reading the reports she'd sent him about the women. She'd already forwarded them on to Dirk.

Joe's laptop sat in his lap, and he was doing his own research, trying to match up the images from the surveillance video with his law enforcement test databases. The man's fedora had obscured his face in every shot. No matter what kind of software Joe used, he wasn't able to turn the fuzzy pictures into an identification.

He'd tracked the man's movements in Grand Central Terminal, from the moment he and the woman arrived in a taxi until he walked off the platform and into the darkness. Not a single frame of the footage was useful. The man must have known where each camera was positioned because he was always looking away, hat pulled low on his face, collar turned up.

Gait recognition proved just as useless. The man walked with a slight limp, but it didn't look like it came from an injury. Joe slowed the film down to watch how he lifted each foot, swung it forward, landed it on the ground, rolled, and stepped again. His left leg had a normal stride—easy, athletic, probably a young man. The right foot was different.

It moved well, but whenever it landed, it hesitated a fraction of a second. Something was wrong with his foot.

That should have been useful, and Joe entered the information into his search. The gait recognition database was much smaller than the one for facial recognition, and he got a quick response. This man's gait didn't match anything in there. That didn't mean much, since the database contained samples from only a handful of criminals and terrorists, plus the odd Pellucid employee.

Joe studied the man's walk again and again. Then it hit him. The man's gait looked odd because he didn't have a real limp. His movements weren't consistent with a hip injury, a knee injury, or an ankle injury. Joe was willing to bet that the man had a pebble in his shoe. He'd either gotten lucky and the stone had fallen in, and he hadn't wanted to stop his walk with the girl to take it out, or he'd put it in there deliberately to confuse anyone who might be watching. A watcher would remember the limp and, once he took the stone out, the man wouldn't have a limp anymore.

Based on what he'd seen, Joe knew better than to underestimate the man. He'd lured intelligent women into the tunnels, sophisticated New York women no less. Then he'd convinced them to stand in the way of an oncoming train and die. After that, he'd left without being suspected of a crime.

Joe watched the man walk down the platform again and again, the woman on his arm leaning against him, never knowing that these were the last minutes of her life. He tried not to look at her, tried to look at the man who led her to her death. Something felt familiar about his long-legged stride, the confident set of his shoulders, but the comparison flew away when he reached the short hitching limp at the end of each step.

He gave up and looked into Salvatore Blue. That man was a ghost, too. He didn't show up in any of the databases where he should, and he wasn't in any criminal databases either. Unlike just about everyone else these days, he didn't have an online profile—no Facebook, no twitter, no pictures posted by drunken friends. Blue sounded like a made-up last name, but the MTA must do background checks, so it probably wasn't.

His cell phone rang from its position on the ottoman. Celeste's face appeared on the screen. His heart lightened. She was calling him. It was far too late for an ordinary call, so she must have heard what had happened.

Vivian handed him the phone. "I'm going upstairs to wash the dog."

He knew she was leaving to give him privacy.

"Thanks," he mouthed silently.

She clucked her tongue at Edison, and he followed her obediently out of the room, tail down in his I-don't-want-a-bath position. He knew the word *wash* as well as well as he knew the word *bath*.

"Hey," Joe said into the phone.

"I heard what happened to the A train," Celeste said.

He'd missed her breathy voice. "Is it in the papers?"

"Maybe," she said.

"Did you get my flowers?"

"I particularly liked the ones where you said I was the sun god," she said. "How are you?"

"A little drunk."

"That bad?"

"She died right in front of me." He didn't want to talk about that. "Remember that room with the lipsticks I told you about?"

"I'm probably not up to date."

He told her about the room and the investigation so far, glad to be sharing it with her, glad that she was pretending that nothing had happened between them.

"So," he finished, "how did he get the key? Do you know if anyone else has copies?"

"That would be illegal." A non-answer, since Joe himself had made a set of duplicates. "The keys were usually hanging on a peg on the wall when we were kids. I never made copies, but I'll ask Leandro tomorrow when he comes back. He might have, or my dad or the servants, or Leandro's friends that go to the parties down there. We weren't careful with the keys."

"Did you guys spend a lot of time down here?"

"Not really." She breathed quietly into the phone. "It was pretty dangerous down there before the September eleven attacks. Lots of homeless people moving around the tunnels before the security sweeps started. Leandro used to throw an underground party every year or so before you moved in, but that was it."

Joe had seen the security at Leandro's parties. Anyone could have taken the keys and copied them. Theoretically, then, anyone could have the key that led to the recently scoured room.

Even if the killer hadn't gotten the key from the Gallos, a locksmith could have made a key. It might be difficult to convince a locksmith to go down into the tunnels, but with enough money, anything was possible.

He took a deep breath and asked his most difficult question. "Are we OK?"

"If you don't push me."

"Your terms, your timing." He sure as hell wasn't going to say anything else any time soon.

"Good," she said. "I have to go sleep now. You should sleep, too."

"I will."

"And be careful out there," she said. "I'd hate to outlive you."

"That wouldn't be so bad," he said.

Celeste ended the connection, and he stared at the artificial flames until Edison padded into the room, smelling of shampoo. He licked Joe's hand, then curled up in front of the fire. Soon the room would smell like wet dog.

Vivian came in after him, rolling down her sleeves.

"Thanks for staying with me," he told Vivian. "You can go home if you want."

"I'm staying till morning."

"I'm safe here in the house." He hoped that was true.

His surveillance program beeped. A quick glance at his laptop reassured him that the latest tunnel trespassers were a group of four track workers heading home at the end of a long shift. Until he'd set up the program, he'd had no idea so many people ventured off the platforms and into the tunnels. He'd always thought he was mostly alone down here.

Clearly, he wasn't.

Not that the surveillance footage was good for much else. He'd already sent the footage he'd collected of the killer to Dirk, but he knew the police wouldn't be able to do much with it either. Vivian had sent him her notes and reports, which were hopefully more useful than Joe's contribution. They couldn't do anything more tonight, but his thoughts kept returning to the dead woman on the tracks. "*Remember*," she had said looking up at him. "*Remember*."

"You should get some sleep," Vivian said. "Do you need help up the stairs?"

"I can manage. Will you be OK going home in the tunnels on your own?" Grand Central Terminal was closed for the night, so she'd have to leave via the tunnels.

"I'm staying through morning," she repeated.

He wanted to argue with her, but her set expression told him that he would lose, and he couldn't deny that her presence reassured him.

31

Ziggy had walked for hours through the sleeping city before returning home. The doorman nodded politely when he arrived. Just another late night for Ziggy. Usually, however, his late nights ended with him in a better mood.

He dropped his ruined shoes down the garbage chute on his floor. Tomorrow was garbage day, so there was little risk they'd be found. Even if they were, they didn't prove anything.

He padded down the hall to his apartment, unlocked his door and stepped inside. Without turning on the lights, he stomped through his front hall into the bathroom.

After doing his business, he washed his hands and caught sight of himself in the mirror. The face staring back at him was tight with rage. Usually, after he liberated a woman, everything became more intense—the colors brighter, the tastes richer, the orgasms overpowering. Every sense in his body gave him heightened pleasure. For days afterward, he had only to close his eyes, touch the lipstick, imagine her face in the last moment, and bliss overwhelmed him, leaving him spent.

When he closed his eyes now, he saw that man screaming and pointing. Running toward Emilia. Shattering their moment together. Tesla had probably watched the last light fade from her eyes himself. He'd stolen Ziggy's moment.

Ziggy smashed his fist against the mirror. Silver glass shattered in a circle around his knuckles. Shards clattered into the sink. His broken image stared back.

A note of pain from his hand told him he'd hurt himself. He opened his fist and looked. A glass sliver protruded between his first and second knuckle. He peeled his lips back in a grimace, then pulled the glass out with his teeth and dropped it into the sink.

Bright blood welled in the puncture. A line of blood traced down his index finger and fell, one perfect drop at a time, into the sink. The vibrant color reminded him of 999.

He brought his hand to his mouth and licked the blood away with quick strokes of his tongue, cleaning it like a cat. The warm softness against his skin was the first thing that had felt right since that man had appeared in the tunnel. He closed his eyes and savored the salty, metallic taste of blood, comforted and able to think.

He sucked on the knuckle without opening his eyes. He knew what he had to do. The fun was gone. It was time for the Finale.

For years, he'd known this time must come. He'd planned it a thousand ways, had been working on it actively for months, but Tesla had never been part of his calculations. In his plans she and he were alone together. They made the decision together, and they died together. They were two people with a single fate, and it was his mission to make her realize it. And he always did. In his fantasies, she always understood.

He'd known she would be his most difficult conquest. She'd always been stronger than the women he met in clubs, and he hadn't wanted to use the drug on her. She must make the choice from her own true soul, unaided by Algea. She'd needed extra preparation, and he'd put a plan into action months ago, working on her intensely for the past few weeks. The process was difficult to watch, but it would be over soon. He wouldn't wait longer for her to take him where he wanted to go.

He could use Tesla to help. He could drive the man to take his own life after he showed him his own bitter memories. Ziggy would remind him of his new suffering, layer it atop the old, until it was too much for him to bear. Then he would make his choice as the others had.

She would watch, and Tesla's experiences would show her the way. His death would make her stop fighting life and embrace death, and Ziggy would go with her. They would both be at peace.

He opened his eyes. He had much to do. As he washed and wrapped his wounded hand, he made a list. He must obtain a powerful tranquilizer. He must find the man alone. And he must take Tesla to her.

32

Vivian gave Tesla a half hour to fall asleep. He'd looked pretty beat when he went up the stairs, leaning heavily on the railing. Plus, he'd drunk more whiskey than he was used to. She figured he'd conk right out.

This was good because she had work to do. While she was washing the dog, she'd checked the rooms upstairs for signs that the home invader had stolen anything or laid any traps for Tesla. Everything looked the same as it always had, but she'd gone over it carefully, wishing that Edison had training in explosives detection.

Then she'd stumbled on Tesla's high-tech stash. He had a handheld explosives detector and a bug sweeper. Expensive gadgets. She hadn't given him enough credit for being paranoid, although she should have. The guy worried about everything.

After giving the dog the quickest bath in history, she'd used her eyes and his tools to check every nook and cranny upstairs while he was talking to his girlfriend. Everything came up clean in the end, including the dog.

That left her the downstairs to sweep, the chamber outside, and the elevator.

Once he was asleep, she started with the kitchen and worked her way forward. She worked the kitchen, the billiards room, the library, and the pantry. If the intruder had come in here, he hadn't left any electronic surprises. Her eyes were gritty with exhaustion. She'd had more cups of tea than she could count, but the caffeine wasn't helping anymore. She needed sleep.

She went outside, glad to see that Tesla's artificial ceiling lightening up. Morning was coming down here and up above.

Painstakingly, she covered every inch of the large room in front of his house. The plants and the LEDs that fed them made it tough going, but she had to admit that she liked them anyway. They brightened the place up, and they also told her that Tesla was settling in. He clearly didn't think he'd be leaving any time soon.

Which meant she had to make this place safe for him. She was in charge of his security, so it was her job, but he was also her friend, and it was her duty. Nobody died on her watch. Slowly, she walked down the tunnel, sweeping left to right. Her shoulders ached. She'd been doing this for hours.

She checked the security systems at both entrances. Both undisturbed since they'd entered.

She decided to head back to the house and see what Tesla had in the way of breakfast. She tiptoed through the front door and back to the kitchen. She set his detectors on the table, so she would remember to tell him what she'd done. Then she went over to the icebox. He had milk in there and cornflakes in the cupboard.

As she reached for the milk, she stopped. What about poison? What if the women on the tracks had been poisoned? That might make their weird behavior make sense.

She took out a large box and began loading Tesla's food into it.

His footsteps sounded on the stairs. Still limping.

He hobbled into the kitchen. His dark hair was wet from the shower, and he wore a pair of clean slacks with a white shirt. "What are you doing?"

He looked better than yesterday. He had dark circles under his eyes, and still looked tired, but the worst of his pallor was gone. "Good morning."

Edison padded over and looked at his empty dog dish.

Tesla rubbed his eyes and yawned. "What have you been up to all night?"

She pointed to the detectors on the table and explained, then gestured to the food. "I think it makes sense to get all this stuff tested. If he did drug those women, maybe he left something here for you, too."

Tesla hobbled to stand next to her, holding onto the counter with one hand. His foot clearly still hurt. "I'll pack that up. You go home."

"I'd feel better taking you to your office first, sir," she said. She'd actually feel better going straight to bed. She had to be up that afternoon to watch Katrinka.

It only took a few minutes for the two of them to pack up the rest of his and the dog's food. He didn't cook much, and didn't have much on hand—just two boxes full.

"You know it's a crime that you only have two boxes of food in your apartment after all these months, right?" she said.

"Only a misdemeanor."

"My mother would call it a felony." If she told her about it, her mother would be over here later today, filling Tesla's fridge.

Tesla laughed and invited her out to breakfast at the Grand Central food court. She'd have preferred to eat at Pershing Square Restaurant. It was just across the street, but it might as well have been on the moon as far as Tesla was concerned.

By the time she got Joe to the elevator, it was clear that his foot was in bad shape, worse than the night before. Vivian left the food boxes with Evaline, the capable woman who manned the information booth, and practically carried Tesla to his office. Miss Kay, the office manager, let them in while Tesla was still fiddling with his keys.

"What are you doing here on a Sunday, Marnie?" asked Tesla.

"What the hell happened to you?" Miss Kay hurried into one of the offices and came back out with a streamlined electric wheelchair.

It was a sign of how much pain he was in that Tesla sat right down in it.

"I'll get Phil in to scan your foot," Miss Kay said. "He lives nearby."

Tesla looked over at Vivian, but she didn't help him out.

"I don't think that's necessary," he said.

"You'll never know what's going on inside that foot unless you look," Vivian said. "It could look like a sock full of marbles."

Tesla glowered at her, but Vivian ignored him. Miss Kay pushed the wheelchair back toward Tesla's office. Vivian followed. She pulled up Dr. Stauss's number on her phone.

"Who are you calling?" Tesla asked.

"Dr. Stauss," Vivian told him.

"He's a neurologist!"

"I bet he knows someone who can set a broken foot." What if Tesla needed surgery? His panicked face told her he'd had the same thought.

Dr. Stauss said he'd be there in an hour, and he'd call in a friend who specialized in sports medicine.

That problem taken care of, Vivian looked around the office. "Anything unusual on the security system this morning?"

"Should I be worried?" Miss Kay asked.

"No," Tesla said.

"Keep an eye out," Vivian said, at the same time.

Miss Kay walked Vivian over to show her the security records. No one in or out since Tesla left the night before, not unusual for a weekend. The surveillance footage was clean, too.

Miss Kay left to get everyone breakfast and coffee. She took Edison with her, and Vivian walked her out. She had to get the boxes from Evaline, and she didn't think that Tesla was at much risk right now.

Nothing seemed amiss in the concourse. A lot of folks heading to work. Still, crowds like that were the best place to hide. Vivian ferried the boxes back and dropped them next to Tesla's desk.

"Go home," Tesla said. "I've got Marnie here, doctors, an MRI tech coming, and police and military personnel on guard in the terminal. I'm safe here."

Vivian waited until Miss Kay returned, took a cup of coffee, and left after extracting a promise from Tesla that he not leave the office until Mr. Rossi sent out a replacement for her.

Instead of catching a subway home and walking, she went straight outside and caught a cab. She needed to get home and get to sleep before she fell over. She intended to sleep all day. With any luck, she'd be so tired that she wouldn't dream about the woman who'd died on the tracks.

33

Joe leaned back in his chair and tried not to think about his foot. It hurt worse than it had the night before. All signs pointed to broken bones. He quailed at the thought that it might need to be operated on. They'd have to take him outside to get to a hospital. He'd have to live in a hospital room, probably without Edison, for days. And the killer would claim his second victim. He took a deep breath. No sense in panicking in advance. Plenty of time to panic later.

Marnie tapped on his office door. She sat down in front of him and waved her coffee cup toward the boxes of food. "Preparing for a siege?"

He brushed the crumbs from his chocolate croissant into his garbage can. "I need to get the food in those boxes tested, to see if it's been poisoned."

"Howard Hughes much?" she asked.

He sighed. Not flattering to be compared to the eccentric, paranoid millionaire who'd ended his life confined to his house, collecting his bodily fluids in jars. Unfortunately, the comparison was more apt than he wanted to admit. "My security cameras filmed a guy breaking into my house."

Her brows creased in concern. "Why was he there?"

He gave her a quick summary of the events of the previous days. If she was near him, she was taking the same risks that he was, and she deserved to understand why.

When he finished, she let out a low whistle. "Things were a lot easier back in California. Corporate espionage. FBI lawsuits. Easy stuff."

"You can always go back there," he said. "No hard feelings."

"Do you know why I came out here?"

He knew a trap when he saw one. He wasn't going to guess. "Why?"

"Because I believe in you, as a scientist and a person. You want to make a difference in the world, make things better." She sipped her coffee. "Back in the Valley, I could help make some app that undercuts taxi drivers or makes photos look retro or whatever. Here I can help people through some of the toughest experiences of their lives, make a real difference. This work matters. You'll make it matter."

He was touched. "I don't—"

"Plus the shoe shopping," she said. "This city is lousy with amazing shoes."

She held up one shoe. It was wine red, with a long heel and a delicate pattern worked into the leather.

"Nice."

"They ought to be with what they cost." She stood and tapped the boxes. "I'll call around and find a lab for these."

"What about the work you came in to catch up on?"

"How important can it be if I left it to Sunday?" She stood to go.

Edison went over and licked her hand as she walked out. A better thank you than Joe's.

Joe called Dirk.

"Norbye." His voice was hoarse with exhaustion. Joe bet that the young policeman hadn't gone to bed.

"Tesla here. Wondering if there was anything new."

"Vivian said you had a break-in. Should we send someone by?"

"Not much point. This guy was wearing gloves. I've checked the surveillance footage, and there's nothing to see. The lights were out."

"I'll come by later," Dirk said. "Never hurts to look around."

"Thanks," Joe responded automatically.

"We do have some interesting news." Dirk cleared his throat. "Vivian asked me to get more tests run on the blood and tissue samples that we retained from Sandra Haines."

Joe was impressed by Vivian's thoroughness. "And?"

"She asked us to check for a certain substance, a drug based on scopolamine. It's not standard, so we never would have looked otherwise."

Joe's stomach roiled. His coffee thought about coming up and spreading itself all over his desk. Edison nudged his leg. "And?"

"They found a fairly high concentration. The medical examiner said it's a designer drug, not one he's seen before. He looked through the database and found it had only showed up in a test once."

"Mine," Joe said.

"Yeah."

"So, the guy who poisoned me has also been poisoning these women?" Joe was impressed that Vivian had thought to look for the drug. He'd mentioned it to her, of course, but he hadn't thought to make that connection himself. Too close to it. He made a note to tell Marnie to have his food tested for that same substance.

"All we know for sure is that the same poison was used in two cases, during both of which the victim spent time in the subway system."

"Is there any way it could be a weird fungus that grows down here? Or a pollutant?"

"It's artificially manufactured, and it was probably ingested, either as a pill or hidden in food or drink. So, no."

Joe thought back to that long-ago party in his underground house. He'd learned of Celeste's ALS and had gotten hammered. Anyone could have slipped him anything. "Do you think he intended to kill me?"

"Maybe."

"Vivian escorted me home the night before my agoraphobia presented. She said I was stumbling around, basically incoherent. At least drunk, maybe more."

"She may have saved your life."

"I'll add that to the tally."

"We all have a tally with her," Dirk said.

Joe listed off the names of everyone who'd had access to his food and drink on that final day, names he'd long since committed to memory. Co-workers at Pellucid, his former company, but not Marnie because she hadn't come out to New York with him. Two FBI agents against whom he'd won a legal battle for control of Pellucid's software. Two investment bankers who'd been helping with Pellucid's initial public offering. Leandro and his socialite party guests.

Dirk interrupted him to get the spelling right, and Joe answered mechanically. His mind whirled. A killer had given him poison. The killer had been in his house. That same killer had prowled the subway system for years, preying on women. Joe might have passed him a hundred times in the tunnels without knowing it. What plan had Vivian interrupted when she dragged him back to the hotel all those months ago?

"Mr. Tesla? Joe?" Dirk's voice came from far away. "Everything OK?"

Joe pulled his attention back to the phone. "Fine."

"Is that everything?" Dirk sounded tired and ready to go.

"One more thing. Are there additional patrols in the tunnels for the A line?"

"There are," Dirk said. "It wasn't easy getting the overtime authorized, but you and Vivian built a compelling case that this was the work of a serial killer and that another woman is at risk there in the next few days."

At least there was that. "I have a... system that monitors tunnel access."

"Is it authorized by the MTA?"

"In a way." It was their cameras he was monitoring, after all. "Could I have the name of someone to contact if I should see the killer heading back into the tunnels with another woman? That could get the patrols to her faster."

Dirk rattled off names and phone numbers that raced by Joe in ribbons of color. Usually, he'd memorize them, but today he wrote them down. The pain in his foot was distracting him, and he didn't want to forget them. Dirk promised to call them and explain Joe's role.

"Should I have Mr. Rossi send someone over to provide security for your office?" Dirk was speaking as Joe's sometime-bodyguard, not a policeman.

"Vivian already did," Joe said. "But the terminal is full of cops, soldiers, and people. I don't think anything can happen to me up here.

34

Ziggy walked around Grand Central Terminal like an ordinary New Yorker, a Mets cap pulled low over his eyes. Facial recognition concentrated on the eyes, and his were barely visible as he wandered around the information booth, looked up at the constellations, and headed over to the shopping arcade.

Tesla's office was there. He'd somehow managed to convince the real estate office to rent him an office space in a sea of retail shops. Money could buy anything, especially in New York.

This was proving to be a good thing. If that man had an ordinary office, Ziggy would never get near it. There'd be security on the first floor, card keys everywhere. Here, he was anonymous. He could walk right by, enter the store across the corridor, smell the expensive soaps and perfumes, and watch the only exit and entrance. The name Lucid looked out at him from the door.

He wondered if he should choose eucalyptus mint soap or grapefruit mint. The eucalyptus was more bracing. It reminded him of a smelly ointment his sister had rubbed on his chest when he got colds as a boy. It didn't make him feel powerful. It made him feel vulnerable. He chose grapefruit mint.

A young guy walked up to Lucid's office and worked the buzzer. He wore the brown uniform of a courier and pushed a dolly. They must be sending something big out.

The doors opened, and Ziggy looked through into the office. A giant glass brain dominated the room, but he was more interested in the man who had taken everything from him. That man sat next to the reception desk in a wheelchair.

Ziggy's heart skipped a beat. The man must have been wounded in the tunnels last night. Maybe the train had hit him. Whatever had happened, he clearly couldn't walk. That simplified things. It simplified things so very much.

The door closed again, but he had seen all he needed to.

He paid for the soap and lingered by the door on the way out, looking through a bin of umbrellas, yellow and black as wasps. He dipped his hand down between the umbrellas and stuck a small black object to the bottom of the bin, careful to make sure that the lens faced Lucid's front door. No one would notice the little camera with all the umbrellas piled on top of it.

He'd be able to monitor the camera remotely and see who entered and left the office. It was Sunday, so the office was likely to be empty already. He'd seen Tesla and a woman through the door, and he bet they were the only ones there, but he had to be sure.

And then there was the dog.

With the man laid up in a wheelchair, he'd have to send the dog out for a walk. That would leave the office practically empty.

Ziggy needed to gather supplies. He could come back as soon as the dog left, disable anyone else in the office, and take Tesla. Then drug him, take him where he needed him, force him to play his part.

In the Finale.

35

Vivian stifled a yawn and shifted in her hard wooden seat. Mr. Kazakov called early and woke her up because he had an unexpected business meeting that took him across town with the weekend bodyguard, so Vivian had to fill in watching Katrinka perform in a school play. This involved a lot of sitting on exactly the parts the ride had tenderized yesterday. She was never going to be a cowgirl.

The show wasn't as bad as she'd expected. The kids on stage were better than anyone in Vivian's high school had ever been. They probably had a professional acting coach. Upscale private school.

Katrinka was a gifted actress, but not gifted enough to hide her disappointment that her parents weren't coming to the show's matinee. Her mother had claimed a migraine and was sequestered in her room, and her father had that meeting. Katrinka had pretended to be too old to care as she put on her makeup backstage. Her red lipstick came in a black and silver case, just like the one Tesla had found. Vivian wondered if the parents of any of the murdered women had gone to their school plays.

Vivian resisted the urge to try to make it up to Katrinka. That would look like pity instead of sympathy. Vivian's mother had missed a few of her events, too, but only when she couldn't move her work schedule around to accommodate them. Usually, she'd moved heaven and earth to be there.

Katrinka wore a Victorian-era blue dress and walked across the stage with affected nervousness. She was playing Dr. Jekyll's fiancé, and her character had started to suspect something was wrong with the seemingly perfect doctor she loved. As worried as she was, she didn't know the half of what was wrong with him.

Dr. Jekyll was a TV-handsome kid who delivered his lines with an assurance that spoke of plenty of time on stage. He'd probably been acting since he was a toddler.

He reminded Vivian of Slade. Or the killer. That guy must be a pretty accomplished actor, too. Sympathetic enough to lure women into the tunnels with him. The women he tricked were savvy, used to living in New York, probably leery of strangers. It wouldn't have been easy to convince them to follow him.

But they had followed him. Earlier in the day, she'd received a text from Tesla telling her that the women were drugged. Considering the time of night when the murders occurred, this probably meant he'd spiked their drinks, which indicated he'd met them at a bar or a club.

On stage, Dr. Jekyll collapsed behind his desk with a moan, and Mr. Hyde emerged. He was played by a smaller kid who leaped onto the desk and squatted there like a monkey. He glared out into the audience and picked his nose.

Nobody would let Mr. Hyde pick them up at a club. Dr. Jekyll, on the other hand, wouldn't have much trouble. Dr. Jekyll looked like he belonged. When Iris and Sandra had been out clubbing, Sandra had abandoned Iris to be with a good-looking guy she met there. He was tall, and he wore a nice suit. She bet Iris knew a lot about expensive suits and the men who wore them. This particular man hadn't raised any alarm bells. He was the kind of guy she would expect to meet at that club. He was still Dr. Jekyll.

Like the kid capering around on stage, maybe the killer only transformed into Mr. Hyde at certain points. In his case, he became Hyde every October to kill two random women. For the rest of the year maybe he transformed back into the innocuous Dr. Jekyll. Or did he become a monster more often, maybe killing women some other way during other months? Vivian shivered at the thought of more victims, of the man moving undetected through the places where he met his victims, because he was above suspicion.

But he wasn't above her suspicions. She'd call Iris to get the name of the club where she'd left Sandra and check it out, but she didn't think the man would be foolish enough to pick up two victims in a row at the same place. If he branched out, that left a lot of clubs. Narrowing it down wouldn't be easy.

On stage Hyde bounced away from Dr. Jekyll's office to the other side of the stage, toward a Victorian bar painted on the backdrop. Hyde had gone off to a club to hunt.

What kind of club would these women go to? Vivian hadn't been to a club in a long time, hating the noise and the crush of people and how, afterward, her hair always smelled like smoke, and she had to scrub some stupid stamp off her arm.

Stamp. Vivian surreptitiously pulled out her phone so as not to seem to be ignoring the performance. She didn't know why she bothered. Half the audience members were openly checking their phones. She flipped through her pictures of the crime scene, hoping that no one was watching over her shoulder. That would take some explaining.

She stopped when she reached the photo of a delicate white hand. The bloody hand rested palm up on a filthy train tie. Vivian zoomed in on the black tattoo imprinted on the wrist.

The black lines formed a palm tree bent into a crescent as if buffeted by a high wind. The design was almost clean enough to be a tattoo, but a slight smudge a quarter inch above the palm trees gave it away. The image wasn't a tattoo. It was a nightclub stamp.

Dirk had probably noticed it, but she texted her supposition off to him and Tesla anyway. If the guy had picked the victim up at a club, there might be witnesses. They might get lucky and find someone who knew the victim or the killer. At the very least they might uncover better surveillance videos than what the subway security cameras had been able to record.

Maybe that waving palm tree would catch a killer.

36

In a drugged stupor, Joe lay on the sofa in Lucid's lobby and stared at his casted ankle. His laptop rested on the coffee table next to him, beeping every time someone left a subway platform to go into the tunnels. Not that there was much he could do about it. He couldn't race to their aid, and he wasn't even sure if the number that Dirk had given him would prove to be useful. He hoped that he wouldn't have to find out.

Dr. Stauss had taken one look at the MRI of his foot and tried to persuade him to go to a hospital to get it fixed. When that failed, he'd doped him up and brought in some guy to set the foot in the MRI room since that was the closest thing they had to an operating room. Encased in a ridiculous plastic boot, his foot was propped up on the sofa's armrest. He was supposed to get regular MRIs, and if the bones didn't mesh together properly, they'd have to perform an operation after all. This was an uncertain reprieve.

He wasn't even allowed to get around on crutches. He was supposed to rest, take pills, and heal. Later, if he was a good boy, someone could take him down to his house in a wheelchair, although how he'd manage the steps was anybody's guess. Right now, he couldn't even touch his nose with his finger. He'd tried right after the drugs had kicked in.

At least the pain was gone.

"If you ooze any further off that couch, you'll be on the floor," Marnie said. "Why don't you go home?"

"Not classing up the joint?" he asked.

"You look like you're plastered."

"Plastered be more fun."

"You sure can't handle your morphine, or whatever they gave you." Marnie laughed. "I'll call Miss Torres to help you to your house. I'd get Mr. Parker here to do it, but he's not on the approved visitor list."

Mr. Parker was the bodyguard sent over by Joe's lawyer, Mr. Rossi, after Vivian had suggested that Joe needed a guard. Like someone would attack him right in his office.

"Not a long list. Security reasons. Sorry, Parker." Joe must not be making much sense, because Marnie gave him an exasperated look. Parker was a guy who looked like a refrigerator or—what was that word. "What are those big guys called in football?"

"Defensive linemen," said Marnie. "And, yes, Mr. Parker does bear more than a passing resemblance to one. Stop pointing at him."

Parker didn't seem bothered, and neither did Edison. The dog was snoozing in front of the sofa. Things couldn't be bad if Edison was sleeping at his post.

The laptop beeped, and Joe looked at it. Track workers again. "Lots of broken track down there."

"Lots of broken track up here," Marnie said.

"The Hyatt," Joe said. "Always the Hyatt."

"I'll get you a room," she said. "Mr. Parker can bring you there."

And so it was that a few minutes later Joe was being wheeled across the concourse to the hotel by a former defensive lineman. Joe's laptop was folded in his lap and Edison trotted along next to the wheels, completely comfortable with the situation. Edison could adapt to anything, even Joe turning into a drug-addled Professor Xavier.

"Good dog," he said, and dropped some treats on the floor instead of handing them to him because his motor coordination wasn't that great. Edison scarfed the treats without breaking stride.

The lineman seemed happier once they were out of the public areas and ensconced in Joe's suite. Good that Marnie had thought to book a suite. He'd no idea what he'd do with a refrigerator-sized bodyguard without adequate space.

Something beeped, and Joe opened up his laptop.

"I think that was your phone, sir," Parker said.

Joe's phone had fallen out of his pocket when Parker had lifted him onto the bed like an infant. Joe was grateful that Mr. Rossi had sent him and not Vivian for that task. Once the drugs wore off, he expected to be embarrassed enough.

The phone beeped again, and Parker handed it to him. It must have synched up with the network when it fell out of his pocket Faraday cage. A text message from Vivian.

He read it twice. It was a picture of the dead woman's wrist. He remembered the mark on her wrist. He probably touched it when he took her hand. He remembered the palm tree, bent over in the wind, looking ready to fall down. He sympathized with being ready to fall down. Vivian's text said that she thought it might be a nightclub stamp.

That wasn't an easy thing to track.

"Too many nightclubs," Joe said. "Or so I read, not being able to go to any of them."

"Maybe when you're feeling better, sir," Parker said.

Such a nice guy. "Even on two feet."

Joe showed him the picture Vivian had texted. "Do you know what nightclub this is for?"

Parker studied it for several seconds. A thorough man, Parker. "I do not."

"Me neither." Joe tapped his phone screen. "I'll find out though."

Hoping to get lucky, he opened up his laptop and tried some easy searches. Nothing useful came up when he tried *new york nightclub stamps* and *palm tree stamps*. Lots of pages with actual stamps for stamp collectors and also some scrapbooking sites.

"I must make a phone call," Joe said. "To a friend."

Parker headed back to the living room, which hadn't been Joe's intent, but he thought it'd be easier to let Parker think it was than try to explain that Joe was stoned and narrating his life.

He called Leandro but it went straight to voice mail. "Calling to see how Celeste is. Are you back from Florida already? I think it's tomorrow, but I'm not sure. It's not tomorrow yet. I guess it never gets to tomorrow, does it? Because then it'd be today. Anyway, call me when you get back. I want to talk about your sister. But I guess I'll see you at Lucid anyway. Because I need to get inside your brain. For the scan."

He ended the call. He was pretty sure the message hadn't gone the way he'd intended. He tried calling Celeste, too, but she didn't answer. He didn't leave a message. He'd learned his lesson with the ridiculous message he'd left for Leandro.

Then he stared at the laptop screen until it resolved itself into a picture of a hand with a palm tree tattooed on the wrist. He'd been working on that. Matching it.

"This will have to be done the hard way, Parker," he said. "I'll create a search that trolls through thousands of Facebook photos tagged in New York and see if the app finds a match."

Parker walked back into the room. "That does sound like the hard way, sir. Maybe not possible right this moment."

Parker might look like a defensive lineman, but he sounded like an English butler. Joe liked the incongruity of it.

"Not impossible, Parker. Nothing's impossible." Joe was already typing away. "I wrote something similar a while ago while trolling for faces. Can't be much harder to troll for palm tree stamps, can it?"

Parker petted Edison instead of answering. Very diplomatic.

It took Joe three times longer than it should have, because he had to keep checking his surveillance app and also because his brain was fuzzy. But, considering the amount of drugs in his system, a performance degradation of a third (black dot red recurring) was a victory.

"I have a result set," he announced.

Parker came to look over his shoulder. Edison wasn't impressed at all. He didn't even look up. Joe would have to search for a steak to impress him.

He flipped through a set of photos. Palm tree tattoos on hands, arms and— "Why would anyone want to tattoo a palm tree there?"

Parker blinked. "To put them in a tropical state of mind."

Joe was already on to the next one, and the one after that. "So many wrong palm trees."

"Stop, please," Parker said. "Go back."

And there it was on screen. The exact palm tree the subway victim had worn on her wrist.

Parker read the text under it. "Hanging with my homeys at Calypso Club, Manhattan."

Bingo, you bastard, Joe thought. "Bingo."

He texted the club name to Vivian and Dirk.

Edison jumped up on the bed and stretched out next to him. The dog wasn't usually allowed to sleep on the bed, but he clearly thought it was a special circumstance.

"You know, Parker," Joe said, "I think I'll take a nap."

"Very good idea, sir," Parker said.

"Would you mind monitoring this app here? If it beeps and you see a man and a woman, probably blond and in evening dress going into a tunnel, wake me up. I have numbers to call."

"You've explained it before," Parker said. "I can manage."

He scooped up Joe's laptop and retreated back to the suite's living room. If he was single, Joe decided, he would have to introduce the man to Vivian. They could go to gun ranges and do martial arts and have tall, capable babies together.

"Did I say that aloud?" Joe asked.

"You did not, sir," Parker answered. "Did you want to?"

"Nope," Joe said, and fell asleep with his hand on Edison's head.

37

Vivian waited to do her official daily check out with Mr. Kazakov. Katrinka was curled up in one of the oversized chairs, looking like a sad little girl, which she probably was. She must have rehearsed that play for months, and neither parent had bothered to come.

"I liked the play," Vivian said.

Katrinka rolled her eyes. "You mentioned that."

Vivian shrugged. The girl wasn't really mad at her. She was just a convenient target.

"Whatever happened with that purse and lipsticks?" Katrinka asked.

Vivian hesitated, deciding what she could tell her. "The police are looking into it."

"I bet you looked into it first," Katrinka said. "For your millionaire boyfriend."

"Not my boyfriend." And probably a billionaire, not a millionaire. "But, yes, I did."

"And? Was I right about the purse?"

"You were. It was a one-of-a-kind, and it led us straight to the woman who'd owned it. She was hit by a subway train under suspicious circumstances."

"There were lots of lipsticks. Doesn't that mean lots of victims?"

"Ten, by my count," Vivian said. "And I think he's not done. I think he'll kill another woman this week. So watch yourself—make sure no one puts anything into your drinks."

"I always do," she said.

That was true. Most women were on guard these days. This guy had to be very convincing to get women to let their guard down.

Vivian's phone rang, and she excused herself to take it. "Torres."

"Dirk here. Are you up for an adventure?"

She was tired from staying up all night, watching out for Tesla, and still sore from horseback riding. "Sure."

"I thought I'd head over to Club Calypso in a while, ask some questions, buy some drinks on the department's credit card. Want to join me?"

"Club Calypso?" She looked at her watch. "When?"

Katrinka perked up on her chair.

"Meet me in a half hour?"

She wouldn't have time to go home to change. "Meet you by the front door."

"They won't let you in like that," Katrinka said. "It's a trendy club."

"I'm not a customer. I'm a cop, or at least with a cop, and they'll let me in."

"You're going with the blond god?"

"Mr. Norbye. Yes."

"Then you definitely can't go like that!" Katrinka scrambled to her feet. "I've got the perfect dress for you. I've never even worn it, and it's a little big on me."

"That wouldn't be appropriate," Vivian said. "But thank you for the kind offer."

"Just let her." Mr. Kazakov spoke from the doorway. "Give her something constructive to do—make someone else up for a nightclub she cannot visit on her own."

From the way Katrinka had talked about Club Calypso, Vivian was willing to bet that she had visited it herself.

"Please," Katrinka wheedled. "It'll be fun."

Vivian thought of the girl's long, disappointing day and gave in.

Katrinka morphed into a no-nonsense stylist. Soon Vivian was dressed in the unworn black dress, and her face had been made up, although she hadn't been allowed to see the results. She was worried about the dress. It clung to her body like a second skin, inky black and shimmering, and it felt expensive.

Katrinka eyed her critically, then flipped the mirror back around so Vivian could see herself.

Vivian did a double take. She didn't recognize the woman looking back at her. The dress was daring—it showed every curve and fell lower in the front than she would have chosen, but she had to admit it flattered her. She twirled around. The back looked good, too.

"You will conquer the blond god before the sun rises tomorrow," Katrinka prophesied.

"Dirk and I are just friends. He'll probably have a good laugh over this... costume."

"No man is going to call that a costume."

Vivian pursed her lips.

"Think of it as a uniform," Katrinka said hurriedly. "To let you fit in at Club Calypso."

Vivian was starting to have some misgivings, but she didn't have time to change back. If she wasn't there on time, Dirk would go in without her.

She splurged on a cab that dropped her at the club's entrance. A long line snaked down the block from the closed front door. Great. A club you couldn't get into unless you were one of the beautiful people.

Dirk's badge should take care of that. Vivian shivered, wishing she'd accepted Katrinka's offer of a jacket.

"Viv!" Dirk called from somewhere near the door. "Over here!"

She hurried over, Katrinka's fancy shoes clicking against the sidewalk.

"I was about—" Dirk stopped midsentence and stared at her, open mouthed.

Vivian felt a blush coming on and hoped that the bad lighting and her dark skin would mask it. "Too much? Katrinka had me basically playing dress up. I can change."

Before Dirk could answer, the bouncer by the door answered for him. "No, ma'am, that is not too much. Looks about right to me."

He stepped aside and opened the door for them, starting a chorus of protests from those in the line.

Dirk put his warm hand on the small of her back and escorted her to the door.

"Wait," Vivian said. She brought up a picture on her phone and showed it to the doorman. It was the woman who had died in the subway. Her face had been cleaned up. "Do you know her?"

The bouncer stopped staring at Vivian's breasts. "Don't recognize her."

Vivian held out her wrist, and he stamped it. She showed the stamp to Dirk—a crescent-shaped palm tree. They were in the right spot.

Dirk followed her into the noisy, dark club. "You look great, Viv."

Vivian smiled. "I got past the bouncer, even at my age."

"He wasn't checking you for wrinkles."

Loud calypso music came from a stage on one side of the room. Sweaty men in Hawaiian shirts played their hearts out, and Vivian's foot started tapping. Like any act in this part of town, they had to be good.

Tall tables littered the edges of the room, and a mahogany bar lined the back wall. Most of the space was given over to the crowded dance floor.

They skirted the dancers and sidled up to the bar, where Dirk showed the roly-poly bartender his badge and the picture of the murdered woman.

"I've seen her before," the bartender raised his voice to be heard over the music. "Name's Emilia."

"Do you know her last name?" Dirk asked.

"No." He shrugged. "Just the first one."

"Maybe from a credit card receipt?" Vivian wondered how he knew her first name.

"She wasn't a woman who had to pay for her own drinks," he answered.

Vivian usually paid for her own drinks, but she didn't say anything.

"Do you have surveillance cameras?" Dirk looked around, his eyes stopping as he spotted the cameras.

"They're monitored in the back." The bartender took them to a wall that had wooden wainscoting below and emerald green paint above. It took Vivian a second to realize that a door was set into the middle, camouflaged to match the wall. The bartender knocked four times, then turned the knob and ushered them inside.

As soon as the door closed behind them, the volume dropped by half. Vivian missed the music.

They went down a short corridor. An open door on one side led to a small bathroom. On the other side was a closed door.

Dirk knocked on the second door, and a chubby guy opened it. He was short and round and dressed in a lemon-yellow suit that would have looked ridiculous on another man, but looked fine on him. "Can I help you?"

"I'm Detective Dirk Norbye." He showed his badge. "And this is Miss Torres."

The guy's eyes ran up and down Vivian's dress, and she restrained an impulse to smack him.

"Ricardo," he said. "Nice to meet you."

"We would like to look at your surveillance tapes from last night. We'll start with from ten to midnight."

"Why?"

Dirk showed the photo again. "Do you know this woman?"

Ricardo peered at the phone like a man who needed glasses but was too vain to wear them. "Can't say I do."

"She was at your club last night, maybe met a man here. Then she ended up dead." Dirk hadn't mentioned how she was hit by a train, or how they had no proof of foul play.

Ricardo gestured back to his computer. "I'll show you what I have."

An hour later, Vivian was regretting agreeing to Dirk's adventure. Her neck hurt, her eyes ached, and she wanted to curl up on Ricardo's none-too-clean couch and go to sleep.

Still, it had been worth it. They'd been through most of the footage, and had seen the murdered woman, establishing that she'd been here. Maybe they'd find someone who knew her. The man she was with wore a straw fedora pulled low across his brow. In the subdued lighting, she couldn't make out a single detail about his face, no matter what angle he was filmed from. He'd either known the position of each camera, or he was the world's luckiest bastard.

Dirk rubbed his temples. "If you could make me a copy of this, I'd like to take it back to the station for analysis."

Ricardo looked up from the couch where he sat reading a paperback. "Can do, but it'll take a while to get them all burnt. Half hour or so."

Vivian straightened up, and her spine cracked in three places. Then she leaned back over the screen. She had five minutes left on the last camera, and she stubbornly watched every frame. Her patience was rewarded.

"Dirk!" she called.

He looked over her shoulder. The camera had caught the man as he pulled up his hat to brush his fingers across his forehead. It was a grainy side view, but it was the best they'd seen so far.

"Maybe Tesla can work his magic on it," she said.

"It's evidence," Dirk said. "I can't show it to him."

"He's got that facial recognition program. Maybe he can get a match."

"It's not through official channels," Dirk said. "I've already bent too many rules for him. Hell, you shouldn't even be here."

"What if you showed it to him to see if it looked like the man he saw in the tunnel?"

Dirk considered this. "Maybe. But I have to ask."

She made a mental note to follow up so Dirk wouldn't try to wriggle out of it.

"Do you want that copy?" Ricardo asked.

Dirk snapped a photo of the man's face, and Vivian was tempted to follow suit, but Dirk gave her a look. The man's profile looked hauntingly familiar. She couldn't tell if she knew him or if her brain was putting together pieces from all the footage she'd seen.

"We'll wait out in the club," Dirk said.

Dirk went to buy drinks, and she found a table. The band played as enthusiastically as they had when she and Dirk arrived. While she waited, she checked out the other men in the club. Lots of blond guys in the right height range. Was one of them the subway killer? Not likely. No hats.

A guy broke out of the pack and headed over to ask her to dance, but he was too short to be the guy she was looking for, so she told him no.

Dirk appeared soon after and handed her a whiskey. "I like your new look."

"Katrinka gets all the credit." Vivian sipped the drink. The New York Police Department had bought the good stuff. She was so tired it went straight to her head. She swayed from side to side in time to the music.

"How about a dance?" Dirk asked.

She looked at him in surprise. They'd gone jogging in the wilds of Central Park. They'd covered each other's backs during more than a few firefights in Afghanistan. They'd schlepped packs through the desert heat together.

But they had never danced.

"Shouldn't we be asking around?" she said.

"We did our work," he said. "I suppose we could use you as bait for this guy, but you're not his type."

"Young, desperate, and hot?" she asked.

"You've got the hot part covered," he said. "But you're not a blond bird with a broken wing."

Like Katrinka. But he was right. Vivian was as far from that description as possible. She had her broken parts, sure, but she would never be a helpless bird—easy prey. She downed her whiskey in one swallow. "Let's dance."

38

Ziggy liked the music—a smoky jazz threaded with longing and despair. The perfect venue to find the next woman, but he turned away from a potential blonde crying into her gin and tonic and settled at an empty table. This wasn't a good time.

The day had been so boring. He'd awoken with a headache, heavy with disappointment from the night before. The pain lingered all day. He'd brought Emilia all the way and then lost her at the last minute. He wasn't even sure that she counted as part of a pair.

Maybe he should find another woman to usher in the Finale. He glanced back to the bar. Orange light fell on blond hair, revealing sad eyes, narrow shoulders, and a black velvet dress.

He stayed put. If he took her, it might fill out the set, and he wouldn't be able to start the Finale until next October. His reluctance must mean that Emilia had counted after all.

Ice cracked in his glass, the sound coming during a pause in the song. He took a long sip of bourbon. He wasn't hunting tonight. He was building up his energy.

He needed it. He'd watched Lucid's office all day. A lot of people came into his office on Sunday. The blonde secretary had gone out for coffee once with the dog, and a huge black guy who looked like a well-dressed tank had arrived. A spindly red-haired man had hurried in, then an Asian guy carrying a suitcase. The redhead and the Asian had left together. They'd looked worried.

Eventually, the tank had come out, pushing Tesla in a wheelchair. The man was obviously high, slumped in the chair with huge, glassy eyes and a leg cast protruding from the front of the wheelchair like a battering ram. The dog had walked next to them. Nobody batted an eye at a stoned man being wheeled around. It was as if the wheelchair gave him an invisibility shield.

A few hours later, the blonde came out and locked up. She was good-looking enough to consider, but she moved with a brusque efficiency that said she had her demons well under control. Besides, he wasn't looking.

That's why he was alone at the jazz club.

He needed patience. The man wouldn't have bodyguards forever. As soon as he sobered up, he'd probably send them away. He was a proud man, and he wouldn't put up with babysitting for long.

Once he gave in to his pride, he'd be unprotected in his home in the tunnels and in his offices. He often worked late, so he'd be alone at both places. Except for the dog.

The dog would have to be walked, and the man couldn't walk him from a wheelchair. He'd have to hire a dog walker to take the dog out. Then Tesla would be alone and vulnerable, confined to a wheelchair. A wheelchair that allowed for invisible transport.

That man had so many demons: troubles with his father, his childhood, guilt about his previous company. Ziggy had heard all about those troubles. He should have walked Tesla into the tunnels a long time ago, let him make his choice with the train. But Ziggy hadn't.

The Hispanic woman had gotten in the way and dragged the man away to safety. At the time, it had angered Ziggy, but now he wanted to thank her. Saving Tesla for the Finale was the way it had been fated to happen.

Ziggy looked toward the bar again. The woman called out with the defeated slump of her slender shoulders, the tears that fell into her drink, and the trembling hands wrapped around her glass. It would be like taking candy from a baby, but he wasn't looking for candy tonight.

He made himself sit in his chair for the duration of the next song without glancing at the bar. After the song was over, he let himself look. She was still there, radiating despair and hopelessness. She needed him. He picked up his drink and headed over to the bar. Nothing wrong with a little window shopping.

39

Joe's mouth tasted like old carpet. He rolled over to get the glass of water he usually kept on his bedside table and realized two things: his foot was heavy and painful, and he wasn't at home.

His eyelids snapped open, and panic coursed through him. A snuffle in his ear calmed him down. Edison was here. He was in a hotel room. The rest of the day before settled back into place.

Time to get up. He maneuvered his leg out of the bed. The pain made him swear, and a figure appeared in the entrance to his suite.

"Do you require assistance, Mr. Tesla?"

Joe couldn't remember his name. A jazz musician. Duke Ellington. Louis Armstrong. Charlie Parker. That was it. "I got it, Mr. Parker. Thanks."

Edison jumped out of bed and walked across to a wheelchair parked against the wall. He released the brake with his mouth, then pushed the empty wheelchair next to Joe's bed.

"You're full of surprises, buddy," Joe said. The breadth of Edison's training always amazed him.

Joe heaved himself into the chair, got to the bathroom, and managed to shower by tying a plastic bag over his cast.

Someone had delivered fresh clothes, a toothbrush, and a razor while he slept. Marnie, probably, since she usually thought of everything.

Edison proved himself again and again, fetching Joe a towel, always knowing where to stand to keep Joe from slipping, and just in general being the best dog in the world. Joe was out of dog treats, too. Marnie hadn't thought of that.

In much less time than he'd expected, he was sitting at work, eating breakfast while Parker walked and fed the dog. It had been tough to convince Parker to leave him alone long enough to take the dog out, but Edison so clearly needed to go that the large man had given in. Edison's brown eyes were persuasive.

Marnie popped her head into his office. "Are you better today?"

"How bad was I yesterday?"

"An eight on the loopiness scale, I'd say."

Eight was purple, a pretty high number. "Did I offend anyone mortally?"

"Luckily, it was a Sunday."

That wasn't a *no*. Joe's foot throbbed, but he wasn't going to take any more pain medication after what he remembered of his performance last night, which wasn't much. "Great."

"The team is at an off-site today, so it's just you and me. I moved your schedule around so you don't have any meetings, in person or on Skype. I thought you might need the time to... err... recover."

He nodded his thanks. "Anything else?"

"You got a call from a Detective Norbye. He said that Salvatore Blue was a transit officer who committed suicide by train about six months ago."

Six (orange). Even if he'd been responsible for the other deaths, he couldn't have been in the tunnel last night. Marnie raised her coffee cup and left him alone.

Joe checked through the names he'd given Dirk the day before—those who'd had access to his food when he'd been poisoned. He'd reviewed those names regularly ever since discovering his condition was caused by poison and not random changes in his brain. He hadn't been able to narrow the list by much, but now that he knew the dates when the murders were performed, he could rule out everyone who wasn't in New York during those times.

He double checked his work calendars, and it was an easy matter to clear everyone at Pellucid. Like him, they had mostly been in California during the previous years. His heart lightened. He'd worked side by side with those people, considered them friends, and he was glad to know that they hadn't betrayed him.

The FBI agents, Bister and Dobrin, were impossible to alibi so simply. He could verify when they were in California meeting with him, but that didn't knock any dates off the list. Other than that, he had no idea where they were on any given date. But he'd always considered them long shots. Sure, they had a grudge against him. He'd prevented them from taking over Pellucid's facial recognition software and turning it into a government secret. But it was a stretch to imagine them poisoning him, and harder to picture them as serial killers.

That left Leandro, his socialite friends, and the investment bankers, Alvin Ross and Thomas Lee. Everyone in that group lived in New York. Eliminating them from suspicion was going to take work.

A quick browse through Leandro's Facebook page showed that he went to Fantasy Fest every year. Although posts could be backdated now, that feature hadn't been around a couple of years ago, so the old timestamps were probably accurate. Fantasy Fest didn't give Leandro an alibi for all the murders, but it did for a couple, and that was enough. Joe was certain that all ten murders had been committed by the same man.

On a whim, Joe looked up Alan Wright's whereabouts during the murders. Alan was a busy man, often in the press, traveling around the world. It shouldn't be that difficult to exclude him from the list of suspects. But it was. Joe was able to track his movements for the last several years pretty easily using information on the Internet. And none of it ruled him out. Alan Wright, billionaire with a busy, international schedule, had been in New York for every single murder.

A rap on his door brought him back to the room and reminded him that his foot still hurt mightily. He was sorely tempted to take the pain meds Dr. Stauss had left for him and abandon himself to loopiness, but he didn't dare. The next innocent victim was still out there.

Parker dropped off Edison and said he'd be there until two (blue). Apparently, he was pulling a double shift. Joe didn't like having a babysitter, but he didn't quibble about the extra security this time.

Joe started checking up on Alvin Ross. The banker had a Facebook page, but he rarely posted, so that didn't help. Ditto for twitter. He showed up at various charity events and was sometimes quoted in news articles about the high-tech industry. Joe dug deeper. Last year, he'd had a regular blog for the *Wall Street Journal.* Unlike many columnists, he responded to comments on his pieces, and those comments were time and date stamped, presumably by the *Wall Street Journal* server and unlikely to be hackable by a financial columnist.

He'd been responding to someone asking about hedge funds at around the time that Sandra Haines was killed. It didn't take him entirely out of the running, but it didn't seem likely that he'd take a break from seducing her to write a hundred (cyan, black, black) word response to a comment posted only twenty (blue, black) minutes before.

Joe pushed back his wheelchair and rubbed his eyes. He was sure that Dirk and his team were already covering this ground, but he couldn't think what else to do. His stomach growled, and he checked the time on his computer. Almost noon (cyan, blue). A long time since breakfast.

"Hungry?" he asked Edison.

Edison jumped up and wagged his tail. Edison was always hungry.

He'd get lunch and then send the dog off with Parker for a quick turn around the block. His regular dog walker, Andres Peterson, could give him a longer walk that afternoon.

His cell phone rang with a number he didn't recognize.

With a prickling in his stomach, he answered.

"This is Genesis Labs," said a woman with a chipper voice and a Bronx accent. "You sent us several samples yesterday for testing."

He was glad that Marnie had followed through. In his pain and drug-induced haze yesterday, he'd forgotten about them. "Yes?"

"We'll email you the electronic results, of course, but I thought you might want a call, being as you paid so much for the expedited testing."

That didn't sound good. "Thanks. What are the results?"

"One of your samples came up positive for a scopolamine derivative."

Joe's foot throbbed, and he felt nauseous. "Which one?"

"The blueberry yogurt."

He wasn't hungry any more. Someone had poisoned him—taken away his ordinary life and driven him underground. Not satisfied with that, he'd tried again. The killer had a key. He'd been in Joe's kitchen. In his ice box. In his yogurt.

And damn near in his bloodstream, too.

Again.

40

Ziggy was cooking. He'd been at it for a while because he didn't have big enough containers and had to work in small batches. Between every batch, he used his laptop to check up on that man.

The man had arrived early in the morning with his dog and titanic bodyguard. The blond woman was there, but the office had stayed curiously empty for a Monday. It looked as if everyone had been given the day off. That made today the perfect day.

He dumped white pool chlorinator crystals into a Schlenk flask. The faint odor of bleach rose from the open top, but the smell dissipated when he put the flask into his makeshift smoke hood. His kitchen fan had been running all morning. That was his only worry, really, that someone would see the leftover tendrils of yellow-green gas escaping out into the New York sky. Plenty of other toxins went out there unremarked, and up to now, no one seemed to have noticed Ziggy's contribution.

He attached a pressure-equalized dropping funnel to the tapered top of the flask, then fitted the hose over the flask's side arm. The hose would deliver most of the gas down to Ziggy's latest storage container.

Then he donned a gas mask, goggles, and gloves. This gas wasn't something to fool around with. Carefully, he lifted the measured hydrochloric acid and poured it into the funnel. He turned the stop-cock to let acid drip down on to the pool chlorine.

The reaction was immediate. The solution bubbled and fizzed and released a pale yellow-green gas. Pressure forced the gas up to the level of the hose and the gas drifted down to the storage container.

He touched the vial in his pocket. He had a dose of Algea ready. He would introduce Tesla to his personal goddess of sorrow and grief.

The chlorine gas he was manufacturing would ensure that the man understood the choice.

He stared at the gas. It was a lovely pale color, like aerosolized gold. It had first been used in World War I, but it had been abandoned because it dispersed with the wind and often ended up killing an equal number of soldiers on both sides.

Ziggy didn't have to worry about that. He'd be using the gas in a contained room, diffusing it at a slow enough rate that it wouldn't get out of control. It would only affect its target.

The gas was impossible to ignore. Tesla would probably recognize it by sight or by smell. Even if he didn't, his symptoms would tell him that he had to take Ziggy's choice.

Either way, his death would be the result.

41

Vivian stood in the immense tiled bathroom, holding a foil pouch in one hand and hating her job.

"I can go to the bathroom by myself," Katrinka hissed.

"Not happening," Vivian said.

Mr. Kazakov had sent a car for Vivian half an hour ago. She'd been woken up by the chauffeur ringing her bell, keeping her from sleeping in yet again. This hadn't improved her mood.

Mr. Kazakov thought it was an emergency. Apparently, someone said Katrinka had drugs in her school locker, and she'd been kicked out of school pending a drug test. Her father didn't want to wait for those results, and had called Vivian.

She had been brought in to monitor the girl's urine test, which meant watching her pee and making certain that whatever liquid got tested for drugs came out of Katrinka's bladder. Vivian had a second test in case of spillage.

On days like this, she missed the Army.

Katrinka put her hands on her hips and glared at Vivian. "I don't have to go."

Vivian leaned against the marble wall. "I'm paid by the hour."

Katrinka unbuttoned her pants. "Do you have to watch?"

"This is no fun for me, either."

"I bet."

As the girl sat down on the toilet, a plastic vial fell onto the marble floor. Vivian pounced on it and grabbed it before Katrinka could stand. The vial contained a straw-colored liquid.

"Three guesses on what this is." Vivian felt disappointed. She'd hoped the girl would be clean, that it was all a misunderstanding. She'd wanted to believe the line that Katrinka was spinning out for her father.

Tears welled in Katrinka's eyes. They looked genuine, but Vivian had seen enough of her acting to doubt them. "Please give that back. Please let me use it. Please."

"You know I can't." Vivian wished she were anywhere else.

Katrinka wiped the tears off her cheeks and sat on the toilet. Vivian handed her the cup.

Katrinka filled it and handed it back. Vivian sat it on the counter, opened the foil pouch, and dipped in the tester sticks. She counted to fifteen in her head while Katrinka flushed and washed her hands. The girl was completely subdued.

"Please," Katrinka said, "you don't understand."

Vivian ignored her. She'd read the instructions and knew that negative results showed up quickly, positive ones took longer. She expected this test to take the full five minutes.

But the test came back negative.

She held the test up for Katrinka to see. "You passed."

Katrinka threw herself on the floor and started sobbing.

Vivian sat next to her and patted her back. "You don't understand. The test says that you're clean. It shows that you haven't been using drugs."

"I know what passed is!" Katrinka choked out.

Vivian took the plastic bottle out of her pocket. "What was the desired result?"

Katrinka sat up and hiccupped. "I wanted to fail."

Vivian stared at her. "Why?"

"So my parents would send me to Montana to live with Aunt Billie. They're always threatening to."

Vivian looked at the bottle in her hand. "You mean the urine you were going to substitute is from a drug user?"

"Just a girl in my class. She's a total stoner."

"I'll talk to your father." Vivian stood. She took the test and the plastic bottle.

"He'll hate me."

Mr. Kazakov was in his study. Mrs. Kazakov was who-knew-where. Vivian had only seen her once and was starting to think she might not even live in the apartment with them.

He looked up from a sheaf of papers. "Positive or negative?"

"It's more complicated than that."

His bristly eyebrows lowered. "I don't see how."

"Do you play chess, Mr. Kazakov?"

"Tell me about my daughter."

She took a deep breath. She wished Tesla were here. He'd be able to explain it properly, show Mr. Kazakov how complicated things were.

"Miss Torres?"

She began.

42

Joe jumped when someone knocked at his door, and a blade of pain arced up his cast. He bit back a curse and gingerly shifted his foot. His foot responded by throbbing at him. Damn foot.

"It's Parker, sir," said a familiar voice. "You have a visitor."

"Marnie cancelled my appointments." Joe didn't say the next three nasty things that came into his head. None of this was Parker's fault. "Who is it?"

"He says he's a friend. A Mr. Gallo."

"Bring him in."

Parker opened the door, and Leandro sauntered in. Edison sat up.

Leandro wore a trench coat and a Mets cap, and he twirled a black umbrella in one hand. It must be raining outside. How long had it been since Joe had felt rain on his skin? He pushed the thought away. He had no time for self-pitying and melancholy. Being in pain always depressed him, and he had to fight it.

Parker came in after Leandro, a question on his face.

"It's OK," Joe said. "I've known Leandro for years. He's not dangerous."

Parker patted Leandro down, and Leandro grinned at him. "Aren't you going to buy me a drink first, sailor?"

"He's clean." Parker said.

"After a fashion." Leandro dropped his cap on Joe's desk and slung himself into Joe's extra chair. He hadn't gotten tanner in Florida, which was kind of surprising. He picked at a bandage stuck on one pale hand, then looked pointedly at the wheelchair. "What happened to you?"

"It's temporary," Joe answered. Celeste would probably tell her brother all the details, since she never seemed to keep anything from him, but Joe had no intention of telling him anything. "How was Florida?"

"Not as good as last year. The homemade bikini contest is always good, though." Leandro raised his eyebrows suggestively.

"Did Celeste send you here?"

"You called *me*." Leandro laughed. "Left a practically incoherent message, reminding me that I agreed to let you scan my brain. Even when drunk dialing, you are such a nerd."

Joe vaguely remembered calling him after they set his foot. He hoped that he hadn't called anyone else in that state, especially not Celeste. He'd have to check his call log as soon as Leandro left.

Joe came out from behind the desk, hands moving the wheelchair forward. "Let's get a peek into that brain of yours."

"How long are you going to be in that chair?" Leandro asked.

"Just a few days," Joe said. Dr. Stauss had insisted on it, saying he should be confined to bed, plus some other more dire stuff that Joe couldn't remember. Dr. Stauss had been angry, that part he remembered clearly.

Parker opened the door. Edison crossed to Joe's left side, which was odd. Maybe he was leaving room for Leandro on the right.

Joe wheeled to the game room with Leandro walking next to him. "We'll do an EEG today. You just have to sit with a cap on your head and watch videos in the best 3-D you've ever seen. Easy stuff."

"Got any porn?" Leandro looked around at the darkened game room and the giant picture of a translucent brain rotating on the screen in front of him.

"It's more like video game scenarios."

"You can make anything boring." Leandro sat in the chair and pulled on the neoprene cap.

Parker checked his watch.

"Don't you go off shift soon?" Joe asked him.

"Fifteen minutes," he said.

Fifteen (cyan, brown). "Would you mind taking Edison for a walk before you go?"

Parker looked between him and Leandro.

"I'm perfectly safe here on my own for a few minutes," Joe said. "Leandro's an old friend. Marnie's at her desk. And the concourse is full of cops. I probably have better security than the president."

Parker smiled and scratched Edison behind the ear. "Yes, sir."

Edison paused at the doorway and looked back, as if asking Joe if he was really sure. Joe smiled at him, and the dog trotted out with Parker.

Joe started Leandro with the walk to the beach, the one that had so terrified Joe. Predictably, Leandro's brain was calm and relaxed when he watched the sun and the waves from his 3-D helmet. It was the opposite of Joe's own reactions, and he envied him.

"Amazing graphics," Leandro said. "All I need is rum. And a naked chick. Or two."

Joe moved on to the next clip, watching Leandro's brain react to a battle scenario that had devastated the soldiers with PTSD. He expected Leandro's amygdala to respond strongly to the battlefield—the amygdala was the area that fired in response to fear, rage, and aggression—and it did. It was more muted than the soldiers' responses, a little more muted than Joe'd expected actually, but it still made sense since Leandro had never been on a battlefield.

"You're a good control brain," Joe said. "Normal and healthy."

"This has to be the worst use I can imagine for this cool gear."

"I'll throw you a bone." Joe pulled up a clip designed to measure sexual arousal. A brunette in a black bikini strolled up from a beach.

"I like where this is headed," Leandro said. "Can you give a guy some privacy?"

Joe studied the onscreen reactions in Leandro's brain. The parts that were lighting up caught him off guard. Joe had observed enough tests to know which parts of the brain should be lighting up—inferior temporal cortex for visual associations, the right insula was probably also involved in sexual arousal, among others. He saw activity in those regions, but it was strangely muted, just as Leandro's response to the battle scenario. Maybe it was nothing. Maybe the brunette wasn't his type.

What was more interesting was Leandro's amygdala. It was going haywire. Joe expected some activity in the amygdala when dealing with sexual arousal, but not this much. Leandro's brain was reacting as if he were terrified. Or furious.

His neo-cortex tamped the responses down, but it wasn't working as well as it should have either. The brains of people with PTSD had that kind of reaction to their triggers, and so did the brains of one other kind of person.

A sick dread grew in Joe, and he froze in his chair, staring at the neurons flashing onscreen, trying to make them mean something else. Otherwise, it was too awful to contemplate. He must be wrong. He wasn't a neurologist. He'd have to ask Dr. Plantec later. She'd have an explanation.

But he knew the explanation. His ears rang, and his eyes teared up, as if he didn't want to take in what he was seeing and hearing.

He'd seen this pattern before in scans that Dr. Plantec procured from a different study. They were different from the scans that Joe wanted, but she'd said they'd provide an interesting control group. He'd never thought he'd see scans like this in real life, especially not in a friend.

Leandro was exhibiting the brain patterns found in many serial killers.

Why had he called Leandro in his drugged state and told him to come here? Could it be the painkillers had lowered his defenses enough for him to process something that he had been denying since he'd compiled the list of people who had access to his drinks that fateful night? A list he'd run through a thousand times. A list from which he'd always discounted a single name.

Leandro Gallo.

But it couldn't be. Not Leandro. Joe had known him for years. He would have sensed something. Celeste would have sensed something. Celeste loved Leandro, and she couldn't love someone like that, not if she thought that he could be capable of such evil. She would be stronger than that. She was always stronger than that.

The pets. Joe remembered a visit to Celeste and Leandro's house in the Hamptons.

Wind whipped Celeste's blond hair across her face, and she pushed it back with one paint-stained hand, a hand that had left paint smears down Joe's back not an hour before.

They were next to a stand of trees.

"Bumble Wood." She pointed to the trees. "Leandro called it that because of the bees."

"Did you guys play there when you were kids? Build a tree house?" Joe only knew what normal children did from books. He'd never stayed in one place long enough to have secret hideouts or tree houses.

He'd gone several steps into the woods before he realized that she'd stopped. Cool shade enveloped him. She stood on the lawn with the sun kissing her hair.

"Come away." Her voice sounded strained. "There's nothing there to see."

He looked around. Green leaves blotted out the sun, and a mat of old leaves covered the ground. It was quiet here. He heard a quiet buzzing and guessed it must be the bumble bees that gave the tiny patch of woods their name.

A line of gray sticks poked out of the ground at regular intervals, like fence posts.

"I'll race you to the beach!" She turned and darted away, running hard.

He looked back at the line of sticks, wondering what had happened to the rest of the fence. In front of each post was a rounded mound of earth, smaller mounds for the far away posts, larger ones for the closer ones.

He dashed back out into the sunshine after Celeste.

With trembling fingers, Joe switched to the next clip. A redhead with deep blue eyes was on Leandro's viewer, taking off a sheer white blouse. Leandro's reaction didn't ebb. If anything, it intensified.

"Marnie, could you come in for a second?" Joe called. Marnie looked like Leandro's victims. She even wore the lipstick they did. If Joe was right, and he hoped that he wasn't, then she would trigger the strongest reaction of all.

"Way to kill the buzz," Leandro said. "Can't you keep quiet so I can concentrate?"

Marnie opened the door. She wore a conservative business suit, nothing provocative. She didn't exude sexuality like the redhead on screen, just quiet professionalism. She shouldn't provoke much of a sexual response in Leandro, particularly with his eyes covered by the 3-D viewer.

She put one expensive shoe onto the carpet. Everything slowed down for Joe, like a film playing at half speed. Her red lips smiled at him, and her head tilted questioningly, wondering why he had asked her to come in.

Leandro's brain activity went haywire, as did his amygdala. Colors flashed across the screen so quickly that Joe couldn't follow them. Marnie had provoked a strong response of arousal and anger.

She crossed the room to Joe, steps so silent that she seemed to be floating like a ghost. She moved so slowly. Time was out of synch.

Her words were perfectly ordinary. "I was going to leave for lunch soon. Would you like anything?"

Joe smelled the floral scent of her lipstick. She was wearing 999. Joe stared at her, unable to speak.

Despair overwhelmed him. His foot and head throbbed with pain, and he wanted to sleep. He blinked, but nothing had changed when he opened his eyes again.

He couldn't deny what was playing out on the screen in front of him. Leandro had the brain of a killer. Leandro's brain had gone crazy when Marnie appeared, probably because he smelled her lipstick. It was his trigger. The lipsticks hidden in the forgotten room made sense now.

He had taken those women down into the subway tunnels, and he hadn't left until they were dead. Then he had taken their belongings as trophies.

Only the lower part of Leandro's face was visible under the 3-D helmet, and his mouth quirked in a half grin. Joe had first seen that grin as a lonely college student. He'd followed that grin to parties. The man with that grin had dragged Joe out of the kitchen to dance and talk to people, showed him that his entire life didn't have to be about mathematics.

Leandro had introduced Joe to Celeste. Celeste. Celeste must know. She couldn't know everything, but she must know something. She must have known her brother wasn't normal. She had been afraid of the woods. She had known what those gray pieces of driftwood were marking.

Celeste hadn't had pets since childhood—she'd told him that once. Their first kitten had died because of some kind of disease in the building, the second one had an accident, and then their parents hadn't let them keep any more pets. She'd only brought it up once, years before. She'd been drunk at the time, and she'd never spoken of it again. At the time, he hadn't thought it important, but he did now.

Killers like Leandro practiced on animals, torturing and killing them, before they moved on to larger prey. Celeste must have known about the kittens.

Genetics loads the gun, and environment pulls the trigger. That's what Alan Wright always said. But Celeste had similar genetics. Celeste had to live in that environment. She must have seen it.

What had she known? About the kittens? About the women? Had she known that Leandro poisoned Joe? Had she wanted him to?

What did it say about Joe himself that these were his closest friends?

"Excuse me." Marnie's voice came from far away, from a place of innocence.

Joe stared at Leandro's brain floating on his monitor.

"Are you all right?" Marnie asked. "Should I call Dr. Stauss?"

"I'm fine," Joe said. "Fine."

"Do you want me to get you lunch?"

"I'm not hungry." Joe needed to warn her.

Marnie tilted her head. She looked between Joe and Leandro, and Joe could see she sensed something weird was going on. She shook her head a tiny fraction, giving up. "I'll be back in an hour, unless I get seduced by a shoe store."

Joe wanted to call out to her as she turned away, but he didn't. He wanted to get her as far away from Leandro as possible. He would let her get clear, distract Leandro, then call the police. The police would sort it out.

"You OK?" Leandro had pulled off the 3-D viewer and the cap that read his brain responses.

"Bumped my ankle," Joe lied. "Hurts like hell."

Leandro reached to put the EEG cap on the desk, but at the last instant, he pivoted his wrist, and an object appeared in his fingers. Joe felt a quick sting in his shoulder. Had Leandro seen right through him, or had he come into the office with the intention of hurting Joe? Not that it mattered now.

His hands fell from the computer mouse and into his lap. He slumped sideways in his chair. Light glittered against a syringe in Leandro's hand.

Joe should have looked deeper, should have recognized the unpleasant truths. Leandro had the keys to the underground. Leandro knew the tunnels. Leandro knew about facial recognition, about gait recognition, about Joe's security underground system. Joe had given Leandro all the tools he needed to defeat him.

"Chemistry." Joe's voice faded at the end of the word. Leandro had majored in chemistry in college. "You made the drug."

"You're the only one who ever remembers that I studied chemistry," Leandro said. "And it's the secret key to every single thing."

Leandro fished a white zip tie from his umbrella. It had been taped up next to the ribs, the syringe too probably. He pulled up Joe's shirt sleeve. Joe tried to move, but his muscles wouldn't respond.

Leandro lifted Joe's wrist and held it against the wheelchair's cold metal armrest. He zip tied it to the wheelchair, then pulled Joe's sleeve back down to cover the tie. He let the other hand rest in Joe's lap. Leandro was posing Joe's body like a manikin.

Celeste. Would Leandro kill her? Ten (cyan, black) women with her face had died in the tunnels. Was Leandro killing her over and over? Or was Leandro killing his mother, not his sister? They looked so much alike. Maybe he wouldn't harm Celeste. Joe knew better than that.

Leandro pushed him deeper into the wheelchair's seat, then dropped his baseball cap on Joe's head, angling the brim low enough that no one could see Joe's eyes, which were rolling around, looking for something, anything, to help him get out of this.

Leandro's sleeve had ridden up, and Joe saw the top of the palm tree that had adorned the wrist of the woman on the tracks. Calypso Club. Not Florida. He'd never gone to Florida. It was a lie, an electronic fakery. The Facebook posts. The phone call.

"You look pale and sickly," Leandro said. "But you'll feel better later when you look better."

He laughed. His laugh sounded high-pitched and wrong, nothing like his regular baritone.

He tilted Joe's head back and grabbed his jaw, forcing his mouth open. Joe couldn't resist him.

A glass vial clinked against his front teeth. A warm liquid dripped onto his tongue. It tasted like hay.

Sadness engulfed him. He had failed. More women would die, and their blood would be on his hands. He would miss Edison and his mother. His friends, too. He'd hoped to join them in the outside world one day, but he wouldn't. He would never feel rain on his face, never see Celeste, never kiss her.

His head drooped forward. Tears fell into his lap.

The wheelchair moved across the room, banging into the door on the way out. Pain flared in his foot, but it felt as if it didn't really belong to him.

His eyelids settled heavily. All was dark, and he fell deep into his own head as he skated across the noisy concourse. People talked and walked and moved around him, but he couldn't see them.

Then, the darkness lightened a shade, and water droplets hit the backs of his hands.

Rain on his skin.

43

Vivian took a deep breath, smelling wood smoke from the fire. It was a homey smell, but nothing about the pristine library was homey. "Katrinka has done some pretty risky things to get sent away—trying to shoplift, making it look like she's doing drugs. Maybe sending her to live with her aunt would settle her down."

Mr. Kazakov scowled at her. "You think you can tell me what's best for my daughter? Only few weeks have you known her."

Vivian knew that she should stop talking if she wanted to save her job. "What's here for her? An empty table at dinner?"

"She's a big girl. Big enough to eat alone." He towered over her, but Vivian wouldn't be intimidated.

"If you can't find time for her in your life, why keep her here? She's an animal in a trap, and she won't stop trying to escape just because you want her to stay." Vivian's phone buzzed in her pants pocket, but she didn't dare take her eyes off Mr. Kazakov.

"An animal, you say?" Mr. Kazakov was shouting now, and he moved closer, his thick jaw thrust out like a boxer's.

She bent her knees and watched his shoulders. If he decided to come after her, she'd see it first there. He was big, and his crooked nose and scarred knuckles meant he'd been a brawler once. But he was probably slower than her. She didn't need to beat him. She just needed to stay out of range.

"Daddy?"

Vivian waited until he turned to face his daughter, then took a few steps backward, putting a chair between her and Mr. Kazakov. But she could immediately see that it wasn't going to be necessary.

His shoulders sagged as he stared at his daughter.

Katrinka stood in the doorway. She perched on the balls of her feet like she wanted to run, but she stood her ground. "Please. Please."

Vivian expected her to say more, but she didn't. She just stood there, twisting a lock of hair with one finger.

He spoke. "Your mother—"

"Doesn't care if I'm alive or dead." Katrinka twitched when she said the word *dead*, and Vivian swallowed hard.

Mr. Kazakov hung his head. Vivian wanted him to go to his daughter, to hug her, to deny what she had said, but he stood still as a statue in the middle of the pristine white room.

"Let me go to Aunt Billie, Daddy."

Vivian's phone buzzed again, but she didn't want to draw attention to herself to answer it. She wanted to fade into the wallpaper and let these two work it out. She wanted to leave, but wouldn't go until Katrinka didn't need her anymore.

44

The sun beat against Joe's closed eyelids. He shuddered in the warmth. His heart raced so fast he knew he would die. His heart would explode soon.

He tried to raise his hand to shield himself from the light, but his arm was attached to something. He lifted the other arm and pressed it tightly against his face. The red light on his eyelids gave way to green and then black. The darkness brought him back. In the darkness he could think.

His immobile hand ached, and a dull pain pressed against his wrist. His ankle throbbed, too, and his head. His body was a catalog of pain.

He struggled through the pain, grasping at something in his memory, but his thoughts were gray and shapeless. His mind felt heavy with sadness and despair. That must have been from the drug that Leandro had given him. He must fight against those effects. He moved his injured ankle. The sharpness of the pain made him nauseous, but after riding it out, his head cleared.

With his eyes closed, he took stock of his body. His right wrist was bound to the wheelchair, and his hand ached. His ankle was broken, still encased in its warm cast. His head throbbed with each heartbeat. His mind felt pixelated and out of focus, as if it had been taken apart and jammed back together by an angry toddler, but at least he could move again.

The air smelled of flowers and bleach like a hospital, not like a subway tunnel or the fume-laden air of New York City. He must be indoors. He would have expected Leandro to kill him underground in the tunnels where the women had died, but this didn't smell right.

He accepted his body's distress and began to listen. A distant hum of traffic, New York's pulse, underlay the stillness. A faraway motor kicked in with a rumble, and a wisp of warm air touched his face. A heater had turned on. He was definitely inside.

A low murmur came from somewhere nearby, then a tinkling laugh, as familiar as his own heartbeat. Before, that sound had always made him smile, but now it filled him with dread. It came again.

Celeste's laugh.

45

Ziggy watched his beautiful sister. Sun caressed her pale cheeks, and a light breeze lifted strands of blond hair off her neck. Her condition had pulled her face out of shape, but the ghost of her classic beauty lingered.

He'd wheeled her onto her rooftop garden and parked the chair facing Central Park so she could look out over the trees and appreciate the colors of the dying leaves. He glanced at the baby monitor in her lap. She used it to communicate with her nurse when the woman was out of the room. Ziggy had dismissed the nurse and left the receiver on so Joe Tesla could hear them, and they him, when he woke up. So far, the man hadn't made a sound.

She shivered. The wind had picked up, and goose bumps ran along her bare arms. He arranged a blanket as yellow as a sunflower across her wasted shoulders. She loved the bright color, said it made her feel like a summer day. Maybe so, but he thought it made her look jaundiced.

"Warm enough?" he asked.

"The cold reminds me that I'm still alive, if only for a little while." Her eyes were fixed hungrily on the far off park, as if she knew that she would never go there again.

He shot a glance over his shoulder and across the garden to the glass-fronted room where he had spent so many afternoons reading to her, playing chess with her, and combing her long hair. Tesla was sitting in a wheelchair parked against the back wall, a few feet from the warm band of afternoon sunlight that fell across the tiles. He had covered his eyes with his free arm but otherwise sat still. He shouldn't be awake yet, but he'd already proved to be an outlier as a test subject for drugs. Ziggy touched a control in his pocket, opening the device he'd hidden in the air ducts.

She tried to see what he was looking at, but he knew that she wouldn't be able to turn her head far enough. It was imperative that she only see what he wanted her to see, move where he wanted her to move. He had positioned her carefully.

"Key West was great." He tried to think of something to distract her from the room behind them, and came up with a lie. "Great sunsets."

"Lots of bikinis, too, I bet." A hint of mischief danced at the edges of her smile.

"I saw a woman with a bikini made out of green paper. She went into the swimming pool, and we watched it dissolve."

She laughed. "That must have been hell on the pool filter."

"Nobody was thinking about the pool filter," he said. "Trust me."

Her blue eyes darkened. "Time was, I would have been the girl with the dissolving bikini."

"I remember." She'd had a bright red bikini when they were fourteen. He still dreamed about it sometimes and woke up slick with shame.

"My last bikini was velvet. And black." She looked toward the faraway orange and gold trees. "That's appropriate when you think about it. My bikini of mourning."

He'd always lied to her in the past, made up some comforting nonsense, but he didn't today. "Have you ever thought about taking it to your grave? Being buried in it?"

Those haunted blue eyes finally met his, and she saw that he was really asking about death, and if she wanted it.

"Every day," she said. "But I can't leave you alone."

"What if you didn't have to, Zag?" he asked.

Their father had called him Zig, her Zag—"Zig and Zag, together forever" was their motto. He hadn't used her nickname in years.

"No, Ziggy," she said.

"Ziggy alone?" He tucked the blanket in more tightly around her shoulder. "I can't picture it."

Her face contorted, and the blanket trembled. She was trying to move her arm, but she couldn't. After a brief struggle, she grimaced. "Take my hand."

He reached under the yellow blanket and held her hand. It was as cool and limp as if she were already dead.

"I don't want you to die," she said.

"I don't want you to die, either," he answered.

"You have things to do. For you. For me."

He squeezed her hand. "Zig and Zag, together forever."

"You need to take care of Joe for me," she said.

Hot rage burned through him. How dare she bring that man into this?

"You're hurting my hand," she said.

He used her hand to pull her wheelchair around to face the floor-to-ceiling glass door that opened onto the rooftop. She drew in a quick breath of pain, but she said nothing.

She stared at the glass, blinked, and looked again. It must have taken her a moment to look across the garden, through the glass, and to make sense of the wheelchair and the figure sitting on it. Then her eyes widened, and she looked up at Ziggy. She'd recognized the man in the chair.

Ziggy watched him until he was certain. Tesla was awake. The man she wanted him to take care of.

He'd take care of him all right.

46

Vivian leaned forward as if that would make the cab go faster. She'd already offered him a fifty dollar bonus to speed, and he swerved between a minivan and another cab, streaking through a yellow light.

She looked back down at her phone, but there was nothing new. As soon as she'd sorted things out with Katrinka and her father, she'd returned Parker's call. He'd told her that Tesla was missing. He'd gone out to walk the dog, leaving Tesla in the office with Marnie Kay and Leandro Gallo, and when he'd returned, the office was locked.

He'd found Miss Kay at the food court, and they'd gone back to the office. She'd used her key to get in, and they'd quickly determined that the office was empty. They'd called the police, and Miss Kay was waiting for their arrival.

Vivian braced herself as the driver screeched to a halt next to Grand Central Terminal. The car behind them laid on the horn and shot past them in the nearby lane. Her driver yelled out the window.

She pushed the pre-counted fare through the sliding window, then sprinted out of the cab without even bothering to close the door. With that fifty buck bonus, he could shut his own door.

Parker met her inside the 42nd Street entrance. Edison was on a leash next to him. The dog barked when he saw her.

"Any news?" she asked.

"Cops are talking with Miss Kay. They're not taking it seriously yet, say he might have gone on a walk."

"Outside?" She gaped at him. "Tesla?"

They were both moving fast, heading through Vanderbilt Hall. Edison was pulling on the leash, urging them forward. He knew something was wrong with his master.

"How did he seem?" Vivian asked.

"In good spirits," said Parker. "He requested I take Edison for a walk. He seemed happy to see his friend. He said they've known each other for years."

"They have." She had already tried to call Leandro Gallo, but it went straight to voicemail. She'd tried his sister's number and Tesla's, with the same results. "He owns the house Joe rents. They've known each other since college."

"I'm wondering if Mr. Gallo was called away, and then someone came and took Mr. Tesla when he was alone. But there was no sign of a struggle."

"Have you checked the house?"

"The house?" Parker shot her a glance.

"The underground house." They'd reached the concourse now, and she jogged toward the clock, sliding between commuters. Parker was already a few steps behind. Maybe Tesla got sick and went home. That'd clear things right up.

Vivian rapped on the glass next to Miss Evaline's window. The woman was talking to a guy holding a tuba case, and she put up one stubby finger to tell Vivian to wait. A line of commuters with questions glared at Vivian, and she ignored them.

Vivian knocked again, and Evaline shot her the kind of look that would have made the average commuter scuttle away in fear.

"It's urgent," Vivian called.

Miss Evaline said a few quick words to the tuba player, and Vivian stepped into his spot.

"No cutting!" said a woman with lavender hair. She looked old enough to be Vivian's grandmother.

"You deal with her." Vivian jerked her thumb at the purple menace.

Parker put on a kindly expression and moved between Vivian and the angry line. Edison looked between the two of them as if not sure which way to go, then pulled his leash out of Parker's hand and came to stand by Vivian.

"Has Joe Tesla or anyone else used the elevator in the last hour?" Vivian asked.

"No one." Miss Evaline looked past Vivian's shoulder at the line behind her.

"Have you seen him?" Miss Evaline kept a good eye out on activities in the terminal. "He might have been in a wheelchair. Without the dog."

Miss Evaline looked down at Edison. He was sitting in front of her door, and as soon as he caught sight of her, he whimpered and cocked his head. Miss Evaline's face softened, and she pursed her lips. Vivian wanted to give Edison a treat—he knew how to melt the hardest of hearts.

"I saw a man pushing a wheelchair, and he came from the same direction as the Lucid office. His back was to me, and I couldn't see the man in the chair either. The man in the chair was wearing a hat and he was kind of slumped over, but he was tall like your Mr. Tesla."

He's not my Mr. Tesla, Vivian corrected automatically, but silently. "How about the man pushing the chair? What did he look like?"

"Tall, blond. There was something familiar about his walk." She pursed her lips again, clearly thinking hard. "It might have been Mr. Gallo."

"Are you sure?" Vivian's heart sped up.

"I just said I wasn't." Miss Evaline crossed her arms. "I said it might have been."

Not much to go on.

Vivian thanked her and headed back outside to get another cab.

"Where are we going?" Parker and Edison kept pace with her. The dog carried his leash in his mouth.

"To Leandro Gallo's house," she said. "I'll call Dirk on the way, see if he can meet us at the door with reinforcements."

47

Joe finally managed to open his eyes. He was in a simple room. Three sides were painted a soft yellow, but the last was floor-to-ceiling glass. A band of sunshine fell across terra cotta tiles. A simple chandelier hung from the white ceiling.

He didn't have the courage to look through the glass, so he studied the rest of the room. A high table stood in the sun. It looked the right height to be wheelchair-accessible. Celeste probably parked there during the day.

The table was empty except for a black tube of lipstick. It looked just like the ones he'd seen in the tunnel. A sick feeling rose in him. Was it Celeste's? Or had Leandro brought a tube he'd stolen from one of his victims? Both thoughts were equally horrible.

In the sun by the glass wall was a baby monitor. That must be why he could hear them so clearly. It probably also meant that they could hear him, too.

One wall held a painting in swirls of red. His heart sank as he recognized it. It was titled, "The Number Three." Celeste had painted it years ago and refused to sell it, even to him. If the painting was here, then he was in her apartment.

He steeled himself and looked through the glass panel at a rooftop garden. Fall flowers bloomed orange and purple. A juniper in a giant pot sat next to a scarlet Japanese maple under a bright blue sky.

He wanted to close his eyes again at the sight of that limitless sky, but he didn't. Instead, he looked at a small figure hunched in a wheelchair, a yellow blanket tucked under her pale chin, her body a shapeless lump. Even so, he would know her face anywhere.

A breeze blew wisps of butterscotch-blond hair around her face. Her head was tilted at a strange angle, and her gaunt face shocked him. She looked so small and frail. Tears sprang into his eyes. He'd seen her again, after all.

"You look like sunshine," he called. "Warm and beautiful."

She smiled and, for an instant, she looked like her old self.

She might look like sunshine, but he was afraid of sunshine, and he could never go to her out there on the rooftop. Even if he could see her, she was as far from him as she'd ever been. Leandro's poison had taken her from him, and Joe would do anything to get her back.

Her brother stood by her side, one hand on the back of her wheelchair.

She looked at her brother. "Why is Joe here?"

"I wanted to bring him earlier, but he wouldn't come."

Lies. But truth lay at the core. Joe hadn't come to her. He'd had so much time to come to her, to share the last months of her life, and instead, he'd cowered underground like a rat. He'd let her suffer alone. Worse, he'd abandoned her to the care of her crazy brother.

"Earlier?" Celeste asked.

"I told him to rent the apartment downstairs." Leandro stood behind her, his fingers inches from her soft, blond hair. She was in danger, and Joe had to go to her. He pushed back at the despair and fear the drug had brought to life in him.

"Why is he here?" she asked.

"I wanted you to see him for what he is," Leandro said. "Before something happens to me."

"What would happen to you?" she asked.

"I won't last forever." Leandro cupped the back of her head. With his thumb, he stroked her hair.

She seemed not to notice his touch, but a flicker of anger at that possessive gesture burned through Joe's despair.

He found the point where the zip tie fastened. He struggled to push the little plastic tongue up to unlock the cuff and free himself, but it wouldn't budge. He could cut it free if he could find something sharp.

He looked around the room again. Just the table with the lipstick and something on the ground beneath the table. A black cap. He ducked his head to see the cap more clearly. He recognized it at once—it was wired with electrodes. It came from the wheelchair that he'd had made for her. She'd used his gift after all.

"I had to risk it, Zag," Leandro said.

She gazed up at her brother. She seemed unafraid. "Risk what, Zig?"

Joe remembered their old nickname: Zig and Zag, the twins.

"I had to risk everything to show you the truth," Leandro said. "The truth will set us free, just like it set them free."

"Them?" she asked.

"The women," Leandro said.

He hooked his fingernail underneath the tab for the zip tie and pushed. His fingernail ripped loose from the nail bed and blood gushed onto the tie. His finger slipped off.

"Your truth," she responded. "Your truth is so dark, Zig. Always dark. It doesn't have to be so dark."

"He killed women, Celeste," Joe yelled. "At least ten."

She looked so sad that he longed to take her in his arms and make everything go away. But he couldn't get to her.

"Really, Zig?" She was talking only to her brother. She hadn't even looked at Joe since the first quick glance. It was as if he didn't exist.

"They wanted my help." Leandro bent down and kissed the top of her head.

"Help?" she asked.

"Help." Leandro touched her hair, and she shifted her head a tiny fraction under his hand, leaning into his touch. Joe felt like he was watching a movie and had missed the first half.

"Why am I here?" Joe's fingers were slippery with blood, and his eyes stung. He coughed.

Leandro smiled then, and Celeste flinched away from him.

"You're both here to make a choice," Leandro said. "Just like the women."

THE CHEMISTRY OF DEATH

48

Ziggy saw a flash of understanding in Tesla's eyes. The man trembled with fear, just as the women had. The drug caused that, and it should have incapacitated him, but his gaze never wavered. Tesla knew what choice he would be forced to make, but he didn't seem too upset about it.

Tesla turned away from the rooftop, stood up as much as he could with his arm tied to the wheelchair, and limped to the door that led back into the apartment. He pulled his wheelchair behind him. He'd not get through that sturdy metal fire door. Ziggy had locked it himself, and he had the key in his pocket.

Ziggy reached down and picked up a weathered pine board. He put it against the roof's parapet. The board was long, and it provided a gentle slope up over the roof's edge. He'd brought the board weeks before, to be part of a privacy fence he'd never need to build now.

He pulled his sister's wheelchair up onto the board and stood balanced on top of the wall that ran around the edge of the roof. That wall designed to keep people from falling off. Far below people crawled like flies across the corpse of New York.

His sister's eyes never left Tesla, and Ziggy hated her for that, even as he loved her so much it hurt.

"Do you smell that?" Ziggy asked. Tesla sniffed, as Ziggy had known he would, and coughed violently. "It smells like bleach, doesn't it?"

"What does he smell?" she whispered.

"Chlorine gas," Ziggy explained. "First used by the Germans in Ypres in 1915. It's surprisingly easy to make in this day and age. Just mix together two common ingredients to create something new and deadly. Simple chemistry."

Tesla coughed again. The gas was acting faster than Ziggy had expected, or perhaps the cocktail of drugs in Tesla's system were increasing its effects.

"It's fast-acting when you get enough of it." Ziggy directed his next words to Tesla. "I've set it to release in small increments to give you enough time to make your choice."

"What choice?" she asked.

"To live or die," Ziggy said. "Just like the women in the tunnels."

"Tell me about them." Her breathy voice was still commanding.

"He brought women down into the subway tunnels, drugged them like he did me, and threw them in front of the train." Tesla spoke between coughs.

Ziggy held tightly to the wheelchair, controlling his anger. "I didn't throw them. Not at all. They chose. Every single woman chose her fate."

"You drugged them?" Her voice broke.

"With my own special drug." He needed her to understand how clever he was. "I invented it myself when I worked with Dr. Bilous. It's a drug that gives you clarity."

"Have you ever drugged me?" she asked. "Did you drug Joe?"

"He needed clarity, and now he has it."

"How long does he have?" she asked.

"Ten minutes, more or less." Ziggy couldn't be any more precise. "After that his lungs will be too compromised. We'll stay and watch."

"What's his choice?" she asked.

"He can walk out through the glass door onto the roof. If he comes outside, the wind will blow the chlorine away, and he'll be safe. Or he can choose to stay in that room and die."

49

Vivian watched the cops jostling for position ahead of her. She was stuck at the back of the pack with stone-faced Parker. Dirk was up there with them, giving orders and making himself useful. But if it weren't for Dirk, they wouldn't have been allowed to tag along at all, and they'd be standing in Leandro's lobby instead of watching the cops get through his door.

Leandro lived in a pricey apartment building. The lobby was clean and open, with a doorman in gray livery and a bouquet of exotic-looking flowers. The concierge, also in a light-gray suit, had accompanied them upstairs after first checking the warrant Dirk had managed to procure with lightning speed.

The paramedic in front of Vivian checked her wristwatch and sighed. Clearly, the young woman had other places she'd rather be. It was Vivian's fault she was there at all. Vivian had requested that Dirk bring a paramedic because Tesla had been drugged by Leandro, and no one knew with what. Assuming he was still alive—her stomach clenched at that thought—he probably needed medical attention.

Dirk took the key off the concierge and motioned that he step back. The concierge didn't move until one of the cops grabbed his elbow and ushered him to stand by Vivian at the back of the line. Where the civilians stood. Five cops up front, four civilians in back.

As if he knew how much it chafed her, Dirk gave her a crooked smile before unlocking Leandro's front door. Dirk pushed the door open, men on both sides with weapons raised, ready to go in.

A cloud of yellowish fog rolled out across the carpet like something out of a horror movie. The cops in front coughed and staggered back. Dirk slammed the door and caught one of his men before he fell. Vivian couldn't remember the guy's name. His face was red, and he slumped against Dirk. Yellow gas churned around their ankles.

The smell of bleach stung Vivian's nose, and her eyes watered. She pointed to the east end of the hall. "Window."

Parker was already moving. Vivian jogged to the window at the west end of the hall and smashed the glass with her elbow. A distant crash of broken glass told her Parker had opened his window, too. A cross breeze blew diesel-scented air down the hall. It smelled way better than the bleach.

That bastard had booby-trapped his apartment. Hopefully not with Joe still inside.

"Don't anybody lie down," called the paramedic. "It's on the ground, probably heavier than air."

Vivian wondered if she'd made things worse by opening the windows.

"Everybody out," Dirk called.

He slung his arm around the red-faced man, who was making a wet, tearing sound when he coughed.

Parker had opened the door to the stairwell at the end of the hall, and everyone stumbled to the stairs, except for the paramedic.

"I wish I could test it," the paramedic said. "It'd tell me what to do."

No time for testing. Vivian's eyes had teared up, and her throat burned. "It smells like bleach. Chlorine."

She hooked her hand around the woman's elbow and frog marched her down the hall to the door. Parker pulled the door closed behind them. It was a good fire door, and it had a tight seal.

Dirk and his team had climbed a flight of stairs and stood on the landing. Vivian let go of the paramedic's arm, and they hurried to join the others.

Dirk was already on the phone requesting a Hazmat team. Vivian did a quick assessment. Parker, the paramedic, and the concierge seemed fine. Dirk wiped at tears with his sleeve, but his breathing seemed OK, except for a quick cough or two. Three of the four other cops were coughing, but only one seemed to be in real distress. He was sitting on the landing, propped against the wall. A female cop sat next to him, one hand on his shoulder.

The paramedic handed him a pocket inhaler. "Albuterol. Do you know how to use it?"

He nodded and took a quick puff.

"He's got asthma," the woman said. "He takes something to control it."

The paramedic fumbled in her bag and pulled out a container of oxygen and a mask. She fitted it over the coughing man's face.

"We need to go back in there," Vivian said to Parker.

"Not without masks and gear." How had Dirk heard her while in the middle of a pitched conversation? "Nobody goes in there."

The two standing cops moved their hands to their weapons almost reflexively.

Vivian looked back to Dirk. "Tesla might be in there."

The paramedic adjusted the oxygen mask. "If your friend is in that apartment, he's already dead."

Vivian recognized the truth in her words and slumped against the wall. She'd failed him. She'd known that he was in danger and had left him with Parker. She'd ignored Parker's call to deal with Katrinka. If she'd been there, she would have stopped Leandro.

"Maybe he's not in there, Torres." Parker sounded like he wanted to believe that Tesla was still alive, that Santa was real.

"I don't know where else he'd be," Vivian said.

Parker shrugged his massive shoulders and looked up and down the stairwell. He needed to be going somewhere, doing something, trying.

Vivian closed her eyes to think. She wondered how many others Leandro had killed. She knew about Tesla and the women in the subway tunnels, but there could have been others. The faces of the women appeared in her mind's eye—blond hair, blue-eyes, delicate features, and the vulnerable look of women who had been wounded.

"I have one more idea," she said. "Another place to look."

50

Joe's eyes burned so much he could hardly see Celeste and Leandro. Every breath scalded his throat and lungs. His body convulsed with coughing, and each cough drew more contaminated air into his lungs. Based on his current rate of decline, he probably didn't have five (brown) minutes left where he'd still be able to function.

He looked to where Leandro stood on the edge of the roof, his hand on the grips of Celeste's wheelchair. After Joe died, Leandro would pull her over the side. She would know that Joe had been too weak to help her. Her last thought as she fell to the pavement would be that Joe had let her down.

"Let her go," Joe yelled. That small effort started another coughing fit, and he fought to keep from doubling over.

"She'll make her choice, too," Leandro said. "I think she'll choose to go with me."

The gas had pooled on the floor now, snaky tendrils of yellow-green wrapped around his wheels. A long ago chemistry class had taught him that chlorine gas was heavier than air. He would die faster on the floor.

Joe stood, bent at a weird angle because his wrist was still zip-tied to the wheelchair. His ankle hurt, and he ignored it. He took a step toward the glass door, but when he got to the band of sunshine across the floor, he stopped as if he had run into a solid wall.

It was ridiculous, but he couldn't take another step forward. His heart beat so fast it was a constant roar in his head. His breaths rushed fast and shallow, drawing in the poison gas. Dread radiated from every cell in his body.

He was trapped.

His choice had been made for him.

51

Ziggy stood with his back to the city. Cold wind buffeted him, and he tightened his hold on the heavy wheelchair. He didn't want to be swept off the roof without her. They must fall together. They had come into the world together, and they must leave it the same way. Their destinies had always been intertwined.

"Is there really poison gas in there?" she asked.

He knew she wanted him to lie to her, to tell that her Tesla was safe, but he wouldn't. Not now. "Of course."

"You can't kill him." A touch of panic, quickly controlled. Zag was always tougher than he.

"He's killing himself. All he has to do to save his life is take a few steps and open the door. It's simple."

"You know he can't go outside."

"The drug makes it harder, perhaps, but who's to say he can't overcome it with enough power of will? That he can't choose to be otherwise?" Perhaps Tesla could succeed in changing his nature, even as Ziggy himself had failed.

She twitched her head violently. It was the biggest movement that he had seen from her in weeks, and it reminded him how trapped she was inside her ruined body.

He leaned down to whisper in her perfectly formed ear. "What about you? What do you choose?"

"I choose for you to save him." She hadn't hesitated before she spoke, and he hated her for it. She cared so much about that man.

"He must save himself. Those are the rules. We will watch to the end, to see if he changes his mind." They would stay because Ziggy longed to watch the life drain from Tesla's eyes, and to make sure she knew that Ziggy was the last man in the world who loved her.

"I'll go off the roof with you." Her blue eyes held no guile. "Gladly."

"I know you will."

"But only if you let him live."

He stroked her cool cheek, and she didn't move away. "You're too stubborn, Zag."

"I want to go off the roof with you," she whispered. "We have reasons for wanting to die, but we can't take Joe with us."

"This is a kindness. If he loved you, he wouldn't want to live without you."

"Nobody else loves me like that," she said. "Just you."

Warmth welled inside him. She loved him, and she knew that he loved her. It didn't matter what that man had told her. She still knew what was most important.

But then he went cold. Her words were true, but they felt like a lie. She would manipulate him to save Tesla. She would do that. Even now, she would do that.

"I won't go to him," he said. "I can't. He has to make his own choice. Just like the women in the tunnels. Just like us."

She rested her cheek against his hand. Even wasted by the disease, she was so beautiful. Suffering had tempered her into something delicate and fine. He smelled her hair and recognized the shampoo she had started using in her teens and never changed, cucumbers and lemon. It smelled fresh and clean in the cold wind.

"Please don't kill him," she said. "Leave him alive to remember me."

He slapped her perfect cheek so hard her head rocked back against the wheelchair's headrest. Tesla wasn't supposed to remember her. That man's memories of her as the artist, the woman, the lover must die, too.

"Please," she said, "let it be just us. Zig and Zag."

The red imprint of his hand marred the alabaster perfection of her cheek, and he couldn't look at it.

52

Joe dragged the wheelchair around to face the door that led back to the house. Maybe he could find another way onto the roof, or at least get some clean air into his lungs so he could think. He pulled at the handle, but the door was locked. It was metal, a fire door installed to let the occupants flee to the rooftop.

He checked for hinges, thinking to remove the pins, but they were on the other side. He coughed again, holding himself upright against the wall. Whatever happened, he wasn't going out that way. That only left the glass door.

He struggled to hold his breath. Breathing was death, and he had to save himself to save Celeste.

Desperate, he looked around the room again. His gaze fell on the EEG cap. It was mostly covered in sunlight, but the tip was still in shade. A small triangle of fabric was within his reach.

"It's the persistence of memory," Celeste said. "That's what I mean."

Joe walked toward it. The cap was only one step away.

"He's getting so close, Zag," said Leandro. "Do you think he'll make those last few steps into the sunshine to save himself?"

He wouldn't be able to make those steps. But he didn't have to.

"He's as rooted as one stark tree," she said.

That didn't make any more sense than her comment about the persistence of memory. His fingers closed on the cap. He snatched it back out of the sunshine and pulled the wheelchair to the back of the room. It was darker there. It felt safer, although he knew it was more deadly. The chlorine smell grew stronger with each step backward, his death pumping quietly out of the heating vent.

"What are you talking about?" Leandro asked Celeste. Apparently, it didn't make sense to him either.

"Just something I saw once," she said. "A tree in front of the sea."

"At the summer house?" Leandro sounded uncertain.

Joe clutched the cap. He didn't know how to work it. He'd had it designed to respond to thoughts in Celeste's mind, and she would have set it up to control the wheelchair using her own images. He had no idea what those were.

"Joe knows what I mean," she said.

He didn't, but her words brought him up short. He replayed the last things she had said. A tree in front of the sea. One stark tree. The persistence of memory.

In a flash, he knew. She was telling him what he needed to know to make the cap work. It was from a conversation they'd had a long time ago. She was talking about Salvador Dali's painting *The Persistence of Memory*, the one with the melting clocks. Clocks were the clue.

It was her code. She and Joe had seen the painting together, in the Museum of Modern Art. She'd talked about one stark tree in front of the sea.

The cap must work like a clock—twelve (cyan, blue) was probably forward, six (orange) backward, three (red) to the right, nine (scarlet) to the left.

"The sky is so bright today," she said. "It's more cyan than blue. It's a good sky for a last day."

Cyan and blue. The numbers one and two. Or the number twelve. The number at the top of the clock. She was making sure that he got it.

Celeste and Leandro were dark figures silhouetted against the bright sky. His eyes streamed and blurred. Any second he would be completely blinded. But he knew what he needed to do. He fitted the cap onto his head, hoping the wheelchair that it controlled was still within range of its wireless technology. He had to hurry, before Leandro caught on and stopped him.

He thought of the number twelve: One (cyan) and two (blue). The chair didn't budge. Had he misinterpreted her code? Maybe she wasn't trying to communicate with him after all. Maybe it was a code for Leandro. Or maybe she'd snapped under the stress.

Then he got it. Just the colors. Cyan, he thought. Blue.

Her wheelchair leaped forward like a horse leaving the gate. She had chosen life. She had chosen him. He smiled with grim determination. Cyan, blue.

The chair pulled free of Leandro. He lurched to the side, and for one hopeful second Joe thought that he would fall off the roof. But he regained his balance.

Celeste's chair rolled down the board toward the door, picking up speed as it went. Cyan, blue, Joe thought again.

He'd get her inside, away from Leandro, and then he could protect her. If he could lure Leandro into the shadows at the back of the room, he could hold the bastard down and let him suffocate in his own gas. Hope rose up in him, and it took away the pain in his lungs. For an instant, he even stopped coughing.

He had to time this just right. He tightened both hands on his wheelchair. If he couldn't get away from the damn thing, then he'd use it.

Behind her, Leandro leaped off the ledge and onto the roof. He sprinted after the runaway chair.

Celeste was closing in on the glass.

Joe lifted his wheelchair and swung it in a wide arc at the glass. He knew his body would panic when he hit the light, but he counted on the momentum of his movement to carry the wheelchair from darkness into light and through the glass.

The impact jolted up both arms.

Tempered glass crumbled into small chunks.

The light would kill him. He gasped and stumbled back against the inside wall.

Celeste's chair zoomed across broken glass toward him.

Stop, he thought, but the chair didn't slow. She would crash into the wall, and it might kill her. He positioned himself to catch her.

Zero, he thought. Black.

The chair stopped an inch away from his outstretched hands.

Sweet fresh air rushed in through the broken door. He drew it deep into his aching lungs.

"I'm sorry," she said. "I'm sorry."

"Are you OK?" He swept off the blanket to see if she was hurt.

"Did Leandro fall off the roof?" she asked.

"Are you hurt?" She wasn't bleeding. Nothing looked broken, but her body was thin and wasted, one shoulder frozen higher than the other and her head tilted permanently to the side. Garish red lipstick made her look like a badly painted doll. He brushed pieces of tempered glass out of her hair.

"Where's Leandro?" She strained to look over her shoulder at the roof outside.

"I'm here, Zag," Leandro called from the broken door. He was so brightly lit that Joe could barely look at him.

Joe dragged himself between Celeste and Leandro. His ankle throbbed.

"Joe," Celeste said. "Let him take me. That's all you need to do."

Joe looked back at her. Her blue eyes pleaded with him. He'd always done what those eyes wanted. "He's going to jump off the roof with you."

"I know," she said. "I want him to. Now that you're safe, I want him to."

Leandro took a step into the room. Glass crunched under his shoes.

"No." Joe couldn't believe her words. She was overwrought. She didn't mean it. She didn't want to die. She couldn't.

"There's nothing for either of us here," she said. "They'll lock Ziggy up for the rest of his life."

"I'm not stopping *him* from jumping." Joe looked back at Leandro.

"I'm worse than dead now," she said. "Can't you see that?"

He didn't see that. He couldn't let her die. He would save her from Leandro, save her from herself if he had to. "You don't understand."

"I understand everything," she said. "But you don't."

"I know what it's like to be a prisoner—" He broke off because Leandro had lunged for him.

Leandro was quicker than Joe had expected, but he managed to throw himself to the side. He came up hard against the wall and pivoted toward the wheelchair.

Leandro charged again, and Joe stepped aside, clipping him on the ear as he went by. Leandro spun to face him. Joe hit him square on the nose. It made a satisfying cracking sound, and blood gushed out.

"Don't hurt him!" cried Celeste.

Then a tearing cough came from deep within her.

The chlorine gas. Even with the fresh air coming in, the gas was too much for her compromised lungs.

Orange (six), Joe thought, even as he dodged Leandro's wild blow. The wheelchair backed across the glass toward the outside. Scarlet (nine) caused the wheelchair to jog to the right, away from Leandro. Black (zero). The chair stopped.

The air was fresher there, but she was in the sunlight, and he couldn't go to her.

Leandro recognized Joe's mistake and started for his sister. Cyan (one), blue (two) bumped the wheelchair away from Leandro and toward Joe.

"Let him take me," she pleaded.

Leandro looked at his sister, then back at Joe. He reached behind his back and came out with a gun. "Let her make her choice."

"I choose you, Ziggy," she said. "Always you."

Leandro's eyes flicked toward her, and he smiled. Joe grabbed the wheelchair attached to his arm, lifted it high, and spun on his good leg. It increased his reach just enough. The chair knocked Leandro to the floor.

Joe fell more than jumped on him and pinned him down. Joe held his breath. Leandro coughed violently. His head was right against the floor, where the gas was thickest. Let him choke on it.

"Don't hurt him!" Celeste gasped, retching.

Orange (six). Joe sent her wheelchair farther onto the roof. She would be safe there so long as he kept Leandro in here.

Leandro bucked under him, and Joe dropped his forearm across his neck, forcing his head sideways. Leandro's face turned red. Tears slicked his cheeks.

Joe couldn't hold his breath much longer. His lungs ached for air, and his eyes streamed. He pressed harder on Leandro's neck. Leandro turned his neck sideways, trying to protect his windpipe.

"Let him up!" Celeste ordered.

Joe wouldn't let him up, not while he had breath enough to hold him down. Hot rage ballooned in his chest.

This man had killed over and over again. He'd taken Joe's freedom. And he'd almost killed Celeste. Joe pushed harder against his neck. Leandro's thrashing weakened.

Strong hands pulled Joe off Leandro. Joe gulped a lungful of gas and retched. His eyes streamed, and he could barely see. Someone set him up on his feet.

A giant figure in black rolled Leandro over and handcuffed him before yanking him upright. Leandro was still alive. Joe felt regret that he had not killed him, and then hot shame. He would have succeeded if he hadn't been stopped. Anger made him as capable of murder as anyone else.

"Got him," said a voice that he recognized as Parker's. Refrigerator Man sounded hollow and far away.

"Hold still, sir," ordered the person holding him up. Vivian, but her voice sounded odd, too.

She righted the wheelchair attached to Joe's wrist. As soon as it was upright, she pivoted and eased him into the seat. It felt good to sit down, to be taken care of. Adrenalin still coursed through him, and he shook. Every tremor reminded him of what he had almost done, who he had almost become.

Vivian knelt to cut his wrist free from the armrest, her face close to his. She was behind glass, her face covered in black. For a second, he couldn't understand what she, too, had become. Then it fell into place. She hadn't changed. She was wearing a gas mask.

"Are you OK, sir?" Her brown eyes were worried.

"Fine." He coughed so hard he couldn't say another word.

She set a gas mask on his face and adjusted the strap behind his head, then nodded to tell him to breathe.

He took a deep breath that tasted like plastic. He would take plastic over bleach any time. He took another shuddering breath. He focused only on the feeling of air going into his damaged lungs. In, then out. Slowly, his lungs stopped their spasms, and his eyes cleared.

He looked out toward the roof. A woman in a blue uniform knelt next to Celeste's wheelchair. Celeste was crying, but she was alive. He'd saved her. She wasn't lying dead in the street, her body entwined with her brother's.

The sun glinted off her golden hair, and she was beautiful.

53

Vivian wheeled Tesla toward the door that led into Celeste's house. She and Parker had done a number on the door with a portable battering ram. The damn door was steel that had been painted to look like wood. It was much harder than they expected, but they'd broken through eventually.

After she'd told Dirk that she thought Leandro might have taken Joe to Celeste's apartment instead of his own, Dirk had called ahead to have cops with gas masks and a ram meet them in front of Celeste's building. The man in charge had let her and Parker break down the door. Nobody wanted to argue with Parker, and she'd coasted along next to him.

She pushed Tesla into a living room that was bigger than her whole apartment. She bet that the custom-designed leather sofa cost more than she made in a year. She headed for the darkest part of the room and parked Tesla facing the corner.

He was sitting up straight in the chair, sucking on the gas mask. His coughing sounded better. Vivian pushed her mask up to the top of her head and looked around for a paramedic.

Two uniforms walked Leandro past. His golden head was sunk against his chest, and he shambled along with his eyes half-closed. A long bruise on his neck showed where

Tesla had nearly killed him. Tesla had been pretty intent on finishing the guy off when she got to him.

"Sir?" She knelt. "Are you OK?"

He gave her a weak thumbs-up, but she raised her hand to call a paramedic over.

The paramedic was a beefy young guy who looked like he spent all his off time working out. He had black hair cut into a buzz and dark eyes. His nametag said his name was Buster.

"Can we get some oxygen over here, Buster?" Vivian called.

Buster fitted an oxygen mask over Tesla's head and turned it on. Vivian wouldn't have minded some of that oxygen herself. Her lungs felt irritated, but not enough that she had to cough. Tesla definitely needed it more.

"Celeste?" Tesla asked through the greenish oxygen mask.

"She's fine." Vivian looked across the living room to where two paramedics clustered around Celeste's wheelchair. She was probably fine.

"I want to see her." Tesla tried to stand, but both Vivian and Buster held him down.

"Let's just do a quick exam," Buster said. "Then you can go."

Vivian liked this brawny young man.

"What's wrong with your ankle?" Buster asked.

"He broke it the day before yesterday," Vivian said when Tesla didn't answer. The woman on the tracks had died only two days ago, but it seemed as if years had passed.

Buster smiled at Tesla. "We'll get you down to the ambulance and get it looked at. Your shoulder, too."

Tesla's eyes went wide with panic.

"He has a private doctor." Celeste spoke from behind Vivian. Someone had pushed her wheelchair over to their wall. "He'll be treated here."

She wore an oxygen mask, too. She had a small cut on her forehead, but otherwise she looked unharmed. Vivian hadn't expected her to be so frail. She'd always sounded so tough on the phone.

"Can we give them a little privacy?" Vivian asked. "I think they have some things to talk about."

54

Joe spread a red-and-white checked blanket across the groundcover. He set the picnic basket smack in the middle and lay down on his lawn. The plants felt strong and springy under his back. They had grown lush in the past few months, and he'd spent a lot of time watching them while his leg and shoulder healed.

Edison rolled around on the ground, yellow legs kicking at the painted sky. Joe turned from his back to his stomach and breathed in the fresh smell of green life. Edison had the right idea.

It was their garden now. The house was legally Joe's. Celeste had deeded it to him and all his descendants in perpetuity. Not that it looked like he'd ever have any descendants. Not at this rate.

His phone rang. Celeste.

"I was setting up for dinner," he said.

He panned the camera around so she could see the painted tunnel and the lush green plants. As always, he ended on the picture of the seagull.

"I only have a minute before I have to go. I don't want to lose the light." She was painting again, in a snug little studio up in snowy Maine.

"How are you feeling?" he asked.

"A seven," she said. "At least."

Seven was slate, a strong number for Celeste. Her ALS had improved since Leandro had been locked away. Joe suspected that her brother had been poisoning her, but she refused to discuss Leandro with him. She said he'd forfeited that right when he almost killed her brother. "Good number."

"It's always good numbers these days."

Maine agreed with her. Before the move, they'd met weekly, usually at the Museum of Modern Art. Joe had become a patron so he could access the museum via the steam tunnels. They had clung together like survivors of a shipwreck, buffeted by cataclysmic events beyond their control. Paradoxically, they hadn't grown closer, but rather farther apart.

The secret pieces of themselves that had been revealed on the roof—her suicidal desires and his murderous actions—had put up a wall neither of them seemed to want to climb. So, they drifted away from each other.

He'd been almost relieved when Leandro had hung himself in prison, and she'd left New York the same day. Now their weekly visits were weekly calls, calls that got shorter and shorter.

"Show me what you're working on," he said.

She fumbled with her phone and nearly dropped it. Her motor control was still compromised, but she could move her left arm enough to paint.

Joe's tiny phone screen zoomed past a snowy outdoor landscape and settled on an easel fitted with a wooden contraption that helped her control the brush when she worked. A stylized yellow and green object was slowly taking form on the canvas.

The image was so abstract that it was difficult to recognize, but Joe knew it by the color, by the way the bright yellow circle lifted itself up to a stippled gray sky. The yellow blob was supported by a slender green stalk that looked too fragile for the bloom.

"A sunflower," he said.

"Just barely," she answered, and that was true, too. The sunflower seemed to recede back into the canvas, as if being pulled into the gray-white sky.

"It's gorgeous," he said. "I want it for my library."

"It could replace one of those fusty Victorian oils," she said.

He liked those oils. "It could."

"I gotta run," she said. "Metaphorically."

Edison bounded across the grass toward the elevator. He gave a happy bark. Joe knew who had arrived.

"Me, too," he said.

There was a long moment of silence between New York and Maine, and then Celeste broke the connection.

Maeve strolled into view with Edison at her side. She'd dyed her hair silver for winter. Silver hair was trendy in New York now, and it looked good above her youthful face.

She carried a potted plant with dark purple flowers. Edison cavorted around her feet until she fished a treat out of her pocket and tossed it to him.

"Who's a good dog?" she asked him.

Edison wagged his tail as if he knew the answer.

"You know we'd both be happy to see you, even without the treats," Joe said.

She made a face. "I pulled this violet out of Macy's window. It was left over and going to be cast out into the snow, so I brought it here."

"Will it live?"

"If you put it in the parlor next to the grow light for the lemon tree, it should have a long and happy life, although it might not flower again." She put the plant into his hands. It had a bright silver pot that matched her hair, and an electric thrill went through his hands when her fingertips touched his.

"I'll do my best with it," he said.

"If it starts to look bad, let me know. I'll nurse it back to health for you."

He set the plant down next to the picnic blanket while Maeve wandered through his yard.

"Just checking on my babies." She bent to caress the tops of the blue star, then picked off a few yellowed leaves. "They look very healthy."

He hated to imagine her reaction if they didn't.

She came back to the blanket and sat cross legged on one side.

He opened a grape leaf picnic basket right out of the Victorian era. She'd bought the basket for him as a lawn-warming present once the ground cover was strong enough to sit on, and he'd invited her to this picnic as a thank you.

"What goodies do we have in here?" she asked.

"I dropped it off at Mendy's Kosher Delicatessen and told them to surprise me."

"Corned beef sandwiches." She held one up. "And pastrami."

He helped her unpack a giant bunch of champagne grapes, a bottle of red wine, a round container that smelled like potato salad, and another that might be coleslaw. At the bottom was a package wrapped carefully in white paper that must have been a steak for Edison. On the sides rested two smaller packages that he suddenly hoped were cheesecake.

"A nice haul." She unwrapped Edison's steak and set it on the ground, using the paper as a plate.

Edison looked over at Joe. He wagged his tail.

"Go ahead," Joe said. "You know it's yours."

Edison downed it in two bites and collapsed on the ground next to Joe. Joe ruffled his ears.

"Winter Wonderland caught on fire again," Maeve said. "The roof started to smoke on Santa's workshop. It's a wonder no elves were melted. We had to do a little triage on a few that got singed. Which makes me an official elf medic."

"I think that puts you square on the nice list," he said.

"How was your day?" she asked.

"I got a weird proposition."

"It's New York. It happens all the time."

He laughed. "A government agent I hadn't seen in a long time stopped by the office."

The silver hair made her blue eyes snap with color. "Did he want you to join a superhero team?"

"Basically. He wants me to work on an anti-hacking task force."

"But I thought you were a hacker." She set out plates and wineglasses.

"That's a problem and a solution, according to the guy." Joe had said he'd think it over, but he'd already known that he would sign up. He'd be able to track down international criminals—pedophiles, terrorists, and who knew what else. He could make a difference.

She ran one hand through her silver hair. It settled again like a cap of feathers. "Sometimes you gotta accept those weird propositions. See where they go."

He splashed wine into their glasses and picked up a sandwich.

She lifted her glass in a toast. "To weird propositions."

He could drink to that.

ACKNOWLEDGEMENTS

So many people work behind the scenes to make sure that Joe Tesla and Edison are at their best. Thanks to Kathryn Wadsworth, David Deardorff, Karen Hollinger, Ben Haggard, Judith Heath, and Joshua Corin for great editing advice and literary butt-kicking; to Peter Plantec, the inspiration for Gemma Plantec, for his advice on Joe's condition; Alexandra and my sister (you know which one) for your sanity and insanity checks; to my scientist friends for their help with crafting the drugs and poison: Dr. Martin Kracklauer, Dr. Christian Schmidt (who is far too cute and fluffy to use his powers for evil), and my son (who, frighteningly enough, knew right away what poison to use); to my wonderful cover designer, Kit Foster; copy editor, Amy Eye; and literary agents, Mary Alice Kier and Anna Cottle.

But, of course, I owe the most to my husband and son—you guys are the best writing family a person could ever have.

And a giant thanks to all my readers! You make it all worth it!

ABOUT THE AUTHOR

Rebecca Cantrell is the award-winning and *New York Times* bestselling thriller author of this book and the other novels in this series: *The World Beneath* and *The Tesla Legacy*. Her other novels include the Order of Sanguines series co-written with James Rollins, starting with *The Blood Gospel* and the award-winning Hannah Vogel mystery series, starting with *A Trace of Smoke*. She lives in Berlin, Germany with her husband.

If you'd like to find out more about her novels, visit her web site, rebeccacantrell.com. All the books are listed there, in order, plus some extra content about researching them and the worlds in which they take place.

If you'd like to receive advance notice of her upcoming books, please sign up for her newsletter at rebeccacantrell.com/newsletter.

Or, if you want to see what she's up to day to day, you can find her on Facebook and Twitter.

AUTHOR'S NOTES

Sometimes it's tough to tell what's fact and what's fiction in Joe Tesla's world. I thought I'd clear that up for you here.

The saddest fact in the book is the statistic that Vivian tosses off early on: someone dies every week in the subway. According to The Atlantic around fifty people die every year in the New York City subways. Even without Ziggy, too many people jump or fall in front of the trains.

When Ziggy talks about his apprenticeship with a chemist who researched and invented many mind-altering chemicals, it sounds too crazy to be true, but there was a chemist named Alexander Shulgin who did just that. He created and tested more than two hundred different mind-altering compounds and was known as the "godfather of psychedelics." The drug Algea exists only, hopefully, in Ziggy's mind.

Joe's research in brain mapping is cutting edge, but it's not beyond the limits of what's going on today. I based the giant brain in his office on the glass brain used to model brain activity by Neuroscape Labs. They even have a video on their web site of an actual "glass brain" thinking.

I did fudge a little bit on the thought-controlled wheelchair, but only a little. Thought-controlled wheelchairs do exist. Here's a video of one that works, complete with cap like in the book. But, as the video states, the user has to spend time training the device to his or her own brainwaves, so it wouldn't work if Joe just picked it up off the floor and put it on.

Research has shown that serial killers do have different brain activity than non-serial killers, although it also shows that serial killers are both born and made—that is, they have a genetic predisposition to be killers, but it is only triggered if they have traumatic experiences in their early lives. I discovered this while reading about James Fallon, a mild-mannered psychologist who was studying the brain scans of serial killers and discovered that one of the scans of the control group was very similar to those killers. When he looked it up, he discovered that particular brain was his own.

I used as many real locations in the book as I could. Joe's office isn't in Grand Central yet, but I called the real estate manager and he said that they would indeed rent him one should he come along with enough cash when there was a vacancy. I guess I'll leave that one up to Joe. Other than that, Grand Central Terminal does have a secret door in the middle of the clock. They say it leads to a storage room, and not a secret elevator, but isn't that what they would have to say?

Joe plays tennis at the real Vanderbilt Tennis and Fitness Club in Grand Central, and he could easily get there without going outside. Likewise, the Campbell Apartment and the Grand Hyatt are within Joe's inside world.

If you ever visit them, take a picture for me!

Printed in Great Britain
by Amazon